HOUGHTON MIFFLIN HARCOURT
CHILDREN'S BOOK GROUP
BOSTON :: NEW YORK

ADVANCE READING COPY

IMPRINT: Harcourt Children's Books

TITLE: Dark of the Moon

AUTHOR: Barrett, Tracy

ILLUSTRATOR:

ISBN: 978-0-547-58132-3

PUBLICATION DATE: 09/19/2011

PRICE: $16.99 / Higher in Canada

TRIM: 5-1/2 x 8-1/4

PAGE COUNT: 320

AGES: 12 and Up

GRADES: 7 and Up

DARK
OF THE
MOON

DARK
OF THE
MOON

TRACY BARRETT

HARCOURT
Houghton Mifflin Harcourt
Boston   New York   2011

ACKNOWLEDGMENTS

As always, deepest thanks to my editor, Reka Simonsen.
Thanks also to my agent, Laura Rennert, and to the members of my critique group:
Shirley Amitrano, Thea Gammans, Cheryl Mendenhall, Candie Moonshower,
Carole Stice, and Cheryl Zach, for their encouragement,
their suggestions, and especially their friendship.

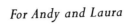

For Andy and Laura

⇥ PROLOGUE ⇤

It isn't true what they say about my brother—that he ate those children. He never did; he didn't even mean to hurt them. He wept as he held out their broken bodies, his soft brown eyes pleading with me to fix them, the way I always fixed his dolls and toys.

Tonight is the new moon, and I dance.

I couldn't fix the children, of course. They were dead, their heads flopping on their necks, their arms and legs pale and limp. My mother ordered the slaves to take them away and give them a proper burial, and I held my brother as he sobbed over the loss of his playmates.

My feet remember the complicated patterns that my mother taught me. She guided me, the cow horns on her head mimicking the shape of the crescent moon above us. She held my hand and laughed encouragement as I followed her, my bare feet marking the black sand strewn over the cold stones of the dancing floor. In the morning, women would crowd around its edge and try to read what our steps had spelled out, the signs made by the feet of She-Who-Is-Goddess mingling with the smaller patterns made by She-Who-Will-Be-Goddess.

When the replacement children died as well, my mother said: no more playmates. My brother wailed and roared in his loneliness, deep beneath the palace, until the Minos took pity and said: just once more. But not children from Krete. The people would stand for it no more, he said.

And so they came in their long ships.

I dance.

CHAPTER 1

THE SHIPS arrived in the spring, shortly before the Planting Festival. I should not have been out watching them, of course. A few years earlier, I would have gone to the harbor with a group of other children, and together we would have played in the black sand, gawked at the foreigners, admired the goods that were unloaded from their ships. Then, two summers before, I had become a woman, and my world had changed, had at once constricted and expanded.

Unlike other girls, I had not found the womanhood ceremony joyful. My mother was happy: that day, I joined her in her sphere, now a sphere encompassing two, where she had been alone since her own mother had died and she became She-Who-Is-Goddess in her place. But as I stood in the palace that day, listening to the chants of the priestesses, responding where appropriate, sweating in the heavy robes that my mother had worn years before when she became She-Who-Will-Be-Goddess, as had her mother and her mother's mother, for as long as time was time, I knew that I was losing almost everything I loved. No more friends, no more playing in the courtyard of the Minos along with his children and my mother's other children. All that was left to me were my mother and my brother Asterion, and although he loved me and I him, he was not good company.

The day of the ships' arrival, when everything began to change, a sweet breeze blew into the palace, announcing that spring was about to arrive. The walls of my home, beautiful as they were with their painted decorations below lofty ceilings, closed in on me. I had overheard one servant telling another that the tribute had arrived from Athens, the principal city of the region of Attika across the sea to the north, and I managed to slip out in the late afternoon, when my mother was sleeping.

I watched from my favorite hiding place, a thick bush halfway up the slope. The ships approached, black and narrow, and pulled into the harbor. People climbed into rowboats that brought them to shore and then disgorged them, some wobbling on unsteady legs, others striding forward as though glad to unkink themselves after the long voyage. I envied those travelers who had come so far, stopping at islands, seeing other lands and other cities, learning what foods other people ate, how they worshiped their goddesses and gods, what clothes they wore.

I would never know what they had seen and what life was like where they had come from. If I crossed the sea, I would cease to be She-Who-Will-Be-Goddess and would become merely Ariadne, priestess and daughter of She-Who-Is-Goddess, but not a deity in training. So I turned my eyes to the newly arrived foreigners and burned with hopeless yearning.

Every nine years, the people of many lands took turns sending tribute to Krete. One year we would receive tin from Tartessos, in another, copper from Kypros, or wheat and ostrich eggs from Aegyptos, or ivory from Aethiopia, or precious amber from the frozen countries to the north. These last lay so far away that sometimes the tall, yellow-haired travelers were delayed a year or even two, and we would have one year with no tribute and then one with double riches.

Eighteen years before, the Minos's oldest and dearest son, Androgeos, had been murdered at the Athenian games. In his rage, the Minos ordered that children of Athens, seven boys and seven girls, must be added to the tribute. Before, the Athenian ships had arrived filled only with luscious green olive oil and the delicate Athenian wine that the Minos particularly liked.

My mother had not interfered. It was her role to order tribute, as well as to direct anything else that affected Krete and its trade, but the right of a father to avenge his son is an ancient and powerful one. She knew how much her brother had loved Androgeos, and further, the people of Athens were led by a king, a warlord who ruled by his might. She knew that they believed, wrongly, that the Minos was her husband

and the ruler of Krete. They would not dare to oppose an enraged father who was also a powerful leader.

In the first shipment, the Athenians had sent sweet, pretty children who would become household slaves and live easy lives, or so the king of Athens evidently hoped. That way, his subjects would not rebel at being forced to pay this precious tribute. Instead, they were sent to work in the mines, where they died quickly. The second time, when I was six years old, the children were made to play with my brother. I don't remember their arrival, although I must have been taken to the harbor as a treat, not yet being She-Who-Will-Be-Goddess. All I remember is their dead bodies. The Minos had been horrified and had relented. The king of Athens was informed that if he included his own son in the next shipment, the Minos would halt the human tribute.

This time I arrived too late to see them disembark, but still I quickly identified the Athenians in the crowd. They were handsome children, well dressed and obviously well fed. The little girls and boys stayed together in a group, some holding hands, some weeping, some laughing and pelting one another with black pebbles. An older boy stood somewhat apart, and I wondered if this was the king's son. A tall girl tried to comfort a wailing boy, who clung to her. I inched forward; they might say something about Athens.

A voice behind me said, "Mistress?" As almost always happened, I had been discovered by a palace servant. It was Iaera, the sister of a girl I used to play with, and she covered her face with her cloak as she spoke. "She-Who-Is-Goddess is looking for you, mistress." I straightened and sighed. It was unthinkable to make my mother wait.

"A woman is in labor," Iaera went on as we hurried up the hill. Before a turn in the road hid the harbor, I cast a look behind me and saw the sun dipping its edge into the sea and the Athenians being led to the palace by the longer but easier road that curved around the slope.

My mother was the only woman on the island of Krete who was unafraid to be outside after dark. Now that I was She-Who-Will-Be-Goddess and any man who touched me would be put to death with unspeakable agony, I, too, could walk under the stars without an escort. This was good, because babies frequently come in the nighttime, and everyone wanted She-Who-Is-Goddess to bless a birth by attending it. My mother and I would often be called in the middle of the night to walk or ride in someone's donkey cart to where a woman was laboring.

Even after I had accompanied her on many of these errands, I was always transfixed by the change when my mother appeared. The laboring woman might be screaming, her damp hair in a tangle over her face as her red eyes glared wildly around the room. Her large belly would convulse as she lay or sat or squatted in a peasant's tiny hut filled with animal smells or a prosperous merchant's house, the thick darkness lightened only by a smoky torch. But when my mother entered, even before her hands moved in a comforting charm, the woman's face would smooth, and then I would recognize her as a fisherman's wife or the woman who sold sandals in the marketplace or the mother of an acquaintance.

Sometimes the laboring woman died, sometimes the baby, but if my mother was there, both usually lived and were well. Even one girl who came out with her skinny bottom first survived. I remember watching as my mother flicked the soles of the baby's narrow feet with her fingertip and vigorously rubbed the chest of the small, slippery thing until she wheezed and then wailed, turning pink in my mother's strong hands. The baby's mother laughed; my own mother and the other women laughed; even I laughed, although I did not know why.

That night, hours after the arrival of the Athenian ships, we walked home from a house that had not been so lucky, where both the mother and her two baby boys, each as small as a fish that I would eat for breakfast, had died. I couldn't put from my mind the sight of those tiny bodies laid out on the dirt floor or the sudden gush of blood that emptied the woman of her life even as she wept over her dead children. Her little son and daughter sat huddled in a corner—the hut was so small that there had been nowhere else for them—the boy stroking his small sister's hair in a vain attempt at comfort as she sucked her thumb. The farmer who was the woman's husband was too stunned to think to offer us the loan of his one donkey. My mother and I slipped out the door, away from the smell of goats and blood and birth, into a night scarcely darker than the windowless shack.

My mother was quiet as we walked, breathing the sweet-scented night air. I didn't try to talk; she was always curt after losing one she had tended, as though angry or disappointed. She knew that the matter was in Goddess's hands, not hers, but each time we saw a mother or a child die, I sensed that she felt she had fallen short of what was expected of her.

I trailed behind. The dust of the road was cool between my toes, and it felt good to straighten my cramped back and legs. My mother stopped and turned, waiting for me to catch up. She slid her hand through my arm and squeezed it, pressing me close to her side, and we continued, hip to hip, my stride nearly matching hers. I took comfort in her warmth.

"They were too small to live, you know." I was surprised to hear her mention the deaths and didn't answer. "Goddess must have changed Her mind about sending the babies into the world. But the mother . . ." She fell silent. It would not do to criticize Goddess, especially when we were walking under Her. I looked up at the cold white eye staring down at us.

"We don't know why She chose to take the woman," my mother said softly. "We can only do our best." She shook my arm gently. "And you are learning so well, my girl. When it comes my time, you will also do your best."

"Your . . . time?"

My mother stopped and pulled her arm out from mine. One of her rare smiles spread across her face, lighting it like the moon coming out from behind a cloud.

"You don't know?" Her smile grew broader. "Look at

me." She turned sideways, smoothing her gown. I felt my jaw drop, and her smile grew to a laugh as I stood goggling at her round belly. How had I not seen?

"Is it . . ." I whispered, and she stopped laughing and shook her head, looping my hair behind my ears.

"Have I taught you nothing? It's been almost a year since the Planting Festival, and the moon will be full three more times before this one comes into the world. No, this baby is not the god's. I was wrong about Ision." The regret in her voice was plain. I, too, missed Ision, the young blacksmith whom my mother had declared the incarnation of the sky god Velchanos at the last Planting Festival. Ision had appeared to enjoy the days that he spent as her consort. He hadn't cried or fought at the end, when his time came to fertilize the fields.

But if this child was conceived months after the Planting Festival, then Ision was not its father, and so he had not truly been the god. This meant that he had died for nothing. I was sorry for that. He had been a sunny and friendly person, and the new blacksmith was sour and silent. I wondered how my mother felt about her error, especially when she saw Ision's wife at work in our laundry.

We resumed walking. We were near the palace now, and dawn was coming, a paler shade of night over the tops of the tall cypress trees that lined the road. The moon followed us, lighting our path. I calculated silently: I was fifteen, my brother three years older. My mother had become She-Who-

Is-Goddess at fourteen. So she was now . . . what? Thirty-three or thirty-four, at least. I had heard of women who had successful pregnancies and deliveries at that age, but it was rare. *Goddess knows what she's doing,* I reminded myself, but I couldn't quench the little flame of fear that tingled in my belly as the sun's edge poked over the top of the palace above us.

It should have been nearly silent, the only sound that of the guards extinguishing the torches that lit the outer walls. But instead there arose the noise of hurrying feet, shouts, the clatter of weapons. My mouth dried until my tongue stuck to its roof. I had never known the palace to be attacked, but late at night, when they thought I was asleep, the women told tales of long-ago raids. We were so strong now, though, that nobody dared. Or so I had always thought.

We ran toward the palace and then stopped, panting, in the shadow of the enormous tree that marked the end of the road. No armed soldiers were running in or out through the wide gate. And now I could hear that the shouts were inter-mingled with a familiar bellowing that echoed off the cold stone walls. I said, "Asterion!" and my mother, her voice tumbling over mine, exclaimed "Your brother!" I scrambled across the big roots, tripped and nearly fell in the semidarkness, and ran toward the gate.

The Minos met us there, barefoot and with his hair disheveled. "Thank Goddess you've returned!" His voice shook as he clutched his cloak. "He has a girl with him and won't let her go."

"What girl?" my mother asked as we hurried together toward my brother's quarters.

"A girl from Athens." I had heard the women whispering that yet another wife for the Minos was among the Athenian tribute. It must be the girl I had seen comforting the little boy down in the harbor. She was pretty, with fine bones and soft-looking brown hair. Asterion liked pretty things, and when Asterion liked something, he sometimes tried to take it apart. I gulped as I imagined what he might do to the delicate girl. My mother, then the Minos, and then I ran down the narrow stairs into the maze of storerooms and corridors under the palace.

The small space outside my brother's chambers was filled with a dozen soldiers, some of them holding blazing torches. Idiots! Hadn't they learned? Some were jabbing their spears through the door, while others shouted and shook their fists. The light from the torches made Asterion's shadow, already distorted, stretch and bob and dance across the wall behind him.

I squeezed between my mother and the Minos, then made my way through the crowd. When I shoved one of the armed men aside, he turned as if to strike me but quickly lowered his eyes at the sight of She-Who-Will-Be-Goddess. Another man noticed me, and then another, and one by one they fell silent.

"Asterion!" I called. He caught sight of me and stretched out one hand in my direction, moaning. His other hand grasped the Athenian maiden's slender wrist. Although she was ashen, no blood was visible. She was even taller than she had appeared from my hiding place above the harbor, although my brother towered over her.

"Go upstairs!" I commanded the soldiers. They hesitated, and a few started to protest. I cut them short. "And take those torches with you! Don't you know he's afraid of fire? Leave me a small lantern." They obeyed. The Minos followed them and then my mother, who shot me a glance that said, "Be careful."

When the small antechamber was empty, I sat down on the floor. "They're gone, brother." He moaned again, and the sound broke my heart. He threw his free arm over his head and roared at the ceiling. I forced myself to sit quietly and wait until his wits, such as they were, returned to him.

My brother had never tried to hurt me. He had not been allowed even to touch me until one day when I toddled away from my dozing nursemaid, Korkyna, and was found, hours later and after a frantic search, asleep on his lap. Asterion had still been a child himself then, though already nearly as tall as a grown man, and he was terribly strong. Korkyna had fainted at the sight of me curled up on my brother's knees, his misshapen head bent over my face. She had thought he was going to eat me, but he nuzzled me and then kissed my forehead.

"What do you have there?" I tried to sound only half interested. Asterion blinked his confusion. I indicated his left arm still stretched behind him, the muscles in his powerful shoulder bulging. The poor girl's wrist would be bruised, if not broken, by that grip.

Asterion looked over his back and seemed surprised to

see what he was holding. She opened her mouth. "Don't speak," I said quickly. "Keep still." She started to nod, then clearly thought better of it and sent me a look of comprehension instead. Good. Intelligence as well as beauty. No wonder the Minos was so eager to have me save her.

"That's not yours," I said. Asterion looked from me to the girl and back again. His face, already misshapen with bulging eyes and bony bumps and ridges, grew even uglier as it wrinkled. The girl closed her eyes.

I knew my brother didn't agree. What found its way into his chamber was his, whether it was food or a rat or an Athenian princess. "No, she isn't," I insisted. "She belongs to the Minos. He wants her back."

Asterion pulled the girl around in front of him, where he clutched her tightly, her face to his chest. I started to rise, then forced myself to sit back down, hoping she could breathe. "When you give her to me, I'll go talk to Cook and see what he can send you." I knew better than to say *if* Asterion released her, which would imply that he had a choice.

He loosened his hold slightly, and the girl tilted her head back to take a breath. "I wonder what you would like." I looked up to the ceiling, pretending to consider. Asterion licked his lips, his gaze fixed on me. "I think I saw some . . ." I drew it out, and he leaned forward, his eyes shining. "I think I saw a pot of honey." His groan was of delight this time. "Yes, I saw some honey, and I think Cook was saving it for the Minos, but when you give me the girl I'll tell him that he has to let you have it instead." Asterion loosened his grip a little more. The girl swiveled her eyes toward me, her brown hair plastered to her head with her sweat or his, or both.

Our mother hated it when Asterion ate honey. He always wound up covering himself in the stickiness, and as he feared water almost as much as he feared fire, it would take me hours to clean it off him. If I didn't, he'd soon be covered in ants, and his roaring as he tried to pull them off with his clumsy fingers would disturb everyone in the palace. But it would be worth it if I could free that girl before he broke something in her slim body.

I stood up and shook out my skirt. "I hope the Minos hasn't eaten it already. He looked hungry when I came in."

Asterion made an impatient sound.

"No, I won't go look. I have to take the girl with me or he'll say that you can't have her *and* the honey. One or the other."

In the end it was that simple. Honey or the girl, and he chose the honey. I held my breath while he considered, afraid that another word or move on my part would make him squeeze her again. But then he released her. He watched sadly as she glided toward me, eyes fixed on the ground. I had been afraid that she would break into a run, but she knew better, and my brother made no attempt to grab her again. She continued through the door.

"I'll be back soon," I promised. Asterion nodded and licked his lips.

"Come on." I caught up with the girl and took her arm,

leading her down a corridor and then around a corner. We passed the stairway that I had used to descend into my brother's chambers and headed for another. The girl trotted to keep up with me.

"Where are we going?" She spoke with a musical Athenian accent.

"To the kitchen." I hurried up the stairs. "I just hope there's some honey."

CHAPTER 2

HONEY THERE WAS indeed, in a small stone pot tightly fitted with a lid made even more secure against insects with a layer of wax. I sat with my arms around my knees and watched Asterion as he ate, dipping his clumsy fingers into the golden stickiness and sucking them, his large, wide-set eyes rolling.

When he had finished, he licked the inside of the honey jar until even he could tell that he had scoured it clean. I stood and put out my hand. My brother looked at the round little pot, evidently decided that keeping it wasn't worth an argument, and extended it to me. He couldn't go any farther, so I stepped closer and took it. His fingers closed lightly around mine, and he made a soft sound.

"You want me to stay a little while?" I asked. He nodded eagerly, his long black curls—his only beauty—flopping over his uneven eyes. Of course our mother had ordered his hair cut when he'd turned twelve, but the shearing had had to be done without the ceremony expected when the god's son reached young manhood. I still shuddered when I remembered his screams as the men pinned him to the ground while the barber worked so fast that both he and Asterion wound up smeared with blood. No one had dared approach my brother with shears since then, and his lustrous black hair now hung past his shoulders.

I moved closer so I could reach my brother's face. I stood on tiptoe and pushed his hair back, off his bumpy forehead. He grinned and shook his head so that the shiny curls once more fell forward. I laughed. This was one of his favorite games, to tease me by undoing some small bit of work I had done.

It must have been the lack of sleep, the sight of the pale dead babies and their suddenly blue-lipped mother, or the shock of the encounter with the Athenian girl, for even in the midst of my laughter, tears stung my eyes. I bit my lip and looked away. If Asterion saw me weeping, he would become distressed, and I had noticed no more jars marked with a bee in the storeroom.

To distract him, I revealed the damp cloth that I had concealed behind my back. Better to be angry at a washing than terrified at the sight of his sister weeping. Asterion grunted a protest but allowed me to get the worst of the stickiness off his hands and from around his mouth. When he had clearly had enough, I stopped. I could finish later.

"Good boy," I said, and he grinned again, his crooked teeth showing. He touched one of the gold earrings that dangled almost to my shoulders. "Gentle," I warned, and he lowered his hand.

I stayed only a little longer, and when I left, he didn't try to follow me. A few years earlier, my mother had had him placed here below the palace, where his roaring wouldn't frighten people. She'd had to recast her binding spell several times, winding the black yarn into one complex pattern after another. Finally, the spell worked; he couldn't move from the two small chambers at the heart of the underground warren of storerooms and corridors, but he was not held so firmly that he felt and fought against his invisible bonds. Now he moaned and then bellowed his version of my name—"Adne! *Adne!*"—as I took one turn and then another, his loneliness following me upstairs and nearly to the women's sitting room.

After the near dark of the underground chamber, the daylight coming in between the columns was almost dazzling. I inhaled deeply to clear my lungs. We kept Asterion as clean as we were able, but a full bath was impossible unless we made him so drunk that he lost either his fear or the ability to fight, and the odors of his dank chamber were never pleasant. Here, the early-spring air mingled with the aroma of warm bread, and I suddenly realized that it was a long time since I had eaten.

The morning light was weak, and the shapes on the walls appeared almost real, not mere figures painted by a long-dead artist in the days when my mother's grandmother had been She-Who-Is-Goddess. The dimness hid the artist's brush strokes on the parade of slim-hipped young women and men who bore platters of springtime fruits and greens and who led tiny white lambs so new that their large eyes appeared to look with wonder at the world they were soon to leave. I almost expected to see the celebrants' legs move in the solemn procession, to smell the heavy scent of flowers in the garlands draped over the columns behind them, to hear their voices lifted in song in praise of Goddess. She stood facing them, bare breasted, a smile on Her lips, clutching two writhing snakes whose painted tongues seemed almost to flicker in and out of their painted mouths.

I caught sight of the Athenian woman. She was seated on a bench near the opening between two large columns, eating the flatbread that Cook made by spreading dough directly onto the coals of the huge kitchen fireplace. At the sight of its crusty top and its bottom darkened by ash, my stomach gave a loud gurgle. Cook, who was entering, laughed and patted the bench where the woman destined to be the Minos's newest wife was sitting. I, too, sat down but wished I didn't feel so awkward. I didn't often see strangers, at least not to talk to, and I didn't know how to behave. Cook handed me my own piece of bread wrapped in a white cloth, along with a pot of fig preserves and a wooden spoon, taking care not to touch me. I knocked off the cinders and took a bite.

That pot reminded me of the honey jar, which I pulled from my robe and handed to Cook. Then I spooned preserves into the crescent that my teeth had left in the bread. The sweetness of the figs combined with the bitterness of the slightly blackened crust was one of my favorite treats.

"Sorry," I said around a mouthful as Cook looked into the jar's emptiness.

"A small price to pay if it kept her safe." Cook nodded at the young woman.

"I'm very grateful." She bit off a piece of bread glistening with golden preserves and washed it down with a swallow of what looked like honey water.

Her musical accent made even these conventional words sound lovely. From close up, she was even prettier than I had thought her before, when she had stood motionless in my brother's grip. Her brown hair, so different from the black ringlets of most of the people I knew, looked as soft as rabbit's fur. Her clear eyes were the nameless blue-green-gray of the sea, and her oval face shone with clear brightness. Her small teeth were white and even.

She was looking at me quizzically. I dropped my gaze and asked, "Why did you go down there, anyway?"

Her laugh was merry. "My mother always says that I'm as curious as a mouse. I wanted to see him—the Minotauros."

I choked on the piece of bread that was halfway down my throat. How dare she call my brother by that name? It made him sound like the son of the Minos and a bull. Cook stood behind me as I spluttered.

Before I had become a woman, Cook would have pounded my back to help me, but of course he couldn't strike She-Who-Will-Be-Goddess, so I coughed and wheezed. When at last I could breathe shallowly without my breath catching,

I glanced up and saw the warning frown that Cook was shooting over my head at the Athenian woman.

She seemed about to say something more, but then one of the Minos's eunuchs poked his head through the door. "He's asking for the new one." He looked from her to me, and I nodded. My pleasure in the girl's company was spoiled, anyway.

My companion rose and straightened her fine linen gown, which was arranged in narrow pleats in the style of mainland women, a thin belt emphasizing her small waist. I stood too and saw that she was examining my clothes as carefully as I was hers. I looked down at my serviceable robe, the one I always wore to childbirths. It fit appropriately but was stained from my work. The dark red smear was new, and once again I thought of that dead woman and her dead babies. I looked back at the girl and opened my mouth to speak.

Then an image rose up and floated in front of her face. I couldn't make it out clearly, but I could tell that it was evil, a miasma that stank of treachery and arrogance and murder.

I closed my eyes and ordered the vision to depart. When I opened them again, it was gone, but so was the girl. She was following the Minos's servant down a long corridor open to the rapidly warming sun, her slender form flickering as she passed through the shadows of the columns. I tried to call out, to warn her to beware of whatever it was that I had seen, but my throat clamped shut and I watched her until she disappeared.

CHAPTER 3

I AROSE after noon, still groggy, and went to find my mother. Iaera stood in her doorway, blocking my way. At my inquiring look, she said, "A messenger from the Pythia— She-Who-Is-Goddess at Delphi—came with the Athenians. She's been in there since midday."

I settled myself on a stool. Every She-Who-Is-Goddess is sister to every other one, although they never meet in person, as crossing the sea would strip them of their divinity and render them mere priestesses. They exchange news and greetings and even spells, I understood. Someday I would be part of that sisterhood as well.

A small woman scurried out. I rose and attempted to greet her, but she hastened away without meeting my gaze.

My mother was seated at a table facing the sun, now low in the sky, with two skeins of yarn in front of her. Instead of joining them together in the complicated series of knots that meant she was casting a spell, she gazed off into the distance, her hands idle. I knew better than to interrupt her reverie, so I stood and waited.

The yarn was of two shades of green and so must have something to do with the Planting Festival. The black ball that kept Asterion confined under the palace lay locked tight in the fragrant cedar chest at the foot of her bed, along with others in which magic was still working. The most precious of them, as large as a baby's head and pure white, lay inside the chest in its own casket made of gleaming dark wood as hard as bronze. It was decorated with very powerful gold symbols whose meaning had been lost to time. More than once I had seen my mother seated at her work table, this box open in front of her as she stared at the white ball. I could tell that she was trying to understand the way it was wound. She did not dare unwind it to find out, of course. It held the power of She-Who-Is-Goddess. Nobody said what would happen if it was destroyed, but it would surely be a catastrophe.

Occasionally, my mother would call me to her and have me hold pieces of yarn as she worked them up, over, and around each other, all the while staring at the white ball as though she would unlock its secret with her gaze.

This white ball was rarely touched. One time in her life, each She-Who-Will-Be-Goddess held it during the ritual in which she became She-Who-Is-Goddess. I had a very hazy notion of what else happened during the ceremony. Only two priestesses remained who had officiated when my mother be-came She-Who-Is-Goddess. They occasionally dropped hints and seemed to delight in making me nervous.

"Child?" My mother's voice sounded tired. "Have you finally slept enough?" Her tone held no rebuke, but her pale and drained face shamed me. I saw that she had one of her headaches, so without being asked I moved behind her and pulled the pins out of her hair. It came down in soft waves. She dropped her work, sighed, and leaned back against me, her eyes closed. I gently rubbed her temples, where a few silver strands showed among the black. After some minutes she asked, "What's she like?"

"Who?"

"The new one." Her voice held no emotion. "The Minos's new wife."

"Pleasant." I fumbled for words. My mother didn't usually show much interest in the Minos's wives beyond making sure they were comfortable and had enough to eat. "Pretty."

"I saw that. As did Asterion."

I stopped rubbing her head. "He can't help it, Mother."

"No, he can't."

I ran my fingers under her hair again and pressed where I somehow could tell it hurt. She sighed and relaxed. "She's from Athens." My mother didn't answer, so I tried again. "Athens, Mother!"

She sat up abruptly and tied back her hair. "And so? Athens is a city like any other."

"How do you know?" Of course, my mother had never left the island of Krete. "I hear it has a mountain right in the middle of the city and the people worship Athena and Erechtheus—they must be very strong if they have two gods! The fields of Attika are beautiful, they say, and the beaches are of yellow sand. Think of it, yellow sand instead of black! You could walk on it all day without burning your feet."

She looked at me gravely but did not respond. She didn't have to remind me of the consequences that would attend a sea voyage.

"The trip must not have taken very long, Mother—she looked fresh and well when she stepped off the boat . . ." I realized I had betrayed myself and stopped. "I mean, I *hear* she looked fresh," I said lamely as my mother's face clouded over.

"What were you doing down by the docks?" I had no answer. "Daughter, don't you know that that is the one place that's dangerous for us—for you and me? All sorts of people are on the ships that come in. Some are decent folk and respect us, but many do not."

"Goddess will protect me," I muttered, and instantly recognized my mistake.

"You know Goddess is angry with me."

What my mother had done to offend Goddess I did not know, but Her wrath had started before I was born and continued despite everything we did to appease Her. My mother and I danced at every new moon, not just before the Festivals; countless snow-white heifers had had their throats slit on

Goddess's altar, their tender meat feeding the twelve priestesses who served Her; my mother tended the white Goddess-shaped stone in the shrine as carefully as a new mother tends to her firstborn, rubbing it with oil until it gleamed, wrapping it in rich robes purchased from traders who traveled from so far away that they spoke a language no one could comprehend.

Yet Goddess continued to visit my mother with punishment, most notably through Asterion. More than one man had offered to sacrifice himself to the wrath of Goddess by killing my brother, but my mother always refused. It was not her love for him that stopped her; the real problem was that no other could take his place. My brother was Minos-Who-Will-Be. Without a Minos, our city of Knossos would fall, and with it, the island of Krete. This we knew as surely as we knew that the sun rose and set once every day and that the moon disappeared and reappeared thirteen times every year.

My mother broke the silence. "I should go to the Minos's quarters and make sure the girl has everything she needs."

"I'll go." I tried to hide my eagerness. "I've been sleeping all day, and you've been working."

"She who is served by all serves all," she murmured.

I nodded at the familiar phrase. "And you have a headache. I'll go and make sure the new one is settling in, and while I'm there I'll see how Glaukos is." The rosy-cheeked child always ran to me when I visited and tugged at my hand to beg me to play with him. His right eye looked to the side as if watching something that no one else could see, something in another world. Worse, he favored his left hand, which made everyone uneasy. It was not natural, but despite his nurses' attempts to make him use his right hand, he persisted.

She-Who-Will-Be-Goddess has to help people, of course, to be kind to them and assure their safety. But she must not grow close to them, not to the children of mortal parents, no matter who those parents were. Glaukos had been conceived by my mother when she was a mortal woman, not Goddess, and his father was a man, not the god Velchanos, so Glaukos was not my brother. If my mother knew that I was growing attached to any one of the children who lived in the Minos's quarters— even if that child was hers—she would forbid me to visit.

"So, may I go to the Minos's quarters and see to the new wife?"

"You liked her, did you?"

I nodded. "I think she might be . . ." I hesitated; it was not a word I said often. "I think she might become a friend." I didn't want to hear what my mother had said so many times before: *You don't need a friend. You have me and Asterion, and if it pleases Goddess, you will have other brothers and sisters. And now you have your duties as priestess. You don't have time for friends.* She gave me permission, though, with a reminder to walk with dignity.

I dreaded going through the palace. It was not only that the dark and twisting corridors took longer than a direct route would have; it was not only that the halls and chambers were tedious in their familiarity. No, the real reason was that it was full of people who would be talking to one another, sometimes laughing, and both the talk and the laughter would cease as soon as they saw me. I always longed to tell them that I, too, liked conversation and a funny story and a hand on my arm as a confidence is told, but of course I couldn't. So I would lower my eyes to the ground, acknowledge their bows with a quick nod, and hurry on.

This time I thought I would be lucky enough to reach the Minos's quarters without meeting anyone. Two women carrying plucked partridges pretended not to notice me and ducked into a chamber until I passed, as though that had been their destination all along. The room they had entered was where the scribes sat all day incising marks into clay tablets, and there was no need for partridges in there. I couldn't resist glancing behind me, and I saw them emerge hurriedly and scurry down to where they were truly going, no doubt eager to tell people of their near encounter with She-Who-Will-Be-Goddess.

A tiny girl lurched out of a room where women were chatting and working on a large loom, and she grabbed my knees as her unsteady legs failed her. I stopped, and she grinned toothlessly up at me, her curls bobbing. As I reached down to touch her smooth cheek, a woman inside the room looked up, gave a stifled shriek, and ran out. She snatched the child away from me, then bowed so low that she folded over the little girl, who wailed in protest as she was squeezed.

"Pardon, p-pardon," the woman stammered, and she backed away, clutching the now-screaming child, until they both disappeared into the weaving room, where the talk and laughter had suddenly ceased.

I stood in the corridor and struggled with myself. I knew that woman; her oldest daughter, Timandra, had been my favorite playmate when we were little girls. She had fed me treats along with her own children, had comforted me when I fell from a tree, had scolded me when Timandra and I wandered too near the pen where the sacred bull was housed. Did the foolish woman really think I would harm my old playmate's sister?

I wanted to stamp into the weaving room and demand that they talk to me, that they not make their children fear me. *There's no reason to be afraid,* I wanted to say. *Even if I wanted to hurt someone, I don't know how. And I* don't *want to.* But this would only frighten them more. So I turned and continued on my way, trying to squeeze the tears back into my eyes.

Then I heard more voices, this time men's and women's mingling. Although it was difficult to tell in those twisting and crisscrossing corridors, the speakers appeared to be coming directly toward me. If it was awkward meeting women unexpectedly, it was a thousand times worse when I saw a man. They would always make a fist with the thumb sticking out between their clenched fingers in the sign that averts evil, and no matter how discreetly they tried to do it, I always saw them pointing it at me.

I didn't think I could bear that now, not after my disturbed night and the deaths of that woman and her children.

Without looking where I was going, I ducked into another hallway, but it turned almost immediately, leading me back in the direction I had come from. I looked around wildly; by now, the desire to escape these unknown people had become an urgent need. Only one remaining corridor led away from them, and I plunged down it.

CHAPTER 4

I RAN DOWN the hall without noticing where I was heading, trying only to distance myself from that merry band. Suddenly I found myself in the Arena of Velchanos. The enormous hall was lit by slanting light coming through windows placed near the high ceiling, and although no bulls were present, their smell lingered in the straw and dirt. A group of boys clustered against the far wall. Some were small, still with the round belly of childhood, and few appeared to have even the beginnings of a beard. Simo, an unpleasant boy I had known since my childhood, surveyed the stands seeming to consider the people soon to be sitting there barely worthy of his notice. Next to him stood his friend Enops, who was a little older than me, and at the end of the line was little Glaukos. I liked Enops, whose easygoing way with me had become tempered with respect when I became She-Who-Will-Be-

Goddess. Glaukos was sweet, and I didn't like the thought of him dancing near the sharp horns of the huge bull that would soon be in this arena.

A man stood with them, his back turned to me. I recognized him from the long white scar that wrapped around his ribs: Lysias, the greatest of the bull dancers in his day, who had survived being chosen by the god. The god had gored him during his first Planting Festival ritual, and now Lysias trained boys who were to put themselves to the test.

I should not have been there. Even though these boys were merely training and were not yet ready to meet the god, preparation for the men's rituals were as sacred as those for the women's, and a violation would cause a great deal of bother, as the area would have to be resanctified. Ever since I had become She-Who-Will-Be-Goddess, my mere presence was enough to disrupt the balance of a sacred space. But so far, I had escaped their notice, and I hesitated to attract attention by moving.

Then I saw that I was not alone in the viewing stands. A man stood a few yards away, resting his elbows on the fence that divided the practice area from the spectators' benches. He, too, had his back to me, and his stocky form and broad shoulders were not familiar. I thought he must be an outlander; Kretan men were almost always more slender than this stranger. At the man's feet lay a large dog with wavy, cream-colored fur. Its long ears hung down, instead of being pricked up like those of our dogs, giving it the appearance of a giant puppy. The dog caught sight of me and rose on its long legs. It trotted to my hiding place and fixed me with its eyes. I am fond of dogs, so I extended my hand. It sniffed my fingers, its plumed tail waving gently.

"Who are you?" I whispered, and the dark eyes looked at me as though wanting to answer. I had just made up my mind to slip away when the dog's head shot out and its teeth clamped on my wrist. A deep voice exclaimed something, and a large brown hand clouted the dog's head away. The dog cringed and squirmed on its belly to its master, licking the hand that had struck it, reminding me of the one thing I didn't like about dogs.

"Did she hurt you?" the man asked. No, it was a boy, but he was mostly grown. He had the darkened skin of one who spends time outdoors. His brown hair and short beard—the beard confirmed that he was not from Krete, where most men are clean-shaven—were streaked with a lighter color where the sun had touched them. His teeth flashed white as he spoke. Despite his hair being cut in an odd way—short in front and hanging down past his shoulders in back—he was handsome. To my surprise he looked directly at me, and I recognized him as the boy I had seen at the port the day before.

I glanced at my wrist. Red marks that would turn bluish purple appeared on both sides, but the skin had not been broken.

"Did the dog hurt you?" the boy repeated, his lilting

voice sounding impatient. I was unaccustomed to being directly addressed by anyone, especially a stranger and a foreigner, and I didn't know how to answer. I shook my head and clutched my wrist in my other hand, trying to think what to say—*Had* the dog hurt me? Was a ring of bruises an injury?—when five of the Minos's guards ran up to us, their long hair flying behind them.

"What happened?" asked Gnipho, the senior of the guards present. Gray streaks ran through the long hair under his cap, which was decorated with two small horns indicating his seniority, and the cloak thrown over his wiry form bore the double stripe of an officer.

"The dog was playing," the boy said gruffly. "Grabbed the young lady's arm in her teeth. No harm done."

"The young la—" Gnipho stopped, looking appalled at hearing me referred to in such an offhand manner. He went on stiffly, his eyes fixed on the ground near my feet, "She-Who-Will-Be-Goddess was not hurt?"

"No," I said.

"I will report as much. Guard, kill the animal."

A younger man grabbed the dog's collar from behind and pressed his knee into her back. He let go of the collar to seize the animal's muzzle, and the dog's body convulsed in an effort to free herself, as a whine escaped her. The guard pulled her head back sharply, stretching the long neck, while reaching for the knife in his belt with his free hand. The boy made a sound of protest and stepped forward, but in an instant the other three guards were holding their spears at his throat.

"No," a voice said. It took me a moment to realize that it was mine.

The men paused in their various tasks and glanced at me before hurriedly removing their gaze to the floor, the air, a point in the distance. Only the dog's owner kept his eyes fixed on me. They were as black as sand, and they glittered as a hint of a smile crinkled the lids.

"I'm not harmed," I said. "The dog was merely playing. Release it."

They hesitated. I let go of my wrist and allowed my right hand to drift up, fingers curling. The guards stared at it, and fear loosened their limbs even as their knuckles turned white with the strength of their grips on their weapons. The men around the dog's owner lowered their spears and stepped back. "Release it," I said again, and this time the guard holding the big dog stepped back and allowed her to rise. She surged to her feet and moved next to her master, pressing against his legs. His hand came down and rested on her head. It looked brown and sinewy among the bright waves.

I dropped my arm. "Leave," I said. The guards bowed and backed away, turning when they were barely seven paces distant, and fled. They stopped and regrouped in the doorway, but at least they were out of earshot. It was the best I could hope for; I could order them to go farther away, but if I did, my mother would surely hear of it.

The boy kept his hand on the dog's head. He looked at me again, this time up and down my whole body, appraising me. I flushed. I knew I should be angry, but instead I felt oddly excited and even pleased that he was looking at me the way I had seen men look at other girls—not at the floor in front of my feet, not at a point somewhere above my head.

"What was it he called you?" His voice was amused, and I flushed again. Now he would behave like the others. Perhaps he would even drop to the ground and lay his forehead on my feet and beg for forgiveness. Somehow, I didn't want to see that broad form bent in humility at my knees.

"I am She-Who-Will-Be-Goddess." I waited for him to stammer an apology at the very least, now that he knew who I was. Instead, his face continued to hold a half smile as his fingers lightly stroked the head of the dog.

"Is that what everybody calls you?"

"What else?"

He shrugged. "What does your mother call you?"

This was where I made my first mistake. My second, really; the first was not withdrawing from the practice arena as soon as I'd seen where I was. Perhaps if I hadn't offended the god by remaining, he would have averted all the disaster that was to follow and tonight I would still be at home, on

Krete, dancing on the ancient floor under the crescent moon while holding my daughter's small hand and showing her the steps that have been passed down from She-Who-Is-Goddess to She-Who-Will-Be-Goddess since time was time.

But that's not how it happened. I told the stranger my name. And at that moment everything began to unravel, the way a tug on an end of yarn makes the whole ball, once firm and round, turn into a meaningless, useless tangle.

CHAPTER 5

ARIADNE," I said. "My name is Ariadne."

The foreign boy bowed. "A fitting name. 'Most holy.' I am Theseus."

The only people whose names can be pronounced with no threat, who can reveal their real names to others without fear, are either so utterly powerless that they have nothing to risk—like small children or my brother—or so strong that nobody would dare try to harm them. It was brave of this Theseus to trust me, a stranger, with his name. I, of course, had nothing to fear by telling him mine, yet out of respect most people avoided saying it.

"But they address you by another name. She-Who-Will-Be-Goddess?" I nodded. "So . . . you will be a goddess one day?" Something in his voice made me squirm. It wasn't quite mockery, but also not the reverence I expected or the fear that would strike most people. I murmured a confirmation.

"And how is that?" The amusement I was certain I heard this time stung. The dog at the boy's side looked up at him and then at me.

"My mother is She-Who-Is-Goddess." I didn't care that my voice was stiff. Let him see that he had offended me. "When she joins our grandmothers, the moon, and becomes Goddess Forever along with them, I will be She-Who-Is-Goddess."

A brief silence, then, "Forgive me. I really am trying to understand. We don't have such goddesses in my country."

"What?" I was astonished. "You have no moon?"

"Of course we have the moon and of course we worship her, but she doesn't walk among us."

How sad, I thought, *to know Goddess only as a light in the night sky that comes and goes!* Even the smallest children in Krete know about She-Who-Is-Goddess and She-Who-Will-Be-Goddess. They know who we are and what we do. They also have some confused ideas about our power, which is why they fear us. Did this Theseus really not know? Were the homes and customs of foreigners so utterly different? If Goddess did not walk among them, how did babies enter the world, and how did the Athenians ensure that their crops would grow?

I thought of the feasting and the merriment of the Planting Festival, and of sweet Ision. He had smiled and waved to his wife and son as the Minos led him out that final morning of last year's Festival. The woman and the boy had clung to each other, as motionless as the stone streaked with dark stains that stood alone in the field under the mild spring sun. The two didn't move while the Minos's men bound Ision's hands to the bolts driven into the stone's corners. The smile stayed on the blacksmith's face even when the shining knife in the Minos's fist came down and opened the doorway to his life. The Minos caught the blood in the bowls used only once a year and handed them to his priests. They ran, letting it splash and drip over the fields, quickly, before it clotted and refused to bestow its blessing anymore. Only then did the skin of Ision's face go slack and the light leave his eyes, and finally the smile slid down until it disappeared.

The memory fled as Theseus asked, "Are you unwell?" and I saw him standing in front of me, solid and strong, the blood beating in a pulse on his temple, his lips red and full, not blueish and withered like Ision's.

Before I could speak, a manservant approached. He bowed, then said to Theseus, "The Minos is waiting."

Theseus started, as though coming out of a dream, and said, "What? Sundown already?" Together we looked out the window, which was placed high in the wall so that the light wouldn't strike the bull dancers' eyes. We were facing east and could not see how far the sun had sunk, but the wisps of clouds were tinged with pink and the sky behind them was darkening. It was too late for me to continue to the Minos's quarters; my mother would forbid me to visit again soon if I appeared to have spent so much time there.

So I inclined my head when Theseus bowed to me, and watched as the guards escorted him out the north door of the arena, which would lead most directly to the Minos's quarters. When his stocky form had disappeared, I hurried back to my mother's room.

She still sat at her table, but now she was strumming the strings of her small lyre. Good; her headache must be better, and when she played music she never noticed the passage of time. I sat next to her. She came to the end of the tune—a song about decorating their homes with green boughs and dancing and feasting that children sing during the Festival of Birth of the Sun—put down her lyre, stretched, and yawned.

"Did you see the Athenian girl?"

I mumbled, "No." She pushed her stool away from the table and stood up, moving stiffly. *If you can keep a secret,* I thought, *if She-Who-Is-Goddess can hide the reason for Goddess's wrath from She-Who-Will-Be-Goddess, I can keep my own counsel too.* So I didn't mention Theseus.

"Come," my mother said. "Let's see what Cook has made for our supper." I reached up to push back the curtain hanging over the doorway, and my sleeve fell back. I saw on my wrist a crescent of red marks, already turning purple, made by the teeth of the dog I had last seen trotting quietly behind her master. We continued toward the sitting room, and through the columns the moon rose, and hung huge and yellow over the city of Knossos.

CHAPTER 6

ARKAS LANDS a blow on my chin, but it hardly shakes me. He's quick but he's small, and if he didn't have two friends with him, he would never have waylaid me. I aim a kick at his groin, but he skips out of the way and jeers, and then his fist connects with my ear. I swear and manage to punch him full in the gut. He doubles over, gagging. I close in to flatten him, and he whips a knife out of some hidden fold of his tunic and waves it at me.

Arkas has never used a weapon before—not a real weapon, anyway. Rocks, sticks, sheep's dung forced into my nose and mouth while four of his friends held me down, yes, but never before something with an edge. The sight of the light glinting off it wakens something in me, and I grab a large piece of driftwood from the ground and block the knife as it flashes.

The blade sticks into the wood, and I hurl the stick far away, the knife with it.

I lunge at him, but his two friends are quicker, and now a fourth boy joins them. They pummel me, as does Arkas when he's recovered his breath, and one of them thrusts out a foot and trips me just as I think I'm about to grab another one by the hair.

I try to get up, but a foot kicks me in the rear and I sprawl forward onto my belly, to the laughter of my tormentors. If I try again, Arkas will just repeat the action, and so I lie flat, panting, and pray for them to go away.

"Bastard!" someone jeers. I don't turn to see who it is; it's what everyone calls me.

"Son of no one!"

It's not fair. I'm hardly the only person in Troizena with an unknown father. Many people live with a crowd of half brothers and half sisters with different fathers, some of them unknown. Yet it is only *my* parentage that causes scorn.

The other women of the village who find themselves pregnant and unmarried are content to admit that they don't know who the father is or to say that he is someone they can't or don't want to marry. My mother, on the other hand, claims that my father was a god—specifically, Poseidon, lord of the sea and of earthquakes—and for this piece of nonsense as well as for what the others call her arrogance for not mixing with them, I must be punished.

Still, it isn't *my* fault. I've never said that Poseidon was my father. If there were something godly about me, surely I would know it. Whenever Arkas or one of his dimwitted followers dared to rub my face in the dirt and twist my arm up behind me until my fingers went numb, I would be able to strike him down—or my father, if he were indeed a god, would come to my aid.

Someone kicks me in the ribs as you would a lazy donkey. They want me to get on my feet. If I do, they'll just knock me down again. I won't give them that satisfaction, so after a few more attempts they give up. They walk past me one by one, spit on me, and leave. Their raucous laughter and shouts continue down the path that leads to the sea, where they will no doubt amuse themselves by tearing the legs off crabs and throwing stones at seagulls.

When I'm sure they've gone, I push myself up and inspect the damage. Not bad, considering how many of them there were. A skinned elbow, a knee in the same condition, a painful red mark on ankle that I know will soon turn blue. My sore sides are the worst, but when I inhale deeply I don't feel the stab of a broken rib. My tunic, which I wear long and belted like the rest of the boys, is filthy. I find a new tear in the cloth under my right arm.

One thing I don't have to worry about is that my mother will scold me for fighting or even for damaging my clothing. If she notices my condition at all, she won't think it worth mentioning. Nor will my stepfather, Konnidas, say anything, although my cuts and bruises will cause his eyes to soften, and he'll lay a hand on my head or shoulder.

So I go home.

Mother is sitting on the stone bench outside the house, spinning fluffy white wool on a hand spindle while ducks waddle past her in a line, their backsides wagging from side to side as they make their way to the pond. A shadow of something flying overhead skims across the yard, and the oldest duck, mother to the rest of them, quacks in alarm, spreading her wings to protect the others, but it's only a swallow, and after shaking their feathers and discussing the matter, the ducks continue on.

My mother glances up and smiles vaguely before going back to her work. "Hello, darling," she says. "Been playing with your friends?" At sixteen, I am much too old to be playing, and I've never had any friends, but she never seems to know this, no matter how many times I tell her. I merely grunt. "That's nice," she says.

"Where's Konnidas?"

"Out, I think. Or maybe inside."

I should have known better than to ask; the odds of her knowing his whereabouts are slim. I duck my head to go through the doorway, and look inside the house. The dirt floor of the one room is packed hard and clean, through my stepfather's efforts, and coals glow in the hearth, ready to flare into flame for the supper that he will cook. The shelves are filled with dried fruit, cheese wrapped in vine leaves, and jugs of wine. Thanks to Konnidas's prudence, we can last out the winter in comfort.

My stepfather isn't inside. The sun is shining, and the air, although cool, is pleasant. He must surely be checking on the olive trees and vineyard, making ready for the spring. I rummage in the bin and find some of yesterday's bread. It's hard, but there's plenty of it, so I tear off a chunk with difficulty and go back outside.

My mother has let her work fall to her lap and is gazing at two red birds fluttering together on the other side of the dirt yard. "Look at them," she says as I drop down next to her and commence gnawing on the bread. "Like dancing flowers."

I glance at them, and they look like birds. "What are you working on?" I ask around the chunk of bread that refuses to soften.

She appears surprised to see the yarn in her hands. "This?" She gives the drop spindle a twirl and feeds in a bit more wool. The lumpy strand of yarn lengthens. "I'm making it as a kindness for your aunt." I know the kindness is all on my aunt's part. She'll pay my mother good money for worthless yarn, and my mother will complain to Konnidas about her sister's stinginess.

Just as I think of my stepfather, he appears, wearing his long gray tunic, as usual, his hair pushed back and falling almost to his shoulders. He is clean-shaven and is tall and thin. At his side paces the largest dog I've ever seen, cream white and long legged, its elegant face framed by long ears.

"Oh!" my mother exclaims as she rises to her feet, her wool and spindle forgotten. "How lovely!"

Konnidas watches her, a fond smile on his lips, as she lifts the dog's slender muzzle with one hand. She rests her other hand on its head, and then strokes the long, silky-looking fur. "A trader was selling her down at the docks," my stepfather says. "She comes from someplace far to the east and far to the north, where her kind is used to hunt wolves."

My mother croons to the animal. Konnidas doesn't seem to notice that she hasn't thanked him. It always makes him happy to please her, though surely he knows that after a few days of treating the dog like a spoiled child, even allowing it into the house, she will forget all about it, and its care will fall to the two of us. She did the same with an orphaned lamb last spring, eventually neglecting it until it became necessary for Konnidas to slaughter the little thing. She ate it as greedily as a child and pretended to have no idea that the meat came from her formerly beloved pet.

As my mother disappears into the house with her new charge, Konnidas turns to me and starts to say something, but he stops and his smile fades as he sees my cuts and scrapes. "The same boys? Arkas and his friends?" I shrug, surprised that he asked. Usually he lets my injuries go unmentioned. "Did you attempt to defend yourself?"

"There were six of them," I say, even though in actuality there were only four. I'm stung: my stepfather made it sound as if I was a coward.

"Still, if you take them one at a time . . . you're bigger than any of them." He's right; I am not tall, but I am broad, and I can plow and cut wood better and faster than the others. It's a little unfair, though, to ask me to stand up alone to six—or even four—boys.

Konnidas has his hands on his hips, and he's staring at me with his lower lip caught between his teeth, as is his habit when thinking hard. He turns to follow my mother.

The bread sits in my stomach like a rock. From inside the house come low voices, first Konnidas's, then my mother's, then Konnidas's again, a little louder and firmer now. I sit up straighter. My stepfather is *never* firm with my mother. I have heard men snicker at him as he goes to the market with their wives while they stay home and work the land, but he never seems to notice, much less care.

My stepfather's next words surprise me: "You must tell him." He can mean only me. Her answer, if it could be called that, is a little ripple of nervous laughter. Whatever he's urging my mother to tell me, I know I won't much like it. Konnidas's next words echo my thoughts. "If you don't, I will. And you might not like the way I tell it." His voice is suddenly clear; he must be standing in the doorway.

"I can't imagine why you're so insistent." She has joined him at the door. I don't turn around, but I picture her laying a hand on his arm. "He doesn't ever really need to know."

"Can't you see how miserable he is?" And then I make out nothing more. Konnidas must have retreated back inside, and the only murmuring after that is in his deep voice, with no reply from my mother.

I know that she'll win. She almost always does, and on the rare occasions when she doesn't, she sheds rivers of tears and then turns silent until Konnidas or I, whichever of us has been the offender, appeases her with apologies and a gift. I once trekked the three miles to the beach and spent all day turning over shells until I found one whose inside was of the soft pink that she adored, only to find that, when I returned, she hadn't noticed my absence. Still, her casual "Thank you, darling" and the accompanying kiss on my forehead made me glow like the shell itself.

So when Konnidas finally emerges and says, "Your mother has something to tell you," I am astonished, and I rise to my feet with dread.

She appears to have forgotten their argument and comes peacefully enough out of the house, the long-legged dog following her. My mother sits down on the bench and picks up her clump of wool and the spindle. My stepfather, however, is clearly determined to discuss the matter at hand. His mild face looks resolute as he says, "Aethra." She makes no answer, although I can tell by the way she doubles her attentions to the misshapen yarn that she has heard. But he will not be ignored. He removes the spindle from her hand, gently but firmly. "No," he says. "You promised."

The few times that my mother has promised something, she has always managed to find a way out of fulfilling it if it was not convenient for her, but I see that for once Konnidas isn't going to relent. I am also aware that whatever she has promised has something to do with me. Altogether an interesting turn of events, and one whose unaccustomed nature makes me nervous.

She sighs and then moves over on the bench, patting it for me to sit next to her. I do so, hanging awkwardly half off the seat. She doesn't seem to notice my discomfort.

"You know, darling, that you are a very special boy." Her tone is one usually used with a two-year-old. "Your grandfather is a king." She pauses as though this is news, but of course I am aware that she is one of the many children of King Pittheus, who rules the small town of Troizena. "And your *father*"—she sounds as if she is about to impart a delightful secret—"your very own father is Poseidon." She claps her hands and nods. "So! What do you think of that?"

"Aethra," my stepfather says again, and I am startled to hear a note of warning in his voice.

"Well, he *said* he was Poseidon!" Her chin juts out. "He came wading out of the water, and darling, there was no ship nearby, so where else could he have come from?" *From farther up the shore,* I think but do not say. "He was surely Poseidon. So tall, so strong and handsome. He stayed for months and months." Her voice trails off, and her eyes are fixed on the ground. When she doesn't go on, Konnidas lays a hand on her shoulder. She looks up at him, tears shining in her eyes.

"I know this, Mother." I try to sound patient. "Don't upset yourself."

"Tell him the rest," Konnidas says gently, paying no attention to me.

My mother wipes her eyes and turns to me with a bright but false smile. "Your father couldn't stay until you were born, although he wanted to, because he had things to attend to." *Oh yes,* I think. *Poseidon is always busy, what with storms to raise and the earth to shake and sailors to drown.*

My mother looks helplessly at Konnidas, who comes to her rescue. "Your father left something for you."

"For *me?*" I look from one to the other. My mother is uncharacteristically grave, and Konnidas returns my stare with his usual equanimity. "What did he leave me?"

Konnidas looks at my mother. "Will you show him, or shall I?"

She rises to her feet and says, "I will show him. *He* told me to." She strides off in the direction of the sea without looking behind her. As soon as I recover from my astonishment, I trot after her, followed at a distance by my stepfather.

CHAPTER 7

"THIS IS it?" I ask. "This is what my father left me?"

My mother has stopped in front of a boulder lying near the sea path. She flutters her hand to draw my attention to it. I have passed this same boulder hundreds of times and have never attached any importance to it. It's just an ordinary stone, squarish, gray and brown, almost as tall as I am.

"Not the *rock*, silly!" She laughs as if I've said something ridiculous. After her earlier reluctance to talk about my father, she now seems eager. She gives the boulder an almost affectionate slap. "He rolled it here himself, a few days before he went back to the sea. He said he left something under it for you, and if the baby was—if you turned out to be a boy, you were to move the rock as soon as you were old enough and strong enough and find it."

For the first time since my mother and Konnidas started

talking about my parentage, I feel a glimmer of interest. If her story is true and my father left me a gift, it must be something hard, not to be crushed by the weight of the boulder, and durable, since it had to last for years. It might be gold. It might even be jewels.

I join my mother and lay my hand on the rough surface of the rock. It's mottled with small orange and green speckles of lichen, and warm where the sun has touched it. I push. It doesn't budge, which is no surprise.

"What was it that he left?" I press my shoulder into it and shove. The rock stands as motionless as—well, as a rock.

"Oh, I don't know. Nothing important, just some things he didn't have use for anymore, I suppose."

"And you didn't tell me about it earlier because . . . ?"

"Why are you ruining such a lovely day?" my mother asks. She is already pouting, and unless I do something to appease her, she will become cold and silent. For once, I don't care. I turn my back as Konnidas puts his arm around her waist. I know I should join him, that as the offender I'm the one who has the power to soothe her, but I'm too angry. Even though I know it's useless, I push against the huge stone again. As I expected, nothing happens. As I also expected, I hear my mother and stepfather returning to the house.

I can't budge the boulder by myself. I doubt that I can move it even with aid, and I know well that nobody but Konnidas will help me. I can do nothing until I come up with a plan. I follow my mother and stepfather up the path and then along the dusty trail that leads back to our house, turning over the possibilities in my mind. An ox—no, the way is too narrow and strewn with rocks. Anyway, I don't know anyone who would lend me such a valuable animal. A group of three or four men might be able to do something. The same problem arises, though: nobody is likely to want to help me.

I eat my supper without speaking. My mother is silent as well, and she merely picks at her food, which is once again lentil stew. It appears that Konnidas has gone to some trouble to make it especially tasty tonight, though whether to soothe my mother or to cheer me up I don't know. He seasoned it with the last of his store of herbs and has grated dried goat cheese over it. I eat mine, and as soon as my mother rises from her stool, leaving most of hers untouched, I take her bowl and eat what remains in it, too.

With such a full stomach I should sleep well, but instead I lie awake, pondering the problem of the boulder. I need a plan. I always need a plan. Sometimes I think life would be easier if I lived day to day, the way my mother and stepfather do.

Before he married my mother, Konnidas was a merchant who wandered all around Attika selling trinkets. He showed up on our doorstep one morning when I was very small, and he never left. He gave my mother the remaining store of his ribbons and earrings and good-luck charms, and for all I know he never gives a thought to the home he left—if he had one—or the people he grew up with.

But I can never stand to leave anything up in the air. I lie on my pallet on the floor, listening to the two of them talking quietly until they drop into sleep and my mother's breathing falls into rhythm with Konnidas's light snore.

I try not to think of the possibility that my mother has forgotten exactly which stone my father showed her and just pointed at the first one she came to after she grew tired of walking. This part of the seaward path is littered with rocks, thanks to the frequent shakings by Poseidon. I could never push over each one of them. No, I have to figure out a way to move only this one boulder, and if there's nothing under it, I'll know that her story was just that: a story. It sounds like one of the tales she used to tell me when I was little.

If my mother didn't just point out some random rock, and *if* the man who was my father intended me to be able to move it (two big ifs), then there has to be a way that someone who is not a giant and not a god can find what is lying under it. My father was not a god (this much is clear now), and if he had been a giant, my mother would have mentioned the fact. Yet he managed to move the rock, if she is to be believed. It's not impossible; after all, the temple in town is made of stones much larger than the one on the path, and they had to have gotten there somehow.

I squeeze my eyes shut and remember the scene. The path is steep, and the rock lies at the bottom of an incline.

Maybe he placed whatever he meant me to find on the ground, then climbed up on a ledge above it and pushed the rock on top of it. That would be difficult, but not impossible.

Even if true, though, that theory won't help me. The boulder now sits firmly on the flat ground. Unless . . .

I have a plan.

CHAPTER 8

I AM UP and out of the house before Konnidas finds me
a chore that will keep me from my task. The air is still chilly,
especially as I draw close to the sea and the winds pick up,
bringing a briny smell and the sounds of far-off gulls. Under a
gray sky that is starting to turn pink, I test several flat rocks
before finding one suited to my purposes, and then I set
to work.

The sun is high when I sit back and survey my efforts. I've
dug a deep trench along the downhill edge of the boulder. My
hands sting; they're already pretty well calloused, but even so,
I've sprung a few new blisters with the unaccustomed work.

If someone indeed tipped the huge rock off the ledge
above me, surely not much of it is buried in the sandy ground.
This means that with some effort I can, in turn, topple it over
into the trench I've dug.

I straighten my stiff legs and poke through the shrubbery until I find a long, stout branch. I plant myself on the uphill side of the boulder and work the end of the stick under it. I push down. Nothing. I press harder, finally leaning so much of my weight on the branch that I'm standing on tiptoe. The branch snaps and I fall backwards, my tunic flying up around my waist. I lie there to catch my breath, and suddenly I hear a giggle. I sit up hastily and pull my clothing down.

Three girls are standing on the path. I know all of them, and I also know that I'm in for an uncomfortable time. For tormenting, girls are even worse than boys. I'd rather be punched in the face by the biggest of my enemies than have to listen to the taunts that girls seem capable of throwing from the moment they learn to speak.

"What is he *doing?*" asks the smallest of them, a pale-faced little thing who I think is distantly related to me. My mother has so many brothers and sisters that I don't try to keep track of who is a cousin, who is married to a cousin, who lives with a cousin's family but isn't related, and all the rest of it.

"Looking for buried treasure," offers an older girl, whose face is heavily marked with smallpox scars. She would be pretty but for that, with a graceful shape, large, dark eyes, and shiny black hair that hangs in braids almost to her waist.

The third, a thick girl with a round face, snickers. "Going to dig himself a hole and hide in it. Then he won't have to worry about Arkas beating him up again." When she laughs, she looks like the Gorgon mask that hangs over the entrance to the temple in town, snaggleteeth and all.

The other girls laugh with her. I stand, resigned to their torment. I'm gratified to see that they shrink back as I rise to my feet, but then, to show that they aren't afraid of me, the two bigger ones straighten. I pretend not to notice them as I search in the brush for a stouter stick.

I find a likely looking pine branch and swing it experimentally over my head. Now the girls scatter, skimming down the path and out of sight. I hear the rattle of loose gravel, then a thud, then an "Ow!" One of them must have fallen. Since they will never know that I took notice of them, I allow myself a grin of satisfaction.

I don't dare to deepen my trench. If I dig too deep, the rock might tip over while I'm in front of it, landing on top of me. Nobody would find me for hours, and when they did, they wouldn't be able to move the boulder any more than I can now. If I survived the impact, that is. Instead, I concentrate on working the end of the long stick under the uphill edge. Once it's in as far as I can push it in the hard ground, I prop a smaller rock under it and then lean on it.

At first, I think nothing will happen, but then the boulder shifts. Not much, but enough to allow me to push my stick a bit farther in, and then farther, and then I hold my breath and heave with all my might. The rock hangs suspended for an instant before crashing over. At the same time, the branch flies out of my hands and whacks me on the right cheekbone. I fall to my hands and knees, dazed and with black mist swirling in front of me. I shake my head to clear it, but that makes me want to vomit, so I stop. I feel something sharp on my tongue and spit out a molar. It lies in a puddle of blood and drool. *That's my offering to whatever god looks after those who seek what is lost,* I think. I blink the tears out of my eyes. Manly tears are nothing to be ashamed of, as when a comrade falls in battle or at news of the death of a great king, but tears of pain and frustration show weakness. I won't allow them, even if no one can see.

When my vision clears, I carefully push myself to my feet. The rock hasn't tumbled all the way over but lies at an angle, leaving a space of the span of two or three hands between its bottom and the ground. It partially reveals a patch of earth that is roughly square, each side about as long as my arm. I survey the damp sand and dirt. Snakes sometimes hide under rocks, and I'm not about to risk being bitten. I bend over, but that makes my mouth throb, so I squat and poke my stick around in the darkness and finally put a tentative hand into the shadow.

Nothing strikes, so I kneel down and reach farther, patting the ground. I hope I'm not supposed to dig; it would be hard to work even a small stone, much less a spade, into the tight area. I wish I knew what I was looking for. I pat the cool earth and dig my fingers into it. I brush aside grubs and many-legged cold things that scurry away from the dim light under the boulder.

It would make a better story if I said that a god appeared

and told me where to look, or even that I had almost given up when I was dazzled by a light that broke out in the narrow space under the boulder, but after only a few minutes I feel something that is clearly not rock or dirt, not plant or animal bones. Somehow I know it's what I'm looking for. I tug at the edge of what feels like a piece of leather barely under the surface. It comes away easily. I sit back on my heels and pull it out into the light.

It's a pouch, perhaps a saddlebag, and something heavy in it shifts as I pick it up. I tuck it under one arm and pat around a little longer, prying clods out of the hard-packed sandy earth. There appears to be nothing else.

Before I have a chance to inspect my find, I hear voices. I hold my breath, listening hard, not even daring to spit out the blood that is pooling in my mouth. If it's the girls again, I have nothing to worry about.

I recognize a harsh guffaw as being in Arkas's tones and, before I've considered what to do, I've scrambled to my feet and am pelting toward home. I should feel disgraced at running rather than staying and fighting, but while I'm defending myself from one of them, the others will surely grab my leather pouch. I'm not about to risk that.

So I run, each step jolting the hollow place in my jaw.

"I found it!"

Konnidas looks up from the patch he's tilling. He's breaking up clods and mixing the leaves from last year's vines into the earth to make it fertile for the spring planting. It's hard work, and boring, but he doesn't act resentful that I've left him to do it alone.

He eyes the pouch in my hands and turns back to his work. "What's in it?" His voice is careful, like he's trying not to show any emotion.

"Don't know yet." I decide not to tell him about fleeing from the boys. Let him think I ran home out of excitement. "Where's Mother?"

"Resting." Konnidas must mean "pouting." I know what will bring her out, though. She's as curious as a mouse. I go to the house and stand in the doorway. I dangle the pouch from my hand. I feel something shift inside again.

"Mother?" No answer, so I say more loudly, pretending to address my stepfather, "Must be asleep. No matter, I'll show her my find after she wakes up."

"I'm not asleep." Her bedclothes rustle, and then there she is, her light brown hair mussed, her cheek creased where it rested on a fold of blanket. The dog at her side shows the pink interior of its mouth in a yawn. "I was waiting for you to come back." My mother eyes the leather pouch. I move aside to let her out, and then both of us sit on the bench.

Konnidas comes up, still holding his spade. He drops it and smacks his hands on his thighs to knock off the worst of the dirt. He looks at my face, appears to be about to say something (I'm sure my cheek is swollen and purple by now), but doesn't. "Show us," he says.

And although I have worked so hard to find this, and although I know—or at least hope—that it will provide me with a way out of Troizena, where everybody knows me as Theseus the Bastard, Theseus the "son" of Poseidon, still I hesitate. *My life isn't so bad,* I think. *Maybe I don't need to change it.*

But then I remember Arkas and his thugs, and the teasing girls. I fumble with the knots holding the pouch closed. I finally break the rotten strings and reach inside, to find two hard packets wrapped in what feels like oiled cloth. One is squarish and light in weight, and the other is long and heavier. I pull them both out and lay them on top of the open pouch. With both my mother and stepfather looking on, I unwrap the smaller packet. I stare at its contents, unbelieving.

"What is this?" My voice sounds harsh as I swallow blood, but I don't try to soften it. "Is this a joke?"

CHAPTER 9

WELL, DARLING," my mother says, anxious, as always, to avoid discord. "Well, they're very *nice* sandals."

I hold one up by its strap. This is a mistake, as the strip of leather has rotted through and the sandal falls to the ground. I pick up the other by its sole and inspect it. Perhaps at one time they were nice, but that time is long past, and lying squashed under a boulder hasn't helped them stay at their best. Still, the buckles are large and solid, and the leather was once thick and must have been stout. Not inexpensive, certainly, but not what I've been hoping for.

"Why would he leave me *sandals?* He must have known that they wouldn't last until I was grown. And how did he know they would even fit me?" I realize I'm whining.

"Open the other one," Konnidas urges. "Maybe there's something more practical in it."

I'm not hoping for something practical. I'm hoping for something valuable—gold or jewels or at least a silver ingot. What I find in the other packet, though, is a long dagger or a short sword, and whatever it's made of has corroded until it's covered with greenish crust. I'm not familiar with metals (anything that rare and expensive seldom comes as far as Troizena), but this must be bronze. I feel a little glimmer of hope. If it *is* bronze, then it's certainly worth something.

Konnidas reaches for it. "May I?" I nod and pass it to him. He holds the hilt in one hand and rests the blade in the other. "A good weight." I'm surprised; I didn't know my stepfather had knowledge of metalwork. With a thumbnail, he scrapes at the crust on the blade, and as it flakes away, a dull yellow gleam leaps out. Konnidas raises his brows and places the sword back on the oiled cloth. "Be worth cleaning." He picks up his spade again and returns to his vines.

I spend the rest of the day rubbing the blade. Konnidas leaves me to it, even though I could be useful in the garden, and I'm grateful to him.

By the time my stepfather heads into the house to prepare our meal, I'm ready to show him and my mother what I've uncovered. I sit at a stool, the sword on my lap. My mother sets a bowl at each place. The fish stew that my stepfather ladles into them smells savory. My hard work with the boulder has made me hungry, and Konnidas, too, seems to have a good appetite. We eat without speaking, occasionally pulling a fish bone off our tongues and balancing it on the edge of the bowl. My mother merely picks at hers and lets the dog lick the broth off her fingers. Both seem to be avoiding my eye.

When I have sopped up the last of my soup with a crust of bread, I clear my throat and put the sword on the table. It looks out of place among the wooden bowls with fish bones perched on their rims.

Konnidas is the first to speak. "A fine blade." I'm still surprised that he knows about metal, and now it appears that he's familiar with weapons as well. I realize with a little jolt that I don't know much about him.

My mother runs a tentative fingertip along the bright figures inlaid in the blade. They appear to be of gold: an owl, with two sparkling dark red gems representing its eyes; a coiling snake whose scales have been picked out minutely by an engraver; and a shape that I don't recognize, a rectangle with one corner cut out of it.

"What does it mean?" I ask. Maybe Konnidas's knowledge will extend this far.

"It means," he says as he picks up the sword and examines its hilt, which I have yet to clean, "it means that our boy here is not only the grandson of a king. He is also the son of a king. The man who left this sword under the stone is—or was—the king of Athens. See, here is the snake. It represents Erechtheus, the first king of the Athenians, and their god. The owl stands for Athena, their patron goddess. This other mark"—his long index finger brushes against the strange shape—"stands for the throne. It means the man who owned this was the king. Those sandals . . ." He pauses.

"Well?" I try not to sound impatient.

"Well, obviously, he means that you are to go on a journey."

"What kind of journey?"

Konnidas looks at my mother, who suddenly becomes interested in feeding her pet. "A journey to find him," he says.

"Is this true?" I turn to my mother. She shrugs and offers a bit of cheese to the dog, who takes it delicately in her white teeth. "Mother! My father wants me to come to him and you never told me so? I could have found some way to move that rock long ago." I stand and pick up the bowls from the table. "I could have been out of here, out of this hole of a town, with a father who could teach me how to be a man . . ." I let my voice trail off when I see the hurt on Konnidas's gentle face. I long to tell him that wanting to know my real father doesn't mean that I esteem him less. I don't know how to say this, so I turn and put the bowls into the washbasin. I start to go fetch water when something Konnidas said makes me turn back.

"Erechtheus," I say, remembering long-ago talk about Athens in the temple. "Isn't he also called Erechtheus Poseidon?" I look over at my mother, who drops her hands and her gaze to her lap. "Mother, did the man—did my father *really* say he was Poseidon? Or did he merely say something about Erechtheus Poseidon?"

"It's so long ago." I detect a tremble in her voice. "I don't remember what he—I don't remember exactly what he said."

"Oh, *Mother.*" A red rage swells in my chest and blocks off my speech. I stalk out and stand in the yard, fuming.

I hear footsteps, but I don't turn around. It can't be my mother; she will take offense at my storming out and refuse to speak to me until I have apologized. When Konnidas clasps my shoulder, I close my eyes and feel my muscles unclench. Until then, I had not known that I had tightened them. He hands me a cloth that he has soaked in spring water, and I lay it against my face, which is hot and swollen.

"Don't be angry." His voice is mild, as always. "She's worried, and that makes her unreasonable." I snort. She has never *not* been unreasonable. Konnidas's next words startle me. "It's time for you to leave, anyway. This place is too small for you."

"What do you mean, too small for me?" I rub my arms against a sudden chill.

My stepfather turns me around and looks into my eyes with his gray ones. I realize that I am almost as tall as he. Konnidas doesn't smile often, but he usually wears a pleasant expression. Now his solemn face strikes dread in my heart.

"What do you mean?" I repeat, and my tight throat makes the last word squeak.

He asks me a question himself. "Why do you think they hate you?"

I don't ask who. It seems that everybody in the village hates me. "Because of what she says," I answer. "Because she insists that my father is Poseidon. They think that I think I'm better than they are."

"Do you?"

"No!"

"Have you ever said that you were?"

"No, of course not." I'm indignant.

"Then why would they hate *you* for it?"

That brings me up short. I look at my stepfather in silence, confused.

"That's not why they hate you," he says. "They wouldn't hold you responsible for something she says. They know her— at least, their parents know her. She's never been—she's always been different."

"Then, what is it? If it's not what she says that makes them angry at me, what?"

"It's you."

"And this is *better*—that they hate me for myself and not for my parentage?"

"Not better. They see something in you that frightens them."

"What do they see?"

"You're too—too big, too strong, for this place. Not"— he raises a hand as he sees me about to speak—"not your body, although that's bigger and stronger than I think you know. No, it's *you*, it's Theseus. Without knowing it, they see that you're greater than any of them, and they're frightened and jealous. So they attack you. It's like wolves—you've seen how the leader has to continually fight to maintain his position?" I nod. "It's the same thing."

This is perhaps the longest speech I have ever heard my stepfather make, and I have no idea how to respond. The silence stretches between us. I hear a *pat-pat-pat,* and the dog comes trotting out of the house. She sits and looks up at me. I look down at her, then across at my stepfather. Both stare back at me.

"All right," I say. "I'll go."

CHAPTER 10

WHEN MY COUSIN Maera was sent to Korinthos to marry an ally of our grandfather, King Pittheus, her mother wept and wailed for days as though Maera had died, and as though she didn't leave behind four sisters to occupy my aunt's time. When Kastor, the son of a fisherman, joined the crew of a merchant ship heading for far-off Lydia, his father threw a feast that lasted all night and into the next day, with wine and roast goat and sweet cakes for all who attended.

When I leave for Athens in search of my father, my mother looks up from where she's arranging dried flowers just long enough to smile and remark that it's a lovely day for a walk.

Konnidas accompanies me to the place where the path to the sea forks and turns into the road running northwest along the edge of the water and thence to Athens. He carries a pack, and before we part he helps me hoist it onto my back. "There's a warm blanket in there." He adjusts the straps and settles it firmly on my shoulders. "And enough food to last you for a few days, if you're careful, and as much water as I thought you could carry."

"Surely there are springs leading down to the sea." I busy myself tightening the buckles and hope he doesn't hear the catch in my voice.

"Maybe. Maybe not. Can't be too careful." My stepfather looks searchingly at my face. "I have tried to be a father to you, Theseus. When I first arrived at your house and you threw rocks at me—remember?" I shake my head. "Oh yes, you were quite the little defender of your home and your mother. I took no offense, and I convinced you that I was harmless. When I stayed, it was as much for your sake as your mother's." At my raised eyebrows, he breaks into one of his rare grins. "All right, then, *almost* as much. I've loved you as I would have loved any son of my own, and I know that this journey is necessary to you. I just ask that you not forget us."

This speech is so unexpected that I have nothing to say beyond, "I never will." A swift embrace, and he thrusts a small pouch into my hand, and then I'm on the road.

The day is chilly, and I know that as I near the sea it will only grow colder. In the weeks I've had to wait for the winter storms to end, the spring has drawn closer but warmth has proven elusive. I'm glad for the cloak that Konnidas bought me, even though my mother pouted when she saw it and accused him of thinking that her weaving wasn't good enough for me (she was right).

I carry the rotten sandals in my pack. My father's sword is belted to my waist, the side with the gold figures toward me so that their gleam won't attract the eye, and the greed, of anyone I might encounter on the road. It slaps against my thigh at each step with a reassuring sound. I'm not expecting trouble, but you never know.

"Why don't you take a boat?" Arkas asked me when I said that I was going to Athens. "It's so much faster."

"Safer, too," said one of his dull-witted friends, unwittingly showing me the honorable way out.

"Do you think I'm a coward?" I asked, feigning astonishment. "Of course I'm going by the overland route. More adventure that way." So, although they must have known that the real reason was that I had no money for boat passage, they had nothing to say.

I haven't gone very far when I hear a soft, high sound behind me. My hand flies to the hilt of my sword, and then I lower it, feeling foolish. It sounds like a baby. *How cruel,* I think. *If someone exposes an unwanted child, they should leave it where someone might find it and care for it, not out here in this wasteland.* The odds of a passerby finding an exposed child are slim, and the hope that someone might adopt such a child slimmer yet, but it's nothing short of murder to leave it where no one is likely to pass for weeks. I poke around in the brush. No baby. I'm about to look further, when I hear a rustling, and the dog that my mother has been caring for these last weeks bounds out of a thicket.

She runs to me on her long legs, her ears streaming behind her, and jumps up, her paws scraping at my waist, her mouth open in what looks like a smile, her tail wagging. If anyone were present I would be embarrassed at how glad I am to see her. I squat and rub her head, scratching her behind the ears, then cup her face in my hands and gaze into her eyes.

"What am I to do with you?" Her tail wags even faster. I consider. My mother has made no effort to train her, and even if she had, I don't know if the dog would obey if I told her to go home. I can't take her back myself; the last thing I want to do is turn around and go slinking into Troizena as though I've changed my mind. Some are expecting that, and the thought of the satisfaction on Arkas's ugly face as he sees me enter the village mere hours after my departure turns my stomach.

I wonder if the dog can keep up with me. She's large but young, and she already appears tired. She'll probably manage for a while and then will lag behind. I can't stand the thought of leaving her alone on the road, hearing her whine grow fainter as I continue on my way. Besides, I have barely enough food for myself, much less a large dog, and I don't carry any hunting weapons. I'm not much of a hunter anyway, and I don't think that she is any better.

I know what Arkas would do. He'd slit the dog's throat without thinking twice and leave her body there for the crows. But I'm not Arkas, and I look into the brown eyes and know that I can't do it. I straighten.

"Come on, then, dog," I say, and take to the road again, accompanied by the sound of her panting and her footsteps.

"I can't keep calling you 'dog.'" We walk for a while as I think. I've heard of a moon goddess called Artemis, a patron deity of the hunt. This Artemis supposedly once asked her father, Zeus, for six lop-eared hunting hounds. I glance down at the cream-colored dog whose ears flap as she paces next to me.

"Artemis," I say. She looks up, still wearing what appears to be a smile, and wags her tail. I shrug. She probably would have done the same if I'd said "seagull" or "cheese." It's as good a name as any, though, so Artemis it is.

The land we're walking over is unappealing—rocky, sandy, difficult to traverse. I am lost in my thoughts and at first don't notice that Artemis has fallen behind. I stop and wait for her to catch up, and as soon as she's reached me she flops down on her belly. Her sides are heaving, and I decide to take my midday meal here—*our* midday meal, rather.

I've just found a relatively rockless stretch of sandy earth and am rummaging in my pack when a loud snort and the tramp of many feet rushing in my direction makes me spring up, sword drawn. A shape bursts from behind a rock, and before I can focus on exactly what it is, it runs straight into my sword and then drops on its side, screaming.

CHAPTER 11

I'M SORRY," I say for what feels like the thousandth time. "I didn't mean to kill your pig. I didn't even know it *was* a pig. I was just holding my sword up at the ready, and it ran right into—"

"She," the old woman says.

"I'm sorry—she?"

"You keep saying 'it.' My Phyllis wasn't an *it*. She was a *she*."

At least, that's what I think the crone says. She's missing most of her teeth, and her words come out somewhere between a mumble and a whistle.

"Sorry," I repeat, feeling inadequate to her grief. I don't know what else to say or what to do about the pig, which lies motionless between us.

"A dozen piglets at each farrowing." She ignores my apology. "Most of them would live to grow up, too, and make fine eating."

I wish she hadn't mentioned eating. I look at the pig and mentally carve it—her—into chops and loins, into fat cheeks and delectable trotters. My stomach rumbles. The old woman looks at me indignantly, and even Artemis lays her ears back as though my hunger, in the presence of this tragedy, is in bad taste.

I end up giving the old woman the blanket that Konnidas packed for me. She is so pleased with it that she becomes friendly and talkative, even recommending an inn farther up the road where I'll be able to sleep in exchange for one of the small pieces of silver from the pouch my stepfather pressed into my hand as I left.

I trudge along the seaside path, first thinking that I should save the silver, then reminding myself that I've been forced to give up my blanket and that the late-winter night is sure to be chilly this close to the water.

The inn is farther on than the old woman said, and it's not much more than a shack, but the old man sitting outside of it chewing on laurel leaves is hospitality itself. "Welcome!" he cries, hauling himself to his feet. He's skinny and wrinkled, and he leans heavily on his staff.

"Sit, grandfather," I say respectfully, but he ignores me.

"Just in time for supper!" he says. "And then you shall have the finest bed in Hellas. What brings a young gentleman so far out into the country?"

"Actually, I'm on my way to——"

"Come in!" He practically shoves me through the doorway. A fire burns in a pit in the middle of the floor, the heavy smoke barely drifting through the hole in the roof. "Sit here." He points at a three-legged stool very like the one that Konnidas must be sitting on at this moment, back in Troizena. He reaches into a bucket and pulls out a fistful of wriggling silver fish, which he proceeds to thread onto long, thin pieces of wood that have been soaking in a barrel next to the fire. He sprinkles the fish with herbs and pops them directly onto the hot coals. They sizzle and send up pungent smoke. After a minute, he turns them, and then he picks up a stick by its end and hands it to me.

I suck the small, salty bodies off the warm twig and wonder if I've ever eaten anything this good. The old man watches me with a satisfied grin, and when my belly is full he takes the three sticks I've emptied and pops them back into the barrel.

"Now, sir, if you're ready for bed?" I look around.

"Where?" I ask.

"Why, right there!" He points to a kind of platform raised about knee height from the floor. There's a sleeping-pallet on it. "Most comfortable bed in Hellas." He puffs out his chest like a dove. "Raised off the floor out of the way of drafts, and to keep the bugs away. Not that there are any bugs here," he adds a little too quickly.

I don't care if the mattress holds a herd of lice the size of sparrows. I'm suddenly so tired that I nod my thanks and tumble into the bed. It wobbles, and I fling myself upright, gripping its edges. I've never slept off the floor before (it has never occurred to me that you *could* sleep off the floor), and I feel as exposed as if I were on a mountaintop.

"Sorry, sir!" He shuffles forward, a wicked-looking blade in his hand. "If you'll step down for a moment?" I'm only too glad to comply, and he hacks off the bottom of one leg and tests the balance of the bed. Now another leg is too long. He trims that one, too. He tests it again, and the bed is still unstable. I'm about to tell him that it doesn't matter, that I prefer a pallet on the floor, when he's finally satisfied. "There's always one either too long or too short," he says as I settle myself in cautiously. "But once they're even, there's no more comfortable bed—"

"In Hellas," I finish for him. "I know. I thank you."

And while he's thanking me back I fall asleep, with Artemis curled on the floor beneath my head.

CHAPTER 12

ELL MY FRIEND here what you just told me."
The guard's pimply face indicates that he is no older than I am, and the mirth that stretches his mouth wide makes my hand itch to strike him. Artemis senses my anger, and a low rumble issues from her long throat. Instead of punching the palace guard, I drop my hand to her head. She falls silent, but I can feel that her every muscle is quivering.

I turn to the older man indicated by the youth. "I'm the king's son," I repeat. "I've come to meet him and to take my place at his side."

"The king's son?" The heavyset man doesn't seem as amused as his companion, but he doesn't move from his spot in front of the door, where he's planted like a tree trunk.

I'm tired. I want to go in and meet the man who supposedly sired me. I'm filthy and I'm hungry, and Artemis is even more worn out than I am. The trip was uneventful, except for the pig that I killed the first day out. A few days later I met a man I thought was a thief, but since I carried nothing of value with me except my sword and my hand rested on its hilt during the whole of our short conversation on the edge of a cliff, I'd had nothing to fear from him.

I should be disappointed by this lack of adventures, but secretly I'm pleased to have made it to my destination in such a short time and with no injuries or loss of more of my meager property than the blanket I had given to the pig-woman. I finished my food quickly, though, and I'm hungry. I can feel Artemis's ribs through her thick coat.

And now that I've come all the way here, and when the man I seek is finally just on the other side of the door, this officious boy and his large friend are blocking my entry. The injustice of it swells my chest, and I want to shout at them. I know it would do me no good and might cause them to throw me out in front of all the people passing on the wide street.

The older man pulls thoughtfully at his lower lip. He lets go of it and it snaps back into place. "What makes you think you're his son, boy?" His tone isn't unfriendly, and even Artemis seems to relax a little.

"He left me something. He wanted me to come to him once I found it."

"Oh, so he left you something, did he? What was it, a golden crown?" The pimple-faced boy's sneering voice is the sardine that broke the pelican's beak, and before I know what I'm doing, I haul back and punch the smirk off his face.

A big hand claps me on the shoulder. I wince, resigned to being tossed out, but instead the hand is steering me forward in a friendly way. "You've just earned yourself entry into the king's chamber." The big man chuckles and pushes the door open. "I've been wanting to do that ever since the oaf joined the guard service. You'll find the king and his lady having their dinner. And boy"—his voice turns serious, and I glance at him, not sure I can believe what I'm hearing—"be careful of the queen. She's a tricky one." He thrusts me forward, and I find myself on the other side of the door.

I'm too dazed at the sudden turn of events to wonder what he means. The chamber is larger than any room I've ever seen before and is so lovely that I can't take it all in. I see a gleaming stone floor laid out in an intricate pattern of blue and red and white and green. The ceiling is open above a pool in the center of the room. White flowers float on the smooth surface of the clear water, and all around the edge of the little rectangular pond, caged birds are singing.

For a moment, I can't make out any people. Then I realize that the men ranged at the far end of the room are not statues, as I first thought, but guards. In the middle of the group is a low table of white stone, and two people are sitting at it on heaped-up cushions, eating something that smells lovely and popping little bits of whatever it is into each other's mouths.

They look up as I approach with Artemis close by my side. I hope that my stomach doesn't growl at the sight of the roasted songbirds and olives and fresh bread piled on platters. The woman, plump and rosy as a baby, is the first to speak. "What a lovely dog!" She reaches out her chubby hand, and Artemis moves closer, and then stretches her long neck and sniffs the woman's fingers politely, her plumed tail waving.

"Thank you, lady." I feel awkward. I don't know how to address her, not certain who she is, though I suspect she is the queen. Artemis, on the other hand, seems perfectly at ease as she goes from the woman to the man, who is also round and smiling.

"Who might you be?" the man asks.

I try to frame my answer. Finally, I squeak, "Theseus" and stop. A proper introduction includes at least the father's name, if not the grandfather's, and so on as far back as the speaker knows. They both smile and nod to encourage me, and I manage to stammer, "Son of Aethra." Somehow, I forgot to ask my mother the name of the king, and in any case I feel shy about using it until I know where I stand. They continue smiling, knowing as well as I do that one who introduces himself by giving his mother's name is the son of an unmarried woman. I blurt out, "Son of Aethra and of the king of Athens."

"Dear me," the woman says, turning to her husband. "Is this another one of yours?"

"Another—another one?" I sputter.

The man seems unperturbed. He tilts his head to one side and looks at me. "Could be," he muses. "He does have something of the look of the House of Aegeus."

The woman nods. "He does indeed. He puts me in mind of Hippon, don't you think? The king's nephew," she explains to me. "He's a nice boy, very strong, broad in the shoulders like you."

My head is whirling. "My mother—"

He frowns. "Who did you say your mother was?"

"Aethra."

The king looks puzzled.

"From Troizena," I explain. "She's the daughter of King Pittheus."

He shakes his head. "I'm sorry, boy, but I don't remember. It must be a long time ago. How old are you, anyway?" Without waiting for an answer, he picks up his cup and drains it, then gestures behind him at a servant, who hurries to pour dark wine into it.

"Sixteen," I say, but he has turned his attention back to his meal.

"Have some wine, dear." The queen passes me a brimming cup.

I begin to feel desperate. It appears the king doesn't believe me. "You left me something." I pull the sword out of its sheath. "You put this and a pair of sandals under a rock, and you told her—"

"Now, *that* sounds familiar!" he cries. He holds out his hand and I give him the weapon. "Ah yes, my old sword. The boulder by the path! I tipped it over on top of this sword and a pair of sandals. You have the sandals, boy?" I tug the straps of my pack and pull out the rotten things. I pass them to him, and he beams. "Move aside, dear," he says to his wife. "Make room for my son—what did you say your name was?"

"Theseus."

"This is my son, Theseus, son of Aegeus. Theseus, my boy, meet the queen of Athens, Medea of Kolkhis."

The words of greeting die on my lips as I turn to face the woman whose notoriety has spread even to Troizena: Medea, the witch, the wife of Iason, leader of the Argonauts. Iason took her away from her home and married her in exchange for her gift of the golden ram's fleece that was the Kolkhians' most sacred object. Then, when Iason decided to take another wife, as was only to be expected of a ruler, Medea flew into a rage, and in her passion and fury she did something unspeakable. To punish her husband, with her own hand she killed her own children, hers and Iason's.

And this same Medea—this woman smiling across the table at me—this is my stepmother.

CHAPTER 13

"HAVE AN OLIVE," says my father.

"Have some more wine," says his wife. She gestures to a guard, who moves like a suddenly animated statue and brings a pitcher and some large cushions. I let him fill the cup but hesitate to sit on the cushions; they are made from a shining cloth of a kind I've never seen before, bright red and blue, marvelously woven into intricate patterns. My clothes are filthy, and I don't smell much better than that pig. Besides, this is *Medea!* If she can kill her own children, gods only knew what she would do to a new stepson.

"Sit!" she says with a beaming smile. But I feel like I've been turned to stone. Medea killed her own brother to steal the Golden Fleece, an act almost as unthinkable as the murder of her children—worse, to some minds. She's still looking up at me, but her smile is beginning to be replaced by puzzlement at my long hesitation.

I sit. The wine poured into my cup is almost purple and has a fragrance that is new to me. I take a sip and then drain it. Before I can ask for more, the guard has refilled it.

Medea heaps bread, olives, small fish bathed in oil, and dried fruit onto a wooden plate and pushes it in front of me. My cup is pointed on the bottom, and I can't put it down while there's anything in it, so I awkwardly scoop a few tiny fish onto a piece of bread with one hand. I close my eyes as I chew; the fish is flavored with herbs and rich with oil, and is delicious. When I open them again, Medea has put broken pieces of bread, a roasted songbird, and some fins and tails of a larger fish into a pile on the floor, and Artemis is snapping it up. As I take a second draught of wine, my dog walks over to the pool, laps up water for what seems an impossibly long time, and then lies down, her head on her crossed paws, and goes to sleep.

"Now," the king says as he puts two plump birds onto my plate, "tell us about your journey here. Any adventures?"

"Nothing to speak of," I say. "I killed a sow the first day— it was being kept by an old woman who . . ." Their faces fall as though they are bitterly disappointed.

I pause.

Nobody knows me here. For all anyone in Athens is aware, I am the hero of my village and a great fighter. Everybody in Troizena seems to think that the road to Athens is fraught with peril, and the king (I still find it difficult to think of him as my father) assumes the possibility of adventures.

To cover the silence and to give myself time to think, I put a songbird into my mouth. I crunch the tiny bones and then wash it down with a large swallow of the dark wine.

"As I say, nothing to speak of." They continue to look downcast. "The sow was the size of a horse." They perk up a little. "It came from the underworld, I think. It spoke with a human voice, and its hooves were as sharp as daggers. It came screaming at me as I walked along the path."

They seem enthralled. I decide to let them wonder, and then the king says, "So, what did you do?"

"Oh, I killed it. Ran it through with my sword." I take another swig of wine.

Artemis has raised her head and is staring at me disapprovingly. "The old crone who owned it flew through the air at me. I had to kill her, too." I'm starting to enjoy this. "And one night I stayed at an inn that had only one bed." I say it casually, hoping they'll think I'm used to something much grander. "The owner of the inn swore that it didn't matter what size the bed was, that everyone was comfortable in it. So, what he did to make sure that everyone fit was to cut off the feet of anyone who was too tall and stretch short men on a rack until they died."

My stepmother gasps. Her round black eyes become even rounder, and she clutches my hand. "What did you do?" she breathes.

"Killed him with his own sword. I left it behind," I add hastily before they can ask to see it. "I'm not a thief, and I didn't want anyone to think I'd killed him for the sake of plunder. It wasn't worth the trouble of taking with me, in any case. It was blunt from all the ankle bones he'd chopped through. And I'm not much good with a sword." I stop, not wanting to remind him of how poor Troizena is. Until I tipped over that boulder, I had never seen a blade longer than a knife like the one Arkas pulled on me.

"What else?" The king leans forward, interest showing on his face.

I cast about for another adventure and remember the man I suspected of being a thief. "A traveler asked me to help him on with his sandals. I was suspicious, because he seemed perfectly capable of doing them up himself, so I was on my guard, and when I was kneeling in front of him he aimed a kick at me." My father shrugs as if to say, "So? A kick?" and I go on hastily, "This was on the edge of a cliff, and if he'd succeeded I would have gone over the edge." He still seems unimpressed, so I go on. "I pushed him off instead." Still not enough. "He fell into the sea, where he was eaten by a . . . by a giant turtle."

"Ooh!" The queen's face is shining. "A giant turtle!" I'm afraid I've gone too far, but she seems completely caught up in my tale. "What else?"

Diabolical animal, thief, murderer. There must be something else I could invent. They look at me expectantly. I open my mouth, hoping that somehow the words will fall out of it. Nothing.

I am saved by the sound of a door opening. A tall girl with brown hair comes in, leading a small boy. The child, perhaps five or six years old, clutches a clay animal of some kind, with wheels where its feet should be. He bends and puts the toy on the floor and then straightens, pulling it behind him with a string. The girl smiles and lets go of his hand. He trots toward us, and his toy rattles across the paving stones.

"Medus, my sweet!" the queen says. "Bring him close, Prokris. Theseus, this is our boy. Medus, precious, this is your brother, Theseus."

"I have a horse," the little boy says. He picks up his toy by its string and holds it out for my inspection.

"It's a fine horse," I say. I have always liked children, at least until they reach an age to join their older brothers in bullying me or their sisters in taunting me. I'm careful to avoid looking at the girl, fearing the derision that I always see in girls' eyes.

Aegeus says, "Prokris, my dear, this is my son Theseus." I rise and bow to the girl, and when I reluctantly raise my eyes to hers, they are as soft as her hair, and all I see in them is curiosity. She's pretty—not striking, but sweet-looking. I smile at her and she ducks her head, but then she raises it and smiles back.

"Your son?" Prokris looks from me to little Medus, who has squirmed off his mother's lap and is now running his toy along the floor, singing to himself.

"Yes, and you wouldn't *believe* the adventures he had on his way here from—where is it you said you come from?"

"Troizena," I say, and instantly the queen launches into a recital of my trek. Prokris gasps at the right moments, and when the tale is over she turns to me with admiration shining in her face.

"Why, that's marvelous! You must be very strong and very brave."

I feel myself turning red. "Well, I—"

"How dull it will seem to you here in Athens."

"Oh, I don't know . . ."

"Surely you long for more adventures?"

I can't say no with her big gray-green eyes shining with admiration. Since she seems to be waiting for an answer, I manage to say, "Oh yes, of course. I'll have to look around a little, see what's up. Not much chance of finding another *Argo*—" I stop in horror at my own words and steal a glance at the queen, wondering how she'll take my mention of the ship piloted by her first husband, Iason. She seems not to have noticed and is fixing Prokris with a quizzical stare, perhaps wondering where the girl is going with her chatter about adventure, as am I.

The girl seems unaware of our attention and claps her hands. "Don't you see what this means?" She turns to the king.

"What *what* means, my dear?" He pauses in the act of putting a sweetmeat into his mouth and gapes at her in puzzlement. Now all three of us are staring at her.

"Don't you see?" She looks from one to the other and then bursts out laughing. "The king's son! And a hero, too."

"Ah!" The queen's face lights up. "My dear?"

The king still looks puzzled, but then he rubs his hands together with a chuckle.

"*What?*" I'm the only one who doesn't understand. I might as well be talking to the little boy's painted horse for all the attention they pay me. The queen has clasped her son in what looks like a strangling embrace, and her face shines.

"Mama, you're hurting me!" The child squirms, and she loosens her grip. He runs his horse back and forth on the floor. The only sound in the room is the scrape of the clay wheels on stone.

The king turns and looks me full in the face. I can't read his expression as he scrutinizes me. Finally, he nods.

"He'll do," my father says. "He'll do very well."

CHAPTER 14

THE QUEEN belatedly realizes that I'm in even greater need of a bath than of food, and as I try to frame a question about what the king means—I'll *do?* Do for what?—she sends Prokris to fetch the child's nurse.

The old woman looks exactly like a bird, with sharp little eyes on either side of a long, thin nose. I almost expect her to flap her skinny arms as she precedes me down a corridor, past weaving rooms full of women who fall silent and peer out the door after us, and storerooms jammed with large earthen vessels of what must be wine and oil, and fat sacks of grain. She wears a most unbirdlike smirk as she waits for me to hand her my clothes. I fumble with them, not sure whether it's decent to strip in front of her. She glares at Artemis, and the dog lowers her head and tail and retires to a corner.

"Come, boy," the bird-woman says, not even trying to

conceal her impatience. "Whatever it is you have under that stinking tunic, I've seen better. I was nurse to Aegeus, and I've had the care of Prince Medus since the day he was born." In my haste I manage to knot the belt even tighter. She shifts her weight and sighs.

At last I lower myself into the steaming water and settle back with a sigh. When I was still small enough for my mother to take an interest in me, my bath was the highlight of my week. She would fashion sea monsters out of shells and wood and make them wiggle through the water, and I would battle them until I emerged clean and victorious.

The woman doesn't leave me to bathe alone, as I had hoped, but rubs sweet-smelling soap into a large sea sponge and vigorously scrubs it on me, tutting through her teeth. "You'll be fit for the king's court when I'm through with you," she says grimly, as if this is a challenge she's taken on. "Although where you're going, it won't make any difference."

"Going?" I sit up, sloshing water over the side of the tub. "I'm not going anywhere. I just got here."

"As you say." Her voice is prim, but I hear a note of sarcasm.

"What do you mean? And why wouldn't it matter how clean I am?"

She pushes me forward and rubs at my back until I think the water will run red with my blood. She yanks up an arm, scrubbing from shoulder to fingertips, and then back down to my armpit. One thing I have to say for her: she's thorough.

Apparently she can't keep from taunting me. "The one you'll be meeting doesn't care what you look like or smell like."

I try to wait her out, but I can't. "Who will I be meeting?"

A dry chuckle, then, "Someone who cares what you *taste* like."

I emerge from the bath wearing a brilliant white tunic, and a silver diadem that holds my hair in place. My feet are encased in sandals so new, they squeak on the stone floor.

The bird-woman has disappeared, and I'm uncertain where to go. I take a tentative step into a corridor, hear muffled giggles, and hastily retreat. I wait a bit and then try again. With the help of a young manservant, I find my way back, Artemis's claws clicking on the stone floor at my side.

The room is empty, and I'm standing in the doorway wondering what to do when I hear a soft footstep. I turn to see the girl Prokris. She lays a soft hand on my arm and asks if I'd like a cup of wine. I accept and follow her into the lofty chamber. I sit on a low stool and notice that the slippery cushions I sat on earlier have been removed. Burned, I wouldn't wonder, trying not to blush as I remember how filthy I'd been. The girl pours two cups of wine and hands me one. The liquid is so dark that I know it hasn't been watered, and I wonder if she's trying to dull my mind, so I take only a sip as she settles next to me.

"I hope you're not angry with me."

So, what she said earlier to the king and queen is some-thing that should anger me. "I didn't understand what you were talking about," I admit. "What did the king mean by say-ing that I would 'do'?"

"It all goes back to the young prince," she says.

"Little Medus?"

"No, no. Androgeos. His father is the king of Krete. Minos. You've heard of him?"

Everyone knows about the powerful King Minos, and ev-eryone in the world sends him tribute. Even small Troizena—when our turn comes every nine years, we send him wine and herbs. "Yes," I say. "I've heard of him."

"His son Androgeos came here to play in our games—the Panathenaic Games. He was a fine athlete, and so hand-some! The king's firstborn, they said, with his first wife. They married when they were barely of age. Androgeos was raised in the palace at Knossos, the first city of the island. Andro-geos was a fine athlete," she repeats, "and that's where all the trouble came from."

"What trouble?"

It appears that the Kretan Prince Androgeos was so good at the games that some drunken Athenians killed him. When word reached King Minos, he was furious, and he added a new tribute to the wine and oil that Athens was already send-ing him.

"Every ninth year, King Aegeus must send seven boys and seven girls to Krete," Prokris says. "At first, he sent pretty children, nobly born, but the Kretans sold them as slaves. Some even went to work in the horrible limestone mines and of course died quickly. That was bad enough, but worse was to come. The second time, the king turned them into play-things for his wife's monstrous son, who tore them apart and ate them."

I have heard of this monstrous son. He is called the Minotauros and is said to be the son of the Kretan queen and a sacred bull.

"This is all very interesting," I say, even as my stom-ach turns at what she has said, "but what does it have to do with me?"

"That second time, almost nine years ago now, Aegeus sent only the children nobody wanted—beggars, mostly, and the ones who should have been exposed at birth. King Minos was furious, and last year he gave instructions that this time, Aegeus must send his son. Medea flew into a rage and said they should never have her son, that she already sacrificed two children and this one would not go to the monster."

I begin to see, and what I see I do not like at all.

"Aegeus had another son, but he died of the fever, and a few years ago, shortly after he married Medea, a boy turned up at the palace claiming that Aegeus was his father." She gazes at me thoughtfully. "You look something like him. You both resemble the king."

"Where is he now?" I ask.

"He disappeared one night, about a moon after he arrived. That was before King Minos ordered Aegeus to send him a son, and Medea—well, Medea saw the boy as a threat to her own child, who had just been born. But now they have a king's son in you." She raises her eyebrows. "Were you about to say something?" I shake my head hastily. "Surely a hero such as you will have no difficulty when you go into the maze and meet the Minotauros."

"*Me?* A hero?" But then I remember the tales I told, about the giant turtle and the innkeeper who cut off his guests' feet and all the rest of it, and I know I am defeated.

And so it is decided. I have arrived in Athens just before the boats are to sail, and the priests agree that this is a sign that the gods have willed me to go—not that the holy men would dare say anything else once the king's mind has been made up.

It's some small satisfaction to learn that Prokris is to be one of the seven girls going as tribute. If I am to be exiled to the strange land of Krete, so is the person who engineered that exile. The king is to make her his wife—one of many, I understand—and since she is a distant relation of Aegeus's, the two kings will become allies after my death has satisfied Minos's desire for revenge.

It is a dark morning several weeks later when we sail, with clouds hanging so low over the horizon that it's hard to tell where they end and the land begins. I stand at the stern of the ship and watch the cliffs retreat, rage against my father battling with the fear in my gut.

CHAPTER 15

T
HE FEW TIMES that I've been to sea, the bobbing waves, the sun beating down on my head, the stink of rotten fish and unwashed fishermen, have sent me to hang over the side, retching. But those were Troizenian fishing boats, and this Athenian ship is something else entirely. Its prow slices through the waves with great speed, whether under sail or powered by oars. The only smell is the clean, briny scent of the ocean, familiar to me since childhood, and awnings and sunshades keep the late-winter sun from being a bother.

I do spend a fair amount of time at the rail, but not in sickness. Instead, I search the horizon for a sign of land. As soon as we put into a port, I'll find some way to escape. The Kretans must think me dimwitted if they imagine that I'll calmly allow them to lead me through the twisting corridors of the maze to be tortured and devoured by that monster.

But we pass by the small islands without stopping.

The sea is so smooth that the children are allowed to play on deck, and I quickly become a favorite among them, as the sailors are uninterested in joining in their games. I knot a piece of rope into a rough ball and show the boys how to kick it into a bucket that has been tipped over onto its side. The game soon turns into one of trying to keep the ball away from Artemis, who romps and frisks on the deck like a puppy. I later find that one of the girls has rescued the rope and tied a piece of sailcloth around it, turning it into a makeshift doll that she sings to and tucks into her pallet next to her when they go to sleep.

The full horror of my situation returns to me at night. I lie awake, trying to imagine what the Minotauros must look like, but without success. I kept a brave face when I walked down to the harbor near Athens, dressed in the finest robe I had ever touched, and oiled and perfumed like a prince—*or a sacrifice,* I thought sourly as I climbed onto the ship. There was no honorable way to refuse to go, and even if there had been, the king's heavily armed soldiers never left me alone from the moment my father decreed my voyage.

My father stocked the vessel with experienced sailors and gave me a fat purse bulging with coins. He was determined to show King Minos that although the king of Athens was subject to the Kretan monarch, Aegeus was a man of wealth and power. He also provided an honor guard, supposedly to escort me, but I suspected that they were really there to make sure I didn't try to escape. Not much chance of that. Out in the sea, I had nowhere to escape to. I raised my hand to the people cheering me for my bravery even as I felt the cowardice in my heart.

Prokris and the six other girls of the tribute disappeared below as soon as they were rowed to the ship. I expected to see her often, but she doesn't show herself until the second evening. I hear that she is not handling the sea voyage well. I step out onto the deck after finishing a supper of fresh fish and dried fruit and see a shape against the rail. I hold back until I'm certain what it is; I've heard of sea nymphs who take human form and lure sailors over the sides of their ships to drown. Then I hear an all-too-human sigh, and so I approach to see that it is Prokris resting her elbows on the rail and her chin in her hands.

I've rehearsed over and over what I'll say when I see her. I plan to ask her what she was doing, interfering back there in Athens, interrupting my very first meeting with the father I'd never known. I mean to accuse her of murder, for suggesting to the king and queen that I be sent to the lair of the Minotauros in the place of their brat. I harden my heart at the memory of the little boy. Yes, he was a handsome child, and yes, he was so small that he would have stood no chance against the monster. Still, he's nothing to me, and I don't see why I should die in his place.

I might even push the treacherous girl into the sea. I feel some satisfaction at that thought, but my heart fails me as I approach, and instead I join her at the rail. Like her, I stare out at the gray-green expanse. The brilliant blue water of yesterday has disappeared along with the sun, and the low clouds allow barely a glimmer of yellow light through.

The girl doesn't look up right away, and when she does, I'm surprised. I expect her to be crying or at least to look sad, but instead her face wears a calculating expression. After a moment, she smiles.

I don't smile back. It was her idea, after all, to send me to the monster to be eaten. My hand strays to the sword that I wear hidden under my cloak. It's short, and nobody has noticed it. Weapons are forbidden on this ship, and I hold a thread of hope that it will give me a chance of survival when I face the monster.

At least she's not weeping. I don't know how to deal with a weeping woman. The silence between us grows uncomfortable, and I don't like the appraising way she's looking at me, or how she appears to have seen the hilt of my sword. I rearrange my cloak around it and cast about for something to say. All I can come up with is the conventional "Are you well?" I curse my stupidity while trying to keep my face expressionless.

"Quite well," she says in a conversational tone. "I've just had to leave my home and I'm crossing the sea to go to a strange place where I'll marry an old man who already has a dozen wives, so as junior wife I'll have to serve all of them as well as him. Oh yes, and this morning one of the girls was sick all over the bag containing my wedding robe, and when I come out here for some peace and fresh air I'm asked if I'm well."

"Sorry I said anything." I try to sound haughty, but I'm afraid it comes out whiny. I firm up my voice. "It's not like *you're* going to have to face a monster that eats people."

She doesn't answer, and I assume she either hasn't heard or doesn't think me worthy of a response. I'm about to leave, when she surprises me with a question. "What do you know of Krete?"

"Not much." I fumble for an answer. "It's an island, a very big island, and it's ruled by a king named Minos. Uh . . ." I think. "They grow saffron. And Zeus was born there."

"The Kretans call him Velchanos," she tells me, "but you're right, it's Zeus. Their Velchanos is also our Apollo and they call their goddess 'Karia.'" I can understand how one god would take the place of two—Apollo rules the sun, and Zeus the sky. But I've never been much interested in religious matters, and I don't know why this girl is telling me about Kretan customs.

It seems that one of Prokris's brothers married a Kretan woman, and Prokris has learned a great deal about the place. "The king's sister must have two children, a boy and a girl. The boy becomes the next king and the girl becomes the priestess."

"What? The son of the king doesn't take over after his father dies?"

She shakes her head.

I've heard of all sorts of ways of running things: rule by conquest, rule by inheritance, even rule by lot, but a leader coming through the female line—I don't like it.

Before I can say anything, Prokris leans close in. She speaks in a low voice, and her words bring me first a chill and then a tingle of excitement.

For Prokris has a plan. If her plan works, everything will change on Krete.

And everything will change for me, too.

CHAPTER 16

I'VE VISITED the palace of my grandfather, King Pittheus, several times. I was always astonished at its twelve rooms—eleven more than any other house I'd ever seen— and its magnificence, with its whitewashed walls and hard stone floors. Then, when I saw the palace of my father in Athens, I realized that Pittheus's palace is as a shepherd's hut compared with that magnificent building. Five or six of my grandfather's palace could fit inside it, and its dining hall is as large as the entire village square at Troizena.

I thought that once I had seen that palace, I had seen the utmost in splendor, but when I catch glimpses of the palace of King Minos in Knossos, I realize that Aegeus is a nothing, a gnat. I can't imagine how such a building as the Knossan palace can exist and how powerful must be the man who lives in it.

It is not only huge, although it certainly is that. It is also magnificent. It sits on top of a hill that isn't as high as the sacred hill in Athens but is much broader. Since I am still working my way up to the palace, I can't see the entire structure at once. The road twists and turns, and by the time we pass through the gate, I've seen enough to know that the Kretan king's residence is as large as an entire city. Enormous, fat red pillars support terrace after terrace, and white steps lead into countless entrances. I wonder which one goes to the maze with its bull-headed monster.

The port of Knossos was jammed with ships and with sailors loading and unloading them when we arrived. Vendors busily hawked roasted meats, fruit, bread, cheap sandals, and local good-luck charms, which are odd clumps of knotted yarn. I bought one. I don't think it will do me any good.

We pushed through the crowd, the king's men keeping careful watch over us. This is pointless, as there's nowhere to run to and we'd be easily discovered. Athenians look quite different from the locals. Most of the Kretan men we pass wear nothing but a white loincloth. They are all short, most of them are slim, and all of them wear their hair in long black tresses. Some are elaborately coiffed; these I take to be the nobles. Others wear white capes marked with one, two, or three black stripes. Soldiers, I find out, most of them palace guards whose rank is indicated by the number of stripes.

"Where are the women?" I ask one of our escorts, whom I suspect to be heavily armed but hiding his weapons under his cloak out of courtesy.

"You saw women down at the dock," he says.

"True. But do none live in the palace?"

He doesn't answer, and as we walk I lean forward to look at his face. He's scowling. "Never mind," I say. "Forget I said anything."

We walk on. It's already odd not to feel my sword under my cloak. It's forbidden for foreigners to carry weapons within the precinct of the palace. Fearing I would be searched, I managed to slip it to Prokris, who has hidden it among her clothes. No one would touch her belongings, and I will need that sword if her plan is to succeed.

The road is steep. Behind us, one of the little girls is whining, and I turn. Prokris is already carrying a small boy who is sucking on his thumb, his head on her shoulder, so I wait for the little girl to reach me, and then I scoop her up and settle her on my shoulders. She grasps my hair with her small fists and stops sniffling.

My guide waits for me at the next turn. "Look," he says, "you're a foreigner, a barbarian." I start to object but think better of it. "Still, you seem like a good sort, and you *are* a prince." He looks at me doubtfully, and I nod in confirmation. "Three kinds of women live in the palace. There are the servants, who are all local girls with brothers and fathers nearby, ready to defend them and to avenge any wrong done to them. Then there are the wives of the Minos. You will not see them, except in his presence, and then only if he invites you." We walk on. Finally, he says, "And then—then there are the others."

"What others?"

"There are two of them. You probably won't see them, but if you do . . ." He trails off and lays a hand on my shoulder. "Well, if you do, be careful. There's no telling what will make them angry, and they are very powerful."

He refuses to say more, and soon we climb steps and pass through wide doors, and we are in the palace. I try not to gasp like a peasant at the sight of the painted walls. Some show leaping dolphins in impossible colors so joyful that despite my dread of what is coming, my heart lifts; some show flowers growing in all directions; others, blue monkeys harvesting saffron blossoms. On one, boats sail on an ocean with waves cresting in every color the ocean never was, red and orange and bright yellow. We pass through chambers decorated with paintings of double-headed axes. My escort tells me that this is a holy symbol called the labrys. It gives its name to the entire palace, the labyrinthos.

Finally, we are in the heart of the palace, where no sunlight falls. Torches are lit, their light bouncing off the shiny stone floor and showing walls painted a solid red. Hands reach up and take the little girl off my shoulders. She clings to my hair briefly, protesting, and then surrenders. She and the five other little girls are led off by women who seem kind enough. In the next room, men coax the little boys along in gentle voices.

"They'll be well taken care of," says my escort as I watch them depart. "Our monster has no need of them."

"He doesn't? Why not?" I blurt before thinking.

The guard turns his unblinking gaze on me. "Why, because he has you."

CHAPTER 17

I HAVE NEVER believed she was the daughter of Velchanos, you know." The thin, sour voice was familiar, but what it said was so strange that for a moment, I wondered if I had dreamt it. It was followed by an answering murmur whose words I didn't understand but which sounded shocked.

I pushed myself up on one elbow, being careful to remain hidden on the long couch in one of the palace's many sitting rooms. I had fallen asleep there after yet another late-night birth. My mother had grown so heavy and awkward that she had allowed me to deliver the baby, a sweet little girl, by myself, and even when we returned to the palace I was so excited that I barely slept.

The first woman went on. "Remember how poor the harvest was before she was born? Velchanos let hardly any rain fall, and the people would have starved if the fish hadn't

been especially abundant that summer. Surely he was showing us that he had nothing to do with her conception." The
speaker was Damia, the oldest of the priestesses now that her
closest friend and ally, Thoösa, had been removed from her
post when I became a woman and took her place.

The other person spoke again. "Have you said anything
about this to She-Who-Is-Goddess?" This voice, too, was now
familiar: Perialla, another of the priestesses. She was close to
my mother's age and was a quiet, somewhat dull woman who
had always been kind to me.

A snort in reply. "More than once. She dismisses the idea,
says she couldn't have been mistaken. She just *knew,* she says,
that she saw the god in Kilix that spring."

"But you don't think so?"

"You know how she is, how she has always been from
girlhood. Can't bear to be wrong. Never could. Velchanos
punished her by hiding himself—still is punishing her."

"Oh, surely not." Perialla sounded almost pleading. "It's
been so long, and she was so young when she offended Goddess. And you of all people should hope that Kilix was the
correct choice."

I held my breath. With any luck, they would talk about
why Goddess was angry with my mother. But luck was against
me, for Damia said only, "Her offense was too grave; it can
never be forgiven. He punished her with the boy, with
Minos-Who-Will-Be. No question about *his* parentage! The
crops have never been so abundant as they were that year. No,

he's the son of Velchanos, all right. Remember the feasting the fall after his conception?"

Perialla must have nodded, for Damia went on, "She-Who-Is never showed the baby, kept him bundled away, and then when she finally had to reveal him on his first birthday, she refused to see what everyone else did, that he was a monster and should have been exposed at birth." Perialla's horrified gasp didn't stop that bitter voice. "That was what the god wanted. It was a test for her, one she failed by keeping him alive, the same as she failed her earlier test."

"What test?" I longed to ask.

Damia lowered her voice, and I strained to hear. "I've heard rumors that the Minos is training an apprentice. Of course, he'd have to keep this secret—if She-Who-Is were to hear of it, she'd say it was sacrilege, since a true son of Karia and Velchanos is alive."

"Who is this apprentice?"

Before Damia could answer, the voice of my mother's maid broke in. "Mistresses, She-Who-Is-Goddess is waiting for you in her chamber." Iaera managed to sound respectful while still expressing urgency. Skirts rustled as the two women rose and hurried out, their shoes tapping on the floor. I knew I should follow after them, but instead I lay back on the sofa.

They doubted me? They thought that I was not the daughter of the god, that my mother had been wrong when she said she saw Velchanos manifest himself in the shepherd Kilix at the Planting Festival before my birth? The crops had been poor in the year of my conception, but so many things could explain that: a misread omen, an irreverent act in the god's cave, even the whim of Velchanos. It didn't have to mean that my mother had chosen wrongly, that the man who was my father had been just that—merely a man, and not Velchanos made flesh. And even if she had made a mistake, no shame falls to She-Who-Is-Goddess; it is up to the god to reveal himself. If he doesn't, She-Who-Is-Goddess must try to guess which man's body is housing Her husband. It's not her fault if he has hidden himself too cunningly. *How like a man,* I'd always thought of the way Velchanos disguised himself. *Capricious, unreliable, wanting to surprise, like a little boy.*

But if she *had* been wrong, then who was I?

I fought back the panic rising in my throat. I had to tell my mother what I had overheard, and she would make it right. She would punish Damia for her evil words and would assure me that I was the legitimate daughter of Velchanos. Then, even as I rose, I remembered that Damia had claimed she had already spoken to my mother, who had denied the accusation. I sank back and chewed on a fingernail.

This was just one more new piece of information that confused me about our customs on Krete. The first had come in my conversation with Theseus. Obviously, our ritual at the Planting Festival was not followed in Athens. Perhaps they did not even sacrifice the god every spring and yet they had fertile fields with a yield of crops in the fall, so why was it necessary here?

Was it necessary here?

And what was my part in it?

The sun moved to a new section of the sky, and one of his rays pierced my vision, reminding me that the day was passing. The priestesses would be waiting for me in my mother's chamber to instruct me in the rituals of the Dark of the Moon. But I couldn't face them now, especially poison-tongued Damia. How many of the priestesses thought that I was merely a girl born to my mother as a mortal woman and not as Goddess, and to Kilix and not Velchanos? That would make Kilix my father, and Kilix's daughter, who worked in the palace as a weaver, my sister.

This was a strange thought, and an even stranger one followed it: if I was the daughter of Kilix but Asterion was the son of Velchanos, he was not my brother.

No. Not possible. *None* of it was possible. I loved Asterion more than I loved anyone except my mother. I could not lose him, and I knew it would be even worse for him to lose me.

This time, I didn't care if other people were in the corridors as I ran, then walked, then ran again to the Minos's quarters. I reached the inner courtyard and stood in its entrance to catch my breath. It was a sunny, open space, large enough for several trees whose fat, tight buds showed how close we were to the Planting Festival. Birds in the small cages that hung from the boughs were singing, their odd little faces showing nothing of what they felt as their beaks opened and shut and notes came out of them. I always wondered if the Minos's birds were happy to be safe from hawks and cranes or if they were sad to be locked in those cages, secure and comfortable though they were.

The courtyard was paved with pale stone polished so smooth that it was dangerous to walk on after a rain. I knew this well; until two years earlier, I had spent most of my waking hours in this place, and every night during the Festivals, I, too, used to sleep in the Minos's compound. I would play with the children of the Minos and the children of She-Who-Is-Goddess and then curl up with my best friends among them in one of the rooms that opened onto the courtyard, snuggling against another warm body. Those were my favorite nights of the year.

But that happy girl was a stranger to me now as I stood and looked at the activity. As always, the Minos was surrounded by children. He sat on a low stone bench, showing the little girl on his lap how to handle her pet rabbit so that she wouldn't injure it. An even smaller boy hung over the Minos's shoulder and eyed his sister or cousin stroking the soft brown fur. At the Minos's feet, two boys laughed as they played some game that involved counting stones, and in a corner, Timandra, formerly my best friend, tuned the strings of a lyre. We had sworn that when we became women, we would still be friends, and after the ceremony, when they had received their new, secret adult names (I had no need of one, as my new name would be She-Who-Will-Be-Goddess), I ran to her. But she turned her back on me and hadn't spoken to me since.

I missed seeing Enops and Glaukos, who, now that they were old enough to dance with the bull, would have moved to the men's quarters. I didn't miss Simo, who also had gone to be trained for bull dancing. Simo had always delighted in tormenting me, and even after I became She-Who-Will-Be-Goddess, he found ways to hurt my feelings that stopped just short of the disrespect that would cause him punishment.

I hung back. Until recently, I had been one of the children petted by the gentle man whose long hair was streaked with gray. Now I wasn't sure of my welcome, especially when I saw Kodros, the Minos's spoiled daughter, approach and whisper something in Timandra's ear. Until I became She-Who-Will-Be-Goddess, Kodros had made my life miserable with teasing and hidden pinches and hair pulling. Now the two of them stared at me, and Timandra giggled.

The Minos caught sight of me, and a broad smile creased his face. "Dear child!" He swung the little boy to the floor and stood, the girl and her rabbit in the crook of his arm. He came to embrace me, shooed children off the bench like pigeons, and settled us together there, his strong arm around my shoulders. The little girl squirmed out of his embrace and ran with her pet to join Timandra and Kodros where they stood whispering together, glancing at me.

I leaned into my uncle gratefully, trying to forget that I was She-Who-Will-Be-Goddess and imagining that I was once more a child who played and slept in a heap with other girls, and ate meals in a rowdy group of children, and sang songs and told secrets and had friends, and quarreled and made up with those friends.

Yet just a few moons away was my second Planting Festival as She-Who-Will-Be-Goddess, and I was looking forward to it with the same ferocity as a child eager for the first taste of spring lamb. It is the holiest time of the year and the most enjoyable, with feasting and dancing and games and laughter. Then there is no difference between She-Who-Will-Be-Goddess, someone to be feared, and the daughter of a shepherdess, someone to join in friendly conversation and games. And of course there was always the chance that this year, Goddess would relent, would forgive my mother for her unspoken offense. That would bring me so much joy that I wouldn't care if I never had a friend again.

The Minos didn't seem to notice my preoccupation. "My bride is lovely, isn't she? And so sweet. Even Orthia adores her." He sounded as eager as a boy with a new plaything. "She applied a liniment to Orthia's shoulders that finally took the ache from them." He shook his head in wonderment. Even my mother had not been able to soothe the aching old body of the Minos's senior wife. Now, in such a short time, Prokris had eased her pain.

When I didn't answer, the Minos looked searchingly into my face. "What is it?" His kindness brought tears, when worry and anxiety and the cruelty of my former playmates had produced only stony hardness. I wept into his shoulder as he stroked my hair. When my tears were spent, he asked, "What's troubling you, little sister?"

I told him what I had overheard and studied his face. He didn't seem surprised. "You knew of this?" I asked.

He nodded. "There are always whispers about She-Who-Will-Be-Goddess. People fear you, and fear breeds all sorts of other things—jealousy, hatred, false flattery."

"But you—you're the Minos! Surely *you* know who I am!"

"I hope I do." His voice, usually merry, was grave. "But Pasiphaë . . ." The sound of her name, so commonplace, so like the name of any woman on Krete, made her seem smaller and vulnerable and made me seem like the daughter of an ordinary woman. I felt as though Poseidon the Earth Shaker had moved the ground beneath my feet. Everything I thought I knew, the person I thought I was, all had changed.

When I could trust my voice again, I asked, "When did people start questioning my—questioning me?"

"Before you were born," he answered. "There was that trouble at the Planting Festival a few years earlier, and then—"

"Trouble? What trouble?"

"Pasiphaë hasn't told you?" I shook my head. "Then I mustn't. But you should ask her."

"Does it have something to do with why Goddess is angry?"

He stroked my hair again and tucked a curl behind my ear. "It has everything to do with it." I waited for him to go on, but he was silent.

I sat up, suddenly resenting the feel of his arm around me, which a moment before had been so soothing. "So, how do I know if I'm She-Who-Will-Be-Goddess or someone else?"

"You can't know it now." His voice was somber. "You won't know for years, I hope. Not until Pasiphaë becomes Goddess Forever and you undergo the Ordeal of the Snakes."

"There's an *ordeal?* What happens?" I had carried snakes into the Goddess sanctuary, and I had seen my mother emerge later, clutching one in either hand, but I had never thought to ask what happened in between.

The Minos patted my hand. I'm sure he meant to be comforting, but I found his touch irritating. "You'll find out," he said quietly. "You'll find out soon enough."

CHAPTER 18

EVERY SPRING, the priestesses carry clay pots pierced with small holes into the shrine in the palace. As soon as I was old enough, I joined them. The pots always felt strangely alive as the weight in them shifted, and rose and fell. Although no one ever talked of it, we knew what lay coiled inside, their scales glittering, their forked tongues flicking in and out, their fangs ready to pierce the skin of anyone foolish enough to reach in without caution.

The priestesses were led by the Minos, who was robed in red and wearing the huge leather-and-bronze bull's head of the Planting Festival. We would disappear from the sight of the waiting crowd, into the small shrine housing the lumpy rock that held Goddess's essence. In that room stood She-Who-Is-Goddess, dressed in ceremonial robes: a heavy skirt that looped from her waist to the ground and an open-fronted jacket that revealed her breasts. Her face was painted stark white, her eyes and mouth looking like the spots on the moon, and her sash was tied behind her in a sacral knot. Gilded cow's horns glinted on her head.

At that point, my mother had not yet fled from her body, and she looked at me with eyes filled with love and concern. "Don't be frightened," her eyes said. "I'm still here."

We deposited our heavy pots on the floor, trying not to breathe the air, which was thick with the smoke of burning herbs that stung our nostrils and parched our throats. My mother stepped forward and shook a wet cypress branch over us, each cold drop of water falling sharp on our faces. Then the oldest priestess—this had been Damia ever since I joined the group—told the story of Goddess and how She came to us.

Long, long ago, before time was time, the island of Krete lay dead. No goddess or god walked our black beaches; no plants grew in our fields; even the fish deserted our shores. In this wasteland, the Great Mother hid her son Velchanos from the murderous wrath of his own father. When Velchanos grew to manhood, he slew his father and became lord of the sky. To thank the land that had kept him safe in his childhood, Velchanos sent down a star to the people of Knossos. This was the Goddess stone, and the people worshiped it, but still the land lay dead. Velchanos was Krete's father, but we needed a Mother. Velchanos saw our despair, so he returned to the land and became a bull, red and white and black. He traveled the earth in search of his wife so that he could bring her to Krete.

"Blessed be Goddess," we all murmured.

He found her—Europa of the mild eyes—and bore her to us on his back. Europa was Goddess, and she chose twelve women of Knossos to attend her. The land grew fertile. Olive groves spread across the hills, and the fields became golden with the sacred crocus. Fish jumped in the sea and in the rivers.

"Blessed be Goddess."

Now time became time. Europa grew old and then died, and the people were frightened. How could they live without Goddess? Would the land return to the death that had gripped it before She came to walk among them?

"Blessed be Goddess."

The very night that Europa died, as the people mourned and wailed, a new light appeared in the sky. It was as large as the sun, but white and pure. It was the moon. The people knew that this was their Mother and that She had returned to Her husband in the sky, and they rejoiced for Her. But the next night, the people saw that She was more slender, and they wondered. Every night, She grew smaller until She disappeared. Shrieks arose from the people, for they thought that Goddess had abandoned them again.

"Blessed be Goddess."

Then the wisest of the twelve priestesses said in the voice of Europa, "Why do you fear, My children? For I am Karia, your Goddess, who formerly inhabited the body of Europa, and I will always be with you. When I am not watching My people from My husband's abode in the sky, I will walk among you."

"Blessed be Goddess."

Goddess chose a girl to take her former place among the priestesses, so again there were twelve attendants. Goddess then showed the people a bull who bore the mark of Velchanos. She instructed them to open the path of its life to free Her husband. The bull's blood flowed, and Velchanos's spirit flew from it to the body of a man of the village.

"Blessed be Goddess."

Goddess took the man's hand and said, "Here is My lord Velchanos." For three days they lived as husband and wife, and then Goddess led the man to the brother of the priestess whose body She inhabited. This man was the first Minos. Goddess told him, "Take My husband's blood and spread it on the fields." The Minos did as Goddess commanded, and again the crocus bloomed and the olives fattened and the fish swam. Goddess returned to the sky but came back to Knossos to bear a child that winter, on the shortest night of the year. "This is My daughter," She said. "She will be Goddess." Velchanos returned again the next spring and took the body of another man, whose blood again caused the fields to be fertile. That winter, Goddess bore a son, once more on the shortest night. "This is My son. He will be your Minos," She told the people. "He will help She-Who-Is-Goddess to find Me each spring and will spread the blood of Velchanos on the fields. So you must do every year, my children, or Knossos will fall and Krete will fall and time will cease to be time."

"Blessed be Goddess," we said. We bowed low to my mother, and when we straightened, my mother was no longer there. The eyes that looked at me were Goddess's eyes, and the heart that beat in her breast was Goddess's heart. One by one, oldest to youngest, we backed out silently to join the rest of the people who had been gathering all day and who now kept their eyes fixed on the door we had just come through. I was the last to emerge. People pressed cups of wine into our hands, and we drank while we waited for Goddess to emerge and find Her husband.

My mother told me that before he became too large to control, my brother had always roamed through the crowd at this time, squeezing people he liked in his strong arms, bumping into or ignoring those he didn't. His grunts and babbling were loud and irritating as the afternoon wore on, but he had seemed unaware that he was causing a disturbance. One year, when he had grown big enough for his behavior to worry the Minos, Asterion had been tethered to a stake on the edge of the crowd, but he roared and bellowed until I let him free. The Minos fed him dried figs laced with a sleeping drug, and when he became meek and biddable, my uncle led my brother down to his chambers.

The next year, Asterion was confined under the palace, along with several boys to keep him company. They were so far away that their screams went unheard, and it was only afterward, when torchlight revealed the bloody horror of my brother's chamber, that we discovered how Asterion had amused himself during the long wait. I was only five years old, but still I comforted him and tried to make him understand that the broken bodies could not be fixed.

For a few years, Asterion was left alone during the ceremony, despite the Minos's warnings that the unhappiness of the god's son might cause our father, Velchanos, to frown on us. The people were made so uneasy at this arrangement, fearing the wrath of the god, that finally the Minos declared that the next time tribute-children were sent from Athens, they would provide Asterion with companionship. That way, he would be kept pacified, and my uncle's fierce desire to avenge the killing of his beloved son would be somewhat satisfied. I tried to comfort myself with the thought that their death would be swifter than if they had been sent to the mines, like the first group of Athenians that had landed on our shore.

Together everyone waited, the crowd of shepherds and fishermen and traders and farmers, women and men, old people barely able to walk and children. We waited in the field, regardless of sun or rain or wind. Sometimes we stood for only a few minutes and sometimes for so long that babies slept and woke and nursed at their mothers' breasts and slept again. Once, the year before I became a priestess, the sun had already touched its lower edge to the horizon before the door opened.

But when it finally did open, it seemed that no time had passed. One figure emerged and stood motionless as everyone leaped and shouted, even the tiny children who could not have known what was happening but who were caught up in the general relief and joy. Discordant sounds burst out as musicians played their instruments without attention to what the others were doing. Women and men laughed and shrieked. Some fainted.

Men ran to smother the flames under the pots where lambs, kids, and calves had been boiled in milk into sweet tenderness. They uncovered the enormous pits where pigs had been roasting since the night before. The Minos scattered red wine over the ground to awaken it and to prepare it for the more vital fluid that would come in just a few days.

In all that noise and in the swirling mass of joy, only two figures never moved. One was me, rooted to the spot in fear and misery, staring up the long stairway. The other stood above me in the doorway, a writhing snake clutched in each fist, as She gazed out at Her people with glittering eyes, a frozen smile on her lips. *What is She doing?* I always wondered. *Counting them, to see who has died and how many have been born since the last Festival? Seeking Her beloved husband, whom She hasn't seen for a year?* Her cold eyes always passed over me as though I were any other girl, or a dog, or even a tree.

For although the figure looked like Pasiphaë, like She-Who-Is-Goddess, She was not. Something had happened, something to do with the cold creatures that had lain coiled up in the heavy pots and that now twisted and squirmed in Her grasp, arching back and gaping, their fangs curving at the black sky, knowing that in a short time they would be chopped into tiny pieces and mixed into the stew that all the people would share.

No longer did that body belong to She-Who-Is-Goddess,

a mortal woman who ate and slept and delivered babies and held me on her lap and sang Asterion to sleep. Tonight She was Goddess, and for the three days until She chose to leave us and return to the sky, Asterion and I would be alone. She was still my mother, but She was also everyone else's Mother, the Mother of each baby and each old shepherd, even of each lamb and rabbit and pig and spring crocus and blade of grass. She looked at me with the same eyes that looked at smelly old shepherds, withered crones, and my childhood tormentor, Kodros.

Everyone else mourned days later, when the first sliver of moon appeared, for it meant that Goddess had departed from among us to be in the sky for the nine long moons until Birth of the Sun, when the days stop shortening and begin to grow long again. I wept along with them. My tears, however, were of relief, not sorrow. Goddess was everyone's Mother, but She-Who-Is-Goddess was the mother I knew, and she was back.

CHAPTER 19

THE ORDEAL of the Snakes?" I asked the Minos. He must have heard the fear in my voice, for he took my chin in his hand and said, "Dearest little sister, has no one told you?"

I shook my head. He clicked his tongue, disapproving.

"I have to go." I stood. "The priestesses are waiting for me, to prepare for the Festival. I still haven't learned—"

He gently pulled me back down next to him. "You don't want to go, do you?"

He took my silence for agreement and beckoned to the eunuch Dolops, a man who had taught me how to whistle and who had once cleaned up after me when I was sickened by a bad oyster. Now he didn't dare to look me in the face.

The Minos told his man to inform She-Who-Is-Goddess that I had been taken ill and would not be able to attend her that afternoon. Then he squeezed my shoulder. "Go into my chamber and rest. I'll have someone bring you refreshment."

The Minos's chamber was opulent, with white marble floors, brightly colored frescoes, and large windows that let in the afternoon sun. It contained very little furniture—a small bed, and a stool by a long, low table that was always crammed with models of the projects that my uncle and his pet architect, Daidalos, were working on. Daidalos had built my brother's dank little chambers, but that was only one of the reasons I hated him. He was so jealous that when his nephew Perdix showed talent in making tools, Daidalos pushed him off a cliff rather than have him cause a stir with some invention. He later claimed that Perdix had turned into a bird and flown away, but nobody believed him. Perdix had been sweet and had made clever little jointed soldiers and horses that Asterion adored. Daidalos's son Ikaros, who swaggered almost as much as his father did, had no interest in "entertaining" my brother, as he put it, and small talent as well.

So I was glad that Daidalos wasn't there, although evidence of his work lay scattered everywhere. I picked up a small, hollow, bronze cow, but its staring eyes made me shudder and I put it down hastily. The model of a mechanism for building what appeared to be a pyramid, such as the Aegyptians are said to bury their dead kings in, stood next to small blocks of stone; elsewhere, metal gears lay locked in complicated patterns, and a waterwheel stood ready to turn when the channel under it was filled with a miniature river. A small figure of a man, carved from ivory and with wonderfully cunning joints that stayed in place except when I moved them, stretched out his arms, to which were attached white doves' feathers, making him look like a winged god. I would borrow this for Asterion, I thought. Nobody would notice it missing in all that clutter, and losing it would serve Daidalos right for killing my brother's toymaker. *Besides, I'll return it someday,* I thought as I pushed it into my pouch, despite the likelihood that Asterion would break it into tiny pieces.

I was examining a seashell with a hole bored in its tip when a voice behind me, familiar yet strange, exclaimed, "Why, it's my rescuer!" The shell hit the stone floor with a *crack.* I should have realized that bringing me refreshment was something between an honor and a chore and that the task would have been delegated to the wife-to-be of the Minos.

The young woman I had removed from Asterion's chamber stood in the doorway, a cup in her hand. I could tell from how she held it, with her fingertips around its top edge, that it contained something hot. I turned to clear a spot and also to give myself time to regain my composure. I piled up a wax tablet, a pair of scissors, and a round piece of crystal polished to transparency that made everything under it look big, and motioned to her to place the cup on the table. She did so with the same grace I had noticed the morning before. Her brown hair was now bound up under a white head covering. No longer wife-to-be, but wife. The Minos had not wasted any time.

I wondered if I should tell the Athenian woman about

what I had seen pass over her face at our last meeting—the shadow of some horrible destiny. No, best not. It could have been merely the result of my disturbed night and not a real warning, and in any case, a warning of what? How could I tell her to be cautious if I didn't know what was threatening her? So I remained silent.

She straightened, watching as I sipped at the steaming cup. It was a simple herb tea, such as my mother and Korkyna often made, and its familiar taste was soothing.

I expected the girl to leave, but she sat down on a cushion. She fingered her necklace of pearls alternating with beads of deep blue lapis. The Minos must treasure her indeed to give her such an extravagant bride gift.

"When the Minos told me to tend to his sister," the Athenian woman said, "I expected a gray-haired old woman with a walking stick. Instead I find *you!* You can't be any older than I am." She looked me up and down in much the same way that Theseus had. "Younger, I would say." I felt myself blushing. I was so thin, I knew that in different clothes, I could be mistaken for a boy. "I must have misunderstood him. You are his niece or his sister-in-law, not his sister."

"I *am* his sister," I said, wishing my voice held the self-confidence that I heard in hers. "And his niece."

Silence. "You're his sister," she finally said, "*and* his niece?"

"We have the same Mother. Goddess is our Mother."

"I thought your goddess was everyone's mother."

"No, She really *is* our Mother. We were born of Her, although at different times, and when she was in different bodies. And our father is Velchanos." She didn't say anything for so long that I thought she hadn't understood, so I tried to explain. "You call him Zeus, I think."

"Oh, you are the girl they call—what is it?"

I swallowed. "I am She-Who-Will-Be-Goddess." For only the second time in my life, it sounded strange.

"I didn't know." She looked at me differently now, as I knew she would, but not with fear—with curiosity, it appeared. "Yesterday, I thought you—well, your dress was stained, and your hair was disarranged, and I thought you were one of the servants." I said nothing. I hoped that the fact that I hadn't looked my best wasn't the only reason she had behaved in such a familiar fashion with me. Now that she knew who I was, would she turn cold and silent? She patted the cushion next to hers. Was she really inviting me to sit with her?

I evidently hesitated too long, because now it was her turn to blush. "I'm sorry," she said, rising to her feet. "I don't know how I'm supposed to treat you—as my sister-in-law or as my husband's niece or as a goddess. Is it wrong for me to sit in your presence?" Instead of answering, I sat on the cushion and motioned to her to resume her seat.

"I know it's hard to understand," I said. I took a breath, trying to remember how I had heard Damia explaining it to another one of the Minos's wives, a girl with skin like ebony who had come from Aethiopia far to the south and who had died just a few months later.

"The body that carried my mother and also carried the Minos," I said carefully, "was my grandmother, She-Who-Is-Goddess before my mother." I looked at her, and she nodded in comprehension. "That means he is my uncle, since my grandmother bore him. But at the time that my mother was conceived, and also when the Minos was conceived, that body was being used by Karia, whom we call Goddess out of respect, and the body of their earthly father was being used by Velchanos."

She nodded again but looked a little less certain.

"Karia and Velchanos are brother and sister. Your Artemis and Apollo are the same as Karia and Velchanos, just as this bowl is a bowl, no matter what you call it in Athens."

"We also call it a bowl in Athens," she said, and I laughed.

"Then, when *I* was conceived," I continued, "Goddess was inhabiting my mother's body, and that spring, Velchanos had chosen to occupy the body of a man named Kilix. So, really, Goddess and Velchanos are my mother and father, just as they are Asterion's, and they are your husband's mother and father, so that means that your husband is my brother and Asterion's, too."

I saw that she was no longer listening and that her pretty face was wrinkled in pain.

"What is it?" I asked.

"Nothing much. Just a bellyache. I always suffer with my monthly flow." So she must be younger than she looked if her flow wasn't yet tuned to the full moon. It wasn't right of the Minos to marry such a young girl; I wondered if my mother knew.

She gave me a brilliant smile. She hugged her knees up to her chest and said, "It will pass soon. Now, tell me all about yourself." At first I was shy, but soon I found myself talking about my life in the palace, about learning the rituals, about how everyone treated me differently since I had become She-Who-Will-Be-Goddess, and how despite my mother's reassurances that one day it would all seem natural and I would treasure my privacy, I still missed having friends and companions.

I had been talking without cease for so long that my throat was dry. I gulped the rest of my herb tea, which was now as cold as river water. "And now tell me about you," I said.

"There's not much to tell."

"You're from Athens," I prompted. She nodded. "And what is Athens like?"

"Large. Grand."

"Larger and grander than Knossos?" The city that sprawled around the palace was all I knew, yet I had heard travelers remark on its size and beauty.

"Different." She leaned back on her elbows and looked up at me with a quick smile. "Every place is different from Knossos."

We talked for a long time. Prokris (I found out that the Athenians had no fear of having their names misused) was older than I had thought. In Athens, women's cycles do not always run with the full moon, and she was surprised that they did on Krete. I managed to forget that I was supposed to be meeting with the priestesses, and I even banished the Ordeal of the Snakes from my mind. Whatever it was, it couldn't be so dreadful, or my mother would never let me do it. She did it at the Planting Festival and came out whole, year after year. The Minos was just being overprotective, as always.

As that day stretched into afternoon and evening and my new friend and I sat together and then walked arm in arm through the courtyard in the cooling air, I didn't think about anything except that I had someone to talk to again.

That must be why I still didn't tell her about my vision. I didn't want to frighten her, to give her cause to avoid me. Would it have made any difference if I had? I like to think not, for that way I can sleep at night, comforted by the idea that Fate or Goddess or Moera Krataia had long ago determined what would be the end for me, for Asterion, for my new friend, even for Theseus, and I could do nothing to change it.

But on the nights when I awaken under a full moon and see my mother's cold white eye staring down at me accusingly, I know that I was mistaken. I should have told my mother and the Minos, and then all would have been different.

CHAPTER 20

I
T SEEMED that whenever I visited the Minos's quarters, I found Prokris seated at his feet, his hand resting on her soft brown hair while she talked and laughed or sang him a song. He adored her, and even the Minos's other wives doted on her. She quickly learned who outranked whom, who liked soft bread and who the crust, which were friends and which loathed each other. The children followed her the way the big dog followed Theseus. Whenever a little one fell or was stung by a bee or stubbed a toe, it was Prokris the child sobbed for and Prokris who could make the hurt go away.

Anytime I could escape from the priestesses' lessons, I fled to the Minos's quarters. I neglected Asterion, visiting him only hastily and infrequently. He was so happy to see me that I felt guilty when I left him looking after me with his huge eyes, and I always swore I would come back and tell him long stories the next day, but I never did.

I had little time at my disposal, in any case, as I often found myself being tutored until night fell. On those days, I imagined Prokris talking and laughing with someone else, and I prayed selfishly that she would not become good friends with one of the Minos's other wives.

Compared with my new friend, the priestesses were dull companions. I had known them my whole life. Priestesses are so powerful that it is allowed to pronounce their names. In addition to the sour Damia and the pleasant but dull Perialla, my mother's attendants were Athis, Meira, Marpessa, Zita, Orthia, Kynthia, Harmonia, Pero, and Kylissa. All were well born. Pero and Kylissa were sisters, born to my mother's mother when she was not Goddess. Orthia and Kynthia too were sisters, and Orthia was the Minos's first wife. She was even older than the Minos, and her mind had turned back into a child's mind, but the ways of Goddess had worn themselves so deeply into her being that she still performed Her rituals flawlessly. Athis had been born to my mother when she was not Goddess and looked very much like her—and like me, I had heard people say.

None of the priestesses were openly unkind to me, but I resented the smile of satisfaction that crossed Damia's shriveled face every time I made a mistake, just as I resented the way Kynthia would roll her eyes and grimace, impatient at my slowness, whenever I had to repeat an action or a prayer.

I loved to make Prokris laugh by telling her about the priestesses. One day, we shared a meal in the shade of the fig tree in the courtyard. Cook had discovered how much Prokris loved squid and octopus. As I hurried through the corridor on my way to meet her, I heard the wet *sploosh-sploosh* of one of Cook's boys slapping a dead octopus over and over against the hard rock outside the kitchen door to break up its tough fibers before Cook stewed it with vegetables and herbs. I hoped the boy kept at it a long time; I wasn't fond of the dish, but I could eat it if it wasn't too chewy.

I had to wait until the Minos settled down for his afternoon nap, as he didn't like Prokris to spend much time away from him. By the time she arrived, I was so hungry that I didn't care if she served me octopus as tough as seaweed.

It was tender enough, though, and there were also cheese and bread, and olives that had come from Athens with the tribute. I liked their foreign taste. If I closed my eyes, I could almost imagine I was on a beach in Attika, with its brilliant yellow sands. I wrapped a few in a vine leaf and tucked them into my pouch to take to Asterion later; he loved olives, and he would enjoy this new flavor.

After lunch, we stretched out on cushions next to the western wall, where a little shade fell in the afternoon. It was warm for early spring, but Prokris always preferred to be outside, even dressed in the finery that the Minos lavished on her. On another woman, the heavy embroidered dress and collar after jeweled collar might have looked garish, but

Prokris carried them with such grace that even the stiff cloth of her overskirt seemed supple. We each had a cup of wine, well watered as was proper for young ladies, and chatted as we lay back on the grass. We fell silent, and I was drifting off to sleep when Prokris spoke.

"What has Damia been teaching you lately?" Prokris knew Damia well; the old priestess constantly came to the Minos's quarters and told the younger wives how to behave.

I cast about for something amusing. "How to dress. She thinks I don't take enough care. She's constantly pulling at my clothes and telling me to wear tighter skirts. When I said that I couldn't birth babies in a tight skirt, she told me that my mother has never had any trouble and I shouldn't either. So, I told her that I can't run in a tight skirt."

I looked at Prokris out of the corner of my eye. She lay on her back, her cup of wine balanced on her belly.

"And then she said, 'Run? She-Who-Will-Be-Goddess must move with dignity!'" I squawked in imitation of Damia. Prokris giggled, and the cup of wine danced. Emboldened, I went on, "And all the while, I can see the bit of food between her teeth and the way her bottom sticks out when she walks as she's telling me how *I'm* supposed to move with dignity!" I hopped up and mimicked Damia, my hips waggling, my face screwed up in her sour scowl. Prokris burst into a merry laugh, and I felt rewarded.

Then another sound made me trip and almost fall. This was a man's laugh, something that should not be heard in the

Minos's quarters, unless it came from the Minos himself, and it was too youthful to be his. I looked everywhere. No one. I couldn't have imagined it, but whoever it was was invisible. I was about to call out, when Prokris leaped up, spilling her wine, and clapped her hand over my mouth.

"Look!" She pointed at the wall above my head. I spun and saw Theseus. He must have been standing on a ladder or on the shoulders of a very tall companion, because his face was at the top of the wall, and he watched us with obvious enjoyment.

"But he—but we—the Minos . . ." I spluttered. I took a deep breath. "Don't you know what the Minos will *do* to him?" She shook her head without concern. I didn't know either, but if Theseus were found here, there would be a great deal of blood and a great deal of pain with that blood.

Prokris held a finger to her lips and slipped behind me, to the door that led from the courtyard to the outer fields. I had not seen that door opened in a long time, and in fact hadn't used it since I had sneaked through it to go to the house of a friend shortly after my womanhood ceremony. The furious scolding I had received when I was found at his farmhouse had been severe, but it was nothing compared to his punishment. No one told me what they had done to him, but he never spoke to me again, and a few months later he shipped out on a trading ship, and I had not seen or even heard of him since.

So I was not eager to repeat the experiment, yet Prokris

pulled the door open with the ease of much practice. I must have looked surprised, because she laughed again and said, "What, did you think that the wives spent all their time locked up in here?" I did, but I held my tongue.

Even as I stepped through the door, I regretted it. Nobody would kill or strike She-Who-Will-Be-Goddess, but even the pretty young wife of the Minos—*especially* the pretty young wife of the Minos—would have no such protection. To meet with a man not her brother without her husband's permission was unthinkable. At least her death would be quick; I didn't know what they would do to Theseus, and I didn't want to know.

No such thoughts appeared to trouble my companions. Theseus, his large white dog at his side, pulled Prokris into the shelter of a large olive tree that was just beginning to bud. In their places, I would have quaked with terror. He beckoned to me to join them, but I stayed where I was and rested a hand on a rung of the gardener's ladder leaning against the wall.

The dog had sat down at her master's side and fixed her intelligent eyes on me. Theseus said, "You needn't fear that Artemis will bite you again." He stroked her head with his brown hand. "She was merely playing."

It was odd to hear an animal referred to by one of the names of Goddess, but it was not an insult. Dogs are holy to Goddess; she is a hunter, after all, and once, when the evil Aktaion attempted to violate her, taking advantage of her weaponless state as she bathed in a forest pool, his own dogs turned on him in horror and tore him to pieces. We honor dogs for that reason.

I looked around. The last time I'd been outdoors was the day the ships had pulled into the harbor, bearing Prokris and Theseus. Spring had come, and the fields were covered in tiny purple and white blossoms, and the air smelled of new grass and clean earth. Birds quarreled in the trees, and a light breeze brought the scent of herbs, crushed under my feet, to my nostrils. The city almost surrounded the palace, but on this side, where the Festivals were held, the fields sloped down toward the sea. I saw farmers preparing their land for planting, turning the earth with plows pulled by huge oxen, or by a lone donkey in the smaller holdings. Some were already planting early seeds. But I couldn't enjoy any of it while sickened by the thought of the danger we were in, meeting out here.

"We have to go back," I said to Prokris, trying not to look at Theseus, who had stood and was stretching. "If they catch you—"

"Oh, they won't catch me." Her voice was confident. "Everyone's asleep. Besides, that eunuch—you know, Karpophoros?" I nodded. He was a quiet and kindly man the size of a Titan. "He likes me. He'll keep everyone away."

"Perhaps she's right," Theseus said to Prokris. "There's no reason to take a risk. We can meet another day."

I turned to thank him, but my mouth refused to open as his shadow lengthened and broadened, like a dark liquid pooling at his feet. I glanced up; he was staring at me quizzically.

I pointed at the ground, my hand shaking. He looked. So did Prokris. "What?" Theseus asked. "What is it?"

The shadow turned from black to red, glistening, sliding smoothly across the grass. It bathed his feet and turned them crimson. I threw my hands over my face and screamed.

Prokris seized my wrist and dragged me back into the courtyard. As she shoved the door shut behind us, footsteps pounded, and two eunuchs burst into sight from the stand of trees. They slid to a halt in front of me, clutching weapons and looking around. "What is it?" panted Dolops, the one who used to be kind to me. I stared at him, wondering how to answer.

Prokris came to my rescue. "She-Who-Will-Be-Goddess was frightened," she said. "A snake." The eunuchs looked bewildered. They knew that I was perfectly accustomed to snakes.

"No, you misunderstood." I willed my voice to be firm. "It was a scorpion."

"A *scorpion?*" Dolops's face mirrored the skepticism in his voice. "Here?"

"Why not here?" I snapped. "But the creature slipped through a crack in the wall without stinging me. You may go now." They hesitated, and suddenly I was furious. I let my hand drift toward the pouch on my belt. At the moment, it held nothing but Asterion's olives, but I could tell by their suddenly widened eyes that they imagined it stuffed with all manner of fearful things: a bird's talon, perhaps, or a moon-shaped rock, or worst of all, a ball of thread with which I could bind a man's heart or his liver until he died slowly and painfully. They bowed hastily and backed away, then fled indoors.

"Didn't you see it?" I asked Prokris.

"See what?" She sounded exasperated.

The door opened a crack, then widened. I clutched Prokris, wondering what bloody monster would come through, but it was only Theseus. He peered to the right and to the left and then stepped through, staying within the shadow of the wall. His bare feet were unmarked, and he left no red footprints.

"I must have been dazzled by the sun." I didn't believe my own words, and Theseus looked similarly doubtful. I moved closer to him. "You have to go now," I said urgently. *"Now."* The effort cost me dearly, though, for my knees bent under me, and I would have slid to the ground if he had not caught me around the waist. I clutched his shoulder until the spots stopped dancing in front of my eyes, and then I pushed him away.

I took a deep breath and turned to Prokris. "Now," I said to her, "I must return to my mother." I forced myself to walk away firmly, my chin held up, and not look back.

CHAPTER 21

I DON'T KNOW what Theseus wants," I said. "The Minos seems satisfied that he's avenged Androgeos, and Theseus could probably leave, if he asked permission. Prokris says he doesn't want to return to Athens, though, where his step-mother will murder him. He told her he doesn't want to go back to that little town he's from, where everybody hates him and nobody believes he's the son of a king." *I know how that feels,* I thought, remembering Damia's words.

Asterion stared at me gravely. He didn't understand, but he was always so flattered whenever I came to talk with him that he stayed quiet and appeared to consider my words thoughtfully. At those times, I could pretend he was an older brother like those my friends had—when I had had friends—a brother who would tease me and bully me on occasion, to be sure, but who would also listen and give me advice, and even fight my tormentors and defend me against threats. Artemis had followed me down the stairs and into my brother's chamber, and now she sat next to him, her front legs like columns in front of her. Asterion's arm, wrapped around her cream-colored neck, looked darker and harder than ever as his fingers toyed with the honey-colored fringe edging her ears. The dog, too, kept her brown eyes fixed on me, with her usual calm. My brother was gentle with her, and she had no reason to fear him.

"And I don't know what he feels for Prokris." I was uncomfortably aware of a jealous pang. Jealous of whom—Theseus or Prokris? "That's foolish," I told Asterion, and he nodded as though I had said something wise. "She's the wife of the Minos. Theseus would be a madman to become involved with her. And she with him." Artemis moved her ears forward a little at the sound of her master's name and then let them fall back.

"Ah!" said Asterion, seeming to agree, and despite my unease and confusion, I smiled. I pulled a handful of nuts from my pouch, and he grabbed them. He offered one to Artemis, but after she sniffed at it and rejected it, he put it in his mouth, his strong jaws cracking the shell, which he then spat out on the floor. He looked at me inquiringly, which meant he wondered if I was concealing any more treats, though I chose to misinterpret.

"How do *I* feel about *him,* you mean?"

My brother chuckled, amused at our conversation game,

and I considered the question. "He's . . . different. He isn't afraid of me, which is refreshing, but at times he seems almost insolent. Oh, not really *insolent*," I said hastily, as though my protective big brother would become indignant at this idea. "He doesn't know our ways and sometimes makes mistakes."

Evidently feeling that something was required of him, Asterion grunted.

"I like him." I didn't know if *like* was exactly the right word. Something about Theseus made me want to touch him, to feel the hard muscle of his shoulder again, to brush my lips against the calluses on his palm. I remembered the pressure of his arm around my waist, supporting me when I nearly fainted after what I had seen, or imagined I had seen, in the orchard outside the palace walls, and I flushed.

Asterion grabbed my hand. This startled me, and I had to force myself not to snatch it away from him, which would have hurt his feelings.

"What is it?" I tried to withdraw my hand, but he grasped it harder and pulled me close to him.

He stared into my eyes, and when I was about to speak, to ask him again what he wanted, he laid a large finger on my lips. "Ahn," he said forcefully. "Ahn, ahn, ahn."

That was his word for no. No what? No talking? Why not? But he removed his hand from my mouth, so that couldn't have been what he meant.

"What is it?" I asked again. "Does something hurt you?" The shaggy head shook a negative. "Are you afraid of something?" He looked away. "Asterion!" He raised his dark eyes to me again, and something in them shook me to my toes. "Brother! What is it?"

For answer, he threw his arms around me and pulled me close. He was trembling.

I stayed with him until he fell asleep, his body nearly crushing me as he relaxed into slumber. I eased his heavy head off my lap and covered him with one of the blankets that became filthy almost as quickly as the servants replaced them. When I reached the doorway, I kicked a small piece of broken pot. I bent to pick it up and glanced back to make sure I hadn't woken him.

My brother lay on his side, his knees drawn up to his chest, in the manner in which dead bodies are laid out for burial. *Don't be silly,* I told myself as I watched his chest rise and fall, rise and fall. *Don't worry about Asterion. No one would dare to harm him.*

But as I turned one corner after another and then climbed the stairs, dread followed me as closely as did Artemis, whose breath I felt, warm on my arm, as I stepped into the darkening upstairs world.

CHAPTER 22

THE MOON grew smaller and thinner and then disappeared altogether. As we priestesses performed the rituals of protection from the darkness and prayed to Goddess to return, I recalled my conversation with Theseus and wondered where She went when She was out of the sky yet not among us on Krete. Twelve other cities were ruled by their own She-Who-Is-Goddess. In Hellas, these were Delphi, Ithaka, and Naxos; in distant Anatolia, the people of the cities of Kolkhis and Ephesos worshiped her; in Aegyptos it was Tel Hazor; in far-off Italia it was Aricia; in Phoenicia, the people of Tyre worshiped her. When I asked my mother the names of the four remaining cities, she always became troubled and refused to answer. I knew better than to press her, as she rarely discussed these secret matters.

I had forgotten many of the Festival's small details over the past year. "No, no!" Damia screeched like a seagull one warm afternoon. "You take thirteen steps from the altar and then turn. Thirteen. Always thirteen." Thirteen for the twelve priestesses plus She-Who-Is-Goddess, thirteen for the cities where Goddess was worshiped, thirteen for the number of moons in the year, culminating in the Planting Festival, after which the year would begin again.

Athis, no longer the junior priestess since I had filled that spot, gave me a quick smile of sympathy. I grimaced at her and rolled my eyes. It had been a long, tedious day, and I was finding it hard to concentrate. "Always thirteen," I repeated, hoping that the yawn I was holding back was inaudible. I think it wasn't, because my mother called me to her. Damia scowled, but She-Who-Is-Goddess was not to be denied. She led the priestesses out.

"Come sit here with me," my mother said, patting the cushion and sliding over. It was getting difficult for her to move; her large belly rubbed against the table in front of her. I felt my forehead pucker; she was so much older than anyone I had ever assisted at a birth. If she could hardly shift her weight to give me a place to sit down, how could she push a child from her body?

My mother noticed where I was looking. "I am healthy and strong," she said, "and it's usually the first baby that causes problems. I had difficulty with my first."

"With Asterion?"

She-Who-Is-Goddess stopped her work. "No, child. Not with your brother. With my first baby."

"But he's your first. Athis is your second, and I'm your third. And then Glaukos." I had never heard of any others.

My mother shook her head. "You're my fifth. Glaukos is my sixth." I must have looked as bewildered as I felt, because she went on. "You didn't know?" I shook my head and swallowed. This meant that she was even older than I had thought. "I had been She-Who-Will-Be-Goddess for less than a year." Her voice trailed off, and I wondered if she was remembering the years that she spent alone, with her mother dead and me not yet born. She had become Goddess after her mother fell ill of an autumn cough that worsened until she died in the winter. "For a day, it looked like the baby would live and would be She-Who-Will-Be-Goddess." I felt a chill at the thought of how close I had come to being only the spare, the extra. My mother sighed and shook her head. "But she lived only until the sun next set." She appeared to have finished her tale.

"You said I'm the fifth," I reminded her. "Asterion was your second?"

She nodded. "Yes, and the god's son. Then another boy, then Athis, then you, and finally Glaukos." She paused before adding, "None of the others were a child of the god." It was no wonder my mother hadn't mentioned the other boy. A boy not the son of the god was of little use to her. That child must have died, as my mother's first baby had done. I barely remembered Glaukos's birth, when I was three. He had immediately gone to live with the Minos. I sobbed when his nursemaid took him away. My mother had been impatient with my tears and reminded me that I could visit him whenever I wanted, but that didn't console me.

"You were too small to help me with them. Now you know more about birthing than other girls your age, even more than some grown women, and you will help me. This time"—she curled the thumb and first finger of each hand into a crescent for good luck—"this time all will go well."

Even She-Who-Is-Goddess was only another woman when giving birth, and whether my mother lived or died was in Goddess's hands. And Goddess was angry with her.

Talking about her children must have reminded her of Asterion, and she asked, "When did you last visit your brother?"

"Just yesterday." This would give me an excuse to leave. I stood. "I'll go see him now."

I stopped long enough to retrieve the small winged man I had picked up in the Minos's room, then slid it and a handful of raisins into my pouch. The store was low, but summer would be here soon and we would have no need of dry fruit.

Lying across the threshold of the door leading to the basement was Theseus's large white dog. I leaned down and stroked her soft head. "Is he down there?" I whispered. Her tail swayed but she didn't move. I stepped over her and felt her eyes on me as I descended the stairs.

I was two turns away from my brother's chambers when I heard a sound. It was a man speaking in a chatty, conversational tone. I paused. I knew who it was, even though the voice was distant. I rounded the final corner and saw Theseus's now familiar stocky form seated on the ground, talking to my brother, who was also seated and was staring at the other boy with his mouth dangling open. I saw to my shame that a string of drool hung from his lower lip.

Asterion saw me before Theseus did, and he scrambled to his feet. "Ah!" he said, and pointed to the Athenian. "Adne!"

"Yes, I know." I hurried past Theseus. I hadn't seen him since the day we had met outside the wall of the Minos's quarters, and the memory of his arm around my waist and of his hard shoulder made me flush. As I crossed the line of white stone that marked the boundary of my brother's chambers, I glanced back and saw, to my secret and confusing pleasure, that Theseus was reaching out to stop me. Asterion took my hand and tried to kiss me, but I wiped his mouth first, and then presented my cheek to him. As he embraced me, he mumbled something, his eyes shining, and his crooked teeth showed in the grin that always melted me.

"Is this your new friend?" I glanced at Theseus, whose eyebrows were drawn together.

"You're not afraid of him?" he asked.

I sat down, motioning to Asterion to do the same. Usually he would have done so eagerly, ready to play whatever game I wanted, but this time he hesitated and glanced at Theseus.

"Don't you want to see what I've brought you?" I patted my pouch, and now he turned his full attention on me. I loosened the drawstring and pulled out the little winged man.

"Ooooh!" Asterion reached for it, but I held it back, and he subsided, hands clasped, as I had taught him. When I knew he wouldn't move again, I held the figure up and moved it as though it were flying, then placed it on his lap. He picked it up, his mouth puckered in a perfect circle.

It always delighted me to please him, as I was never sure what he would like and what he would stomp to bits in disappointment. I watched as he turned the little man over, bending the toy's knees, twisting its arms backwards at an impossible angle, cocking its head so the painted face looked over its own back. He rocked and laughed in glee.

Seeing him absorbed, I addressed Theseus. "What are you doing here?"

"Came to see the monster."

I was lucky that Asterion was engaged in twisting the limbs of his new toy, or he would have been upset at my indignant gasp. "He's not a—"

"I know, I know," Theseus hastened to assure me. "I know he's not that. Anyone can see it. People call him one, though, don't they? But I don't think he's so bad." He rose to his feet—slowly, I noticed. I was pleased that he had learned so quickly how to keep from startling my brother. "I don't see why they don't let him out. He seems fearfully bored here."

"Oh no!" This time my exclamation penetrated Asterion's awareness, and he paused in his play. I forced myself to smile at him and patted his hand. He went back to what he'd been doing, but now he seemed to be listening. I went on more calmly, as though talking of the weather. "No, he can't be let out. You wouldn't say that if you'd seen—"

"Tomorrow, I'll talk to the Minos about it. I'll see what he has to say."

Before I could answer, my brother burst out in a high-pitched wail. I leaped up and was horrified at the blood dripping from his mouth. "Open!" I commanded. He shook his head. I squeezed his large jaw until it gaped, revealing the broken pieces of a wing of his little toy. I pulled out the ivory splinters from his tongue. When I had finished, he bellowed, throwing his arms around me and drenching me with red-stained slobber. He pulled me down to the floor with his weight, so I sat with his large head on my lap. I sang him one of my mother's lullabies, but he didn't appear to hear me, so I stopped and stroked his hair, feeding him raisins one by one until they were gone. "Hush now," I said again and again. "Hush now."

Theseus watched silently. When Asterion's sobs finally subsided and he lay sniffling, clutching the painted head of the now armless figure, Theseus spoke. "What I want to know is why he wasn't exposed at birth. Would have been the kindest thing for him. For everyone."

"But he's—"

"He's your brother." That wasn't what I had been going to say, but it was true, so I kept silent. Theseus evidently wasn't satisfied, though, and he leaned forward and scrutinized my face. "You were going to say something else, weren't you?"

"Asterion is . . ." I swallowed. "He's the firstborn of Goddess and Velchanos." Surely Theseus understood by now what that meant, but his face didn't show any enlightenment, so I was forced to go on. "He's the firstborn son of Goddess and Velchanos," I repeated, "and he is Minos-Who-Will-Be. When the Minos dies, Asterion will take his place." Still silence, but I knew what Theseus must be thinking: *How could Asterion perform the duties of a high priest?* Theseus might be unfamiliar with the ways of Krete, but any priest, anywhere, would have to know how to perform rituals, say prayers, make sacrifices—a whole series of things that were unthinkable to anyone looking at my brother as he sat on the floor popping the head of his toy into his mouth and out again, laughing with delight at the sound it made as it flew from his lips.

"Goddess will take care of it," I said. "She always does. She always will. We must trust in Goddess." I was echoing my mother's words, and like her I curved my thumb and first finger into a crescent to lend force to what I said.

"How do you know he's the son of Velchanos?" Theseus asked. A few days earlier, I would have been shocked, but because I had overheard Damia's doubts about my own parentage, I stopped the indignant reply that sprang to my lips.

"He was born at the right time, at the Festival of Birth of the Sun, nine months after the Planting Festival. And the crops were especially plentiful that year."

Theseus looked dubious. "I know something of this. I was told that I was the son of a god, and as it turns out, I'm not."

A grunt from Asterion made both of us look at him and then back at each other. For the first time since we'd met, Theseus seemed to have lost his self-confidence.

"Your father is king of Athens, though, is he not?"

"He is."

"Well, then . . ." I didn't know much about kings. I knew that in Aegyptos, the king ruled by right of having married the daughter of the previous king and that frequently a brother and a sister would wed to keep the royal line pure. Mykenae's king ruled by conquest, a barbarian system, I thought. In Athens and some other cities, the oldest son of the king took the throne—sometimes, I'd heard, even killing his own father if he was impatient. "Well, then, someday you will be king as well, will you not?"

He gave a wry smile. "If your brother doesn't eat me first."

"He doesn't hurt people on purpose," I said, but Theseus wasn't listening.

"It was my father and his wife who sent me here." I had heard of stepmothers who killed their husbands' children, but it was more commonly stepfathers who were murderous. I didn't understand that. Exposing a child at birth—yes, this was difficult, and it made everyone sad, but nobody had grown to know and love that child, and it was usually the best for everyone.

Before I could answer, Asterion lifted his head and said, "Huh!" He pointed to the doorway.

"What does he mean?" Theseus asked.

"Someone's coming." This was a rare occurrence, and I felt curious. Theseus scrambled to his feet, almost tripping on the hem of his robe, and clapped his hand to his waist as though looking for a sword.

Asterion always seemed to know who was coming. If this were my mother or the Minos, he would be on his feet making eager barking sounds. If it were someone he was afraid of—almost everyone else—he'd be whimpering. But he was squatting, his enormous knees almost up to his ears, and rolling the little ivory head along the floor. Its painted face, the features blurry now, flashed up and down and up and down before coming to rest with only the smooth, white back of its head visible.

Was it merely by chance that the little man hid his face from me? I later wondered. *Or was it an omen, a warning sent by Goddess?* If it was a warning, it was a useless one. I didn't recognize it as such, and even if I had, I wouldn't have known how to change everything that was about to happen.

CHAPTER 23

I KNOW from the first moment I see the Minotauros that I have nothing to fear from him. He's very tall and hideously ugly, but really he's nothing more than a child in a misshapen body. He seems painfully lonely and bored. The people who attend him wait until he's asleep to leave his food and to empty the bucket that he uses (badly) for relieving himself. He grins, showing crooked teeth, when I first come down to his dark, smelly chamber. I keep an eye on him, but I soon relax.

His sister, Ariadne, is quite different. She's small, and like all the Kretan women I've seen, she has black hair hanging in waves almost to her waist. She is not merely pale, like the rest of the noblewomen here; she has an unhealthy pallor. Her face looks, I think, like the mushrooms that appear in the deep forest after rain and glow against the dark earth. I understand that she rarely sets foot out of doors.

Her eyes are her most striking features. They're large, and so dark that the pupil is invisible in their depths, and long black lashes form a fringe around them. She is not pretty, but in an odd way she is beautiful.

I haven't admitted it to Prokris, but her plan now makes me uneasy. It was different when we were on the ship, sailing who knew where, with a hideous monster waiting to eat me on the other shore. It seemed logical then that once Prokris was established as queen, we would somehow kill the monster, liberate the Kretan people, and take over the country. She promised that she would marry me in exchange for my help, and I would become the island's ruler.

She never doubted that she would become the king's favorite wife, and indeed, the Minos does seem fond of her. But we were wrong about the rest of it. The Minos is not a king. He is the chief priest and some kind of lawgiver, but he is the subject of his sister, and she is the human incarnation of the moon goddess. Prokris can't make such a claim. She's obviously a mere woman, a mortal.

I have also found out that the people here are not ruled by fear of the Minotauros. They call him "*our* monster" with an air of pride. Most of them, anyway. Killing him wouldn't cause a great outpouring of gratitude and support. We certainly wouldn't be liberating anybody.

Prokris is very daring and manages to slip out of the women's quarters frequently, mostly because she has charmed the eunuchs who serve as the Minos's guards. One day, we sit in the crook of a tall cypress just outside the wall. Prokris likes being up this high. She can see into the compound where the Minos lives with his wives and children.

"They took all my things," she says. "Those women went through my bags and chests and took away my clothes and everything else I brought. They sneered and said they were fit only for barbarians. Imagine, these people calling *Athenians* barbarians!"

I'm about to agree, when I realize what she's said. "*All* your things? What about my sword?"

"They took that, too." She sounds glum but not alarmed. "Don't worry; they don't know you brought it. I said Aegeus had given it to me as a parting gift. They gave it to the Minos."

I suddenly feel vulnerable. It's not like I actually had the sword in my possession, but knowing that Prokris had possession of it had given me a sense of security.

"They did let me keep my wedding dress," she goes on. "But they took it away after the ceremony, and I think they cut it up and divided the fabric among themselves. The Minos didn't seem to care, but the women were just vicious."

Prokris tells me that Ariadne thinks she'll be a goddess one day. "She's mad," she asserts.

"Completely mad," I agree. But I wonder.

"It just isn't natural for this whole island to be governed by a woman," Prokris says. "Once you show them what a *real* ruler is like, a real king, they'll come to our side. How could they not?"

I understand her reasoning. A woman can't command an army—no soldier would take orders issued in a female's high voice—and the tasks that women are good at, spinning and weaving and tending to babies, take all their time. Still, I hesitate. The fields of Krete are fertile, and the trade ships stop here regularly, leaving all sorts of goods and departing heavy-laden with limestone and precious saffron. Tribute comes in punctually from the many subject lands. No one seems to fear attack. The maze of storerooms under the palace, except where Ariadne's befuddled brother spends his lonely days, is bursting with grain that the queen doles out evenhandedly to her subjects. They are well fed and seem happy.

My status here is unclear, now that it's become obvious that Ariadne's brother isn't going to eat me. I don't know if I'm an honored guest, a playmate for the Minotauros, a slave, or something else. I don't even know if they'd let me go if I asked, so I don't ask.

Prokris dismisses my concerns and counsels patience. "I'll be able to tell when the time is right," she promises. "You continue charming the little princess, and I'll lull the old man into trusting me completely. I'll know when it's time to move."

So I wait, trapped in her schemes.

CHAPTER 24

MY MOTHER'S servant Iaera ran into the inner chamber. Usually the servants avoided the dark, twisting corridors under the palace like the mouth of Hades, so I was already on my feet with surprise at the sight of her when she grabbed my wrist. The shock of her touch made my throat squeeze shut. "What is it?" I managed to squeak.

"You must come." Iaera dropped my arm as though it had burned her. But her urgency propelled me forward, and I ran out, forgetting Asterion, Theseus, everything except the unknown danger that had alarmed the maid enough to touch me. Iaera was close behind. "Your mother—She-Who-Is—it's the baby."

"What baby?" I asked stupidly.

"*Her* baby. It's coming."

"No, it isn't," I insisted, even as I took the stairs two at a time, holding my robe up out of the way. "It's not due for more than another moon." Iaera was silent, which chilled me more than a contradiction would have done. I flew down the corridors and threw open the curtain at the doorway of my mother's chamber.

I must have taken a wrong turn, I thought. This was not where my mother and I lived and worked and slept. This must be some other room, this place where priestesses stood in silence, each holding a candle whose light illuminated her white face, making a circle around the high bed where something writhed.

I don't know how long I stood in the doorway trying to take it in, that my mother, not Goddess, not She-Who-Is-Goddess, but a woman like any other, was delivering a baby and that Goddess was sending the baby much too early.

Damia spoke from her place next to my mother's head. "Come now. Only She-Who-Will-Be-Goddess may touch her at this time." The familiar odor of birth, of blood and something else sharp that I smelled only when a baby was coming, made me almost forget who it was that looked at me with reddened eyes, her black hair stuck to her sweaty cheeks, and I got down to work.

I knelt, rolled up my sleeve, and felt for the baby. My stomach wrenched; I couldn't understand what I was touching. It *was* the head, wasn't it? I pushed my hand farther in and winced as my mother gave a little whine. Where were the eyes, the nose? *Dear Goddess, is this a child without a face?*

Then I realized something almost worse. The child was the wrong way up. My mother and I had once safely delivered a baby who was looking toward the heavens, like this one. My mother had said it was a wonder that Goddess had not killed both the child and the woman. I didn't trust that Goddess would allow such a wonder to me, especially after She had allowed me such a short time to train.

Almost the worst part of the long night—as I tried to turn the baby over, as I gave up on that and tried to pull it out by force, as the floor grew slippery with blood, as the candles flickered and shadows moved like imps around the room— was the silence. My mother made no sound after the whine that I had ripped out of her, and the priestesses stood like trees. Many of them were experienced midwives, but when I asked them to help my mother sit up, they looked through me as though I were crystal. When I screamed and knocked the candle from Perialla's hand, she didn't wince. She picked it up and relit it at the one that Damia clutched in her own white claw.

When at last I held the tiny baby, wet and squalling, the priestesses blew out their candles—I had not noticed that pale light was coming in through the columns—and bustled about. One took the child from my arms and wrapped her in a white fleece. Another dipped a cloth in a basin of water and sponged my mother's face, clucking and murmuring.

Perialla rubbed the birth slime and blood from the child and held her up for me to inspect. The tiny thing was purplish, but as she screamed, she brightened to pink and then red. She was covered with fine black hair, and I recoiled. Had my mother given birth to a monster?

"Just like my son, my firstborn." Perialla's voice was tender. "Furry as a little squirrel at birth. He lost it all in a few weeks, as she will too." The words "if she lives" hung in the air between us. I knew her son; he was large and handsome, with no more hair than any other man. Perialla put the baby in my arms. I wrapped her snugly, and her screams turned to whimpers and then silence as she looked around with large, milky-gray eyes.

My mother was lying so still. Didn't she want to see the baby? I brought the child around, and my mother didn't move as I held the tiny bundle up to her.

"She's small, but she's strong," I said.

My mother turned her face away. "Call her Phaedra," she said. Why didn't she say, "I'll call her Phaedra"? I picked up her hand. It seemed small and thin, and she hardly returned the pressure of my fingers. I pressed my face into her palm, my tears mingling with her sweat.

"Phaedra," I agreed. It was a pretty name, and one I had not heard before.

One of the priestesses did something to the bedding that caused my mother to gasp and catch her lower lip between her teeth. I looked back sharply, ready to scold the woman, when I saw that she was carrying away a blanket so heavy that it dragged on the floor, leaving a dark smear behind it. I handed the baby to the nearest woman and stood to see what I could do to stanch the bleeding.

"Stop." Something in the way Damia spoke halted me. She turned to my mother and said, "You must tell her." My mother's head moved back and forth, back and forth, on her pillow in a firm negation. "Pasiphaë." The use of my mother's name startled me, but Damia repeated it. "Pasiphaë, you must tell her now."

Still nothing.

"If you do not . . ." The old woman's voice faltered, and then she went on more firmly, "If you do not, I will."

"Let me stop the bleeding first," I pleaded. Damia moved aside, and I inspected the damage that the baby had caused. That *I* had caused. I did what I could to slow the flow of my mother's life from her body, but I had only given her another hour, if that. When I finished, I went back to her side and picked up her hand once more. It was cold, but I felt a weak pulse in the wrist.

The silence lasted until my heart squeezed at the thought that she must have died, but then she whispered, "Leave us."

Damia hesitated, looking from me to the white face surrounded by black hair unloosed from its usual knots and coils and spread over the sweat-soaked pillow. The priestess pressed her thin lips together, bowed, and withdrew out of earshot, but still within the chamber. *Why can't the old turtle leave us alone?* was my miserable thought, but then my mother's fingers tightened almost imperceptibly on mine, and I bent in closer.

I knew that I was about to hear the answer to the question that had plagued me ever since I could remember—*Why is Goddess punishing my mother?*—and, I fervently hoped, to the new one that had been brought up by Damia and Perialla—*Who am I?* Yet, suddenly, I didn't want to know. If my mother revealed the secret she had guarded for so long, it meant that she knew that Goddess was taking her.

I smoothed a lock of damp hair off her face. She opened her eyes with a great effort. "Come closer," she said. "I know you have wondered why Goddess is angry with us."

"I don't need to know, Mother," I said, but she stopped me with a look that had something of her usual command.

"You do need to know, and you need to hear it from me. I must make clear to you what I did, so that you don't do the same." The dread that settled in my chest threatened to sicken me, and I didn't dare speak again. I merely bowed my head.

"Long ago," she said slowly, "when I was your age . . . I had been She-Who-Is-Goddess for only one year. It was the Planting Festival and I—oh Goddess, there is so much you don't know!" Her lips were as pale as the moon behind a cloud. I chafed her cold hand between mine; surely if I could warm her, she would return to herself. But she pulled away.

"Listen to me," she said hoarsely. "Soon I will be Goddess Forever and you will be She-Who-Is-Goddess. No!" she said as she saw me starting to speak. "This is how it must be. Look to Damia for anything you need to learn. She will not dishonor Goddess by leading you incorrectly. It should be

Thoösa, who will return as senior priestess, but she harbors too much ill will."

And Damia doesn't? I thought, but all I said was, "I will, Mother."

Her breath was shallow. "Damia would never dishonor Goddess, as I did."

"No," I protested. "No, Mother, you never—"

"Hush. It was long ago, so long ago." Her voice faded, and then grew stronger. "I had undergone the Ordeal before, but sometimes it is more powerful, sometimes less. This time—the time of which I speak—I was Goddess, yet I was not. I was also, in some way, Pasiphaë. I saw with Pasiphaë's eyes, and I heard with Pasiphaë's ears." A pause; then, so faintly that I could barely hear her, "And I loved with Pasiphaë's heart."

"No, Mother," I whispered. "I don't want to hear."

"You *will* hear. When I stepped out of the shrine, the people rejoiced that Goddess had returned. I wanted to tell them that they were wrong, that I was still She-Who-Is-Goddess, still Pasiphaë, and that the Ordeal had failed. But Goddess stopped my tongue. And I suppose that in some way I *was* Goddess. But there was more woman than Goddess in me, and the woman in me failed my people. I knew my husband. I saw Velchanos. He had taken the body of Nikanor." Her voice lingered over the name, a new one to me.

"Who is Nikanor?"

She squeezed her eyes tight, and a tear slid from the outside corner of each. Her breath barely stirred my hair. "He was—he was a man. A simple man, really, a carpenter who had grown up near the palace, my playmate as a child. He was the one I loved above all others. And so, even though I saw that he was Velchanos, even though I knew I had to choose him to be my consort until the Goddess in me returned to the moon, I could not. I could not bear to watch my brother open the pathway of Nikanor's life and give him to the fields." Silence. The gray sky outside was growing brighter, but darkness hung heavily around me.

"No," I said. "No."

My mother went on as though she hadn't heard me, and I think in truth she had not. She seemed to be speaking to someone else—to herself, or perhaps to Nikanor. "How could I? How could I spill the blood of my sweet one, my darling? We would have three days together, and then I would see my own brother open his neck, and for all that year, whenever I saw a plant, I would know that it had grown on his blood. How could I eat bread, knowing that the wheat grew and gave me life only through the death of the one I loved most in the world?

"So," went on her inexorable voice, "I chose another. He was a good man, glad to give his life for the people. He did not know that his death was wasted. I rewarded his family richly after the small part of Goddess in me returned to the sky, and they have never wanted for anything. Yet his life was gone for no purpose." The silence returned and lengthened.

"I don't know anyone named Nikanor," I ventured.

"He was . . . he died. One moon after the Festival. A beam in a house he was building fell on him. He knew what I had done, and he knew that Goddess was killing him in a shameful way, making him waste his death, instead of honorably on the stone altar. He died cursing me.

"But then I thought I had finally been forgiven when you were born—you, my lovely Ariadne, who learned Goddess's dance the first time we stepped it together; you who have the skill of our grandmothers in helping babies into the world and in casting charms." She licked her cracked lips, and I moistened them with a cloth dipped in cool water. Her head fell back on the pillow. "Do you understand?"

"I understand." I finally did. I finally knew what made my mother weep in the night, why her eyes were dark with terror as she surveyed the crowds at the Planting Festival.

"And you know what you must do when you become Goddess?"

"I must be true to Velchanos. I am to choose the man whose body he inhabits, no matter who it is." I shuddered. Velchanos might decide to test me by taking the form of a sick old man or a stinking farm boy. No matter. I would do what was required.

Even as I looked to her for confirmation, my mother's eyes closed and her grip on my hand slackened. "No," I said again, but the other priestesses, alerted in some way that I did not understand, filed in. One loosened the ties of my mother's robe while another gently sponged blood from her legs and belly. I wiped away spittle from the corners of her mouth.

Her hand moved, and I could tell that she was trying to form a blessing. I curved her thumb and finger and pressed it to my forehead. Her eyelids opened a crack, showing eyes as lifeless and flat as a dead fish's. "Never dishonor Goddess." And then they closed.

"Come, child." Damia's creaky voice was unexpectedly gentle. "Come. She has joined your grandmothers."

"No!" I screamed, but the priestesses ignored me and even pushed me aside. I could not watch them treat her body like that of any other woman taken by Goddess, so I went to the window. My legs shook under me, feeling as limp as the tentacles of a dead octopus.

The stars were no longer visible. Damia stood behind me, and together we watched the moon set. I shook to the rhythm of the earthquake within me.

"She has gone home," the old woman said softly. "Karia has returned to Her husband, and already he has forgiven and cherishes Her."

CHAPTER 25

OF THE NEXT DAYS I remember little, and that little is in pieces that don't connect with each other.

The Minos ran into my mother's chamber for the first time in my memory, calling her name. The women scurried away like birds at the approach of a hawk. The sight made me laugh, bringing concerned frowns to the priestesses' faces.

The baby cried. I went to tend to her, and at first I was restrained by Perialla, who seemed to think I would harm the little thing. Did she imagine that I blamed Phaedra for my—our—mother's death? No, Goddess had killed her, and Goddess now tormented me. She had tortured my mother for years, and then She took her from me. Goddess had sent the baby early, when I would be unprepared and before I had a chance to learn more of what I needed to know.

No, Phaedra wasn't responsible. Poor little thing; if she lived, she would grow up without knowing our mother. I finally convinced Perialla to release me, and I picked up the tiny body. The red face, screwed up to cry, smoothed as I crooned to her. Something wet splashed onto her face. I realized it was my tears.

That first night, a whine at my door made me sit up and look; in the darkness, I could make out a large white shape. My heart leaped—with joy or fear?—at the thought that it was the spirit of my mother, but the next instant I saw that it was Theseus's dog. Artemis came to me, her head and tail down as she ambled across the stones, her nails clicking. She sighed and flopped down. I wrapped my arms around her and buried my face in her warm fur, inhaling the animal scent that finally drove the stench of the birthing room from my nostrils.

The body of She-Who-Is-Goddess, washed and dressed in finery, was shown to the people outside the shrine. Damia later told me that I was present when the ancient stone burial chamber in the cleft between two hills was opened and her body was put into it, but I don't remember that. I do remember Theseus telling me that she had returned to her mother, which was true, but I think he meant the earth. Strange people, the Athenians, who think the earth, and not the moon, is our Mother.

For three days, mourners screamed and wailed. Were they frightened because there was only me left, and I was still only She-Who-*Will-Be* until the Festival? Did they fear that I would fail when the time came to lead the ritual?

If they were frightened, they were not half as frightened as I. Thoösa was reinstated as priestess to make the full complement of twelve, and my lessons with Damia changed. No longer was I being reminded how to serve as a priestess—I had to learn how to officiate. I needed to do all this without ever having seen the most secret rituals, without repeating the words after my mother until they were firm in my mind, the way she had learned them, as had her mother before her, since time was time.

"She should have taught the girl." Damia's bitter voice sounded like reeds scraping together in the wind. "It wasn't right that she left it for so long."

I was in the women's sitting room. Cook set bread and preserves in front of me, but I couldn't bear the sight of food. I pushed the plate aside and took a sip of warm honey water. It briefly chased away the bitterness in my mouth. I took another sip and picked up Phaedra, who lay on a large pillow looking at me solemnly. I rocked back and forth. The baby had no need of comfort—she rarely cried—but holding her made the hard feeling in my chest ease.

Thoösa said, "You know how she was. Thought she knew everything. Thought she'd live forever. No need to teach She-Who-Will."

I couldn't bear to hear them blaming my mother for what Goddess had done. But my mother was now Goddess. Would She continue punishing me for being the child of a lovesick woman who had killed a man for no reason, a man who thought his death meant life for the people? "Hush!" I called out, and instantly they fell silent.

Theseus told me about his journey to find his father, when he encountered bandits, murderers, and wild animals. I couldn't help thinking that he was embellishing the tale to amuse me and stop my mind from dwelling on my troubles. It was a kind thought, but it didn't help.

The worst of the splintered memories is of sitting next to my brother in his fetid chamber, which no one had thought to clean since my mother died. He was whimpering with hunger when I arrived carrying bread and cheese and fresh water. He ate and drank, tears and snot running down his face, and when he had devoured everything, I tried to make him understand that our mother would never come to see him again. "Ama?" he asked hopefully over and over, using his word for her. "Ama?" It shredded my heart.

"Ama is no longer here." How could I make him understand? "Ama is in the sky." I pointed upward, and he turned puzzled eyes to the ceiling, where a fat spider had caught a buzzing fly.

"Ama?" His astonishment surprised me into laughter, even while tears ran down my face.

Through it all, there were endless lessons about when to hold the white ball of yarn, what to do with it, what to say to the priestesses. How I must fast for three days before the dark of the moon to make a hollow inside me for Goddess to enter, how to acknowledge the people, what words to say at what times. I repeated the chants after Damia and Thoösa, and they seemed pleased, but I had no idea of the meaning of the words.

They told me that the Minos would wear the head of a bull through the ceremony and that when I found Velchanos, the bull's head would be transferred to that man to show that the god's spirit had entered him. "I know that," I said, impatient that they thought I had not been to Planting Festivals every spring of my life. They exchanged glances. "What?" I asked, but they didn't answer. An odd quality to their silence filled me with dread. I wondered if it was something to do with the Ordeal of the Snakes, but of that I heard no mention, and I did not ask.

And night after night I stood between the columns of the Great Hall and looked at the moon as She reached her full roundness and then dwindled, nearing the time when She would disappear and Goddess would come to me. Would I somehow know the moment that my mother and her mother and all our Mothers entered my body? Would I recognize my mother's presence?

I won't fail you, I thought every night as I watched Her. *When the time comes, I will see the god. I will. And no matter whose body he has chosen to inhabit, I will acknowledge him.* "Are you really there?" I whispered, searching the gray spots to try to find something of my mother, but the blank, white eye stared down at me coldly without answering, and I returned to my chamber, where I lay sleepless until dawn.

⇥ THESEUS ⇤

CHAPTER 26

HE DAYS march past each other in a tedious procession. I could lounge on cushions all day, eating and drinking, and find a different girl in town every night if I chose, but I'm not used to such idleness. Konnidas would show one of his rare smiles if he were to learn that I look for something to do—he used to have to chase me down to make me help him hoe a field or gather firewood.

The palace guards seem bored too. Everyone in the world rightly fears the Kretan navy, so the chances of an enemy slipping past the ferocious-looking warships that circle the island are slim. The Kretans are good swordsmen, and I manage to pass some time learning how to fence. They give me only a wooden practice sword, but it's well balanced and easy to use. I improve rapidly, but compared with the soldiers, I am incompetent. When I feel foolishly inadequate, I offer to wrestle them. My size makes up for my lack of skill—the men here are generally small, and they're quite slender until they reach middle age, when lack of exercise and the excellent Kretan food turn them soft and wide.

Everyone is courteous, but the men seem wary of me. Some of the younger boys are friendlier, and I enjoy giving a fuzzy-headed youngster named Glaukos wrestling lessons. He's talkative and cheerful and would be well-looking if not for one eye that refuses to follow the other one and a bad habit of using his left hand.

One of the boys I saw training to dance with the bulls early in my stay in Knossos has offered to show me the rudiments of this sport. He's named Simo, and he reminds me of Arkas. He's small and quick, like my tormenter back home in Troizena. Even though practicing with a real bull is prohibited—it would be a sacrilege, I think—and Simo holds a board with bull's horns nailed to it, I quickly learn that someone as large and slow moving as I has no business being in the bullring. I trip over my own feet, and Simo grazes my back with the horn tip. On the next pass, I dodge him but accidentally tread on his foot hard enough to make him curse.

"Sorry," I mumble. He hands me the board.

"You take a turn." He limps off to the side of the ring. Despite my misgivings, I run at him. He waits until I'm close enough that I worry I'm going to gore him, and then he trips me. I sprawl in the sand, and he is astride my back. "Ha!" he says, and smacks me between the shoulder blades. I stand up and shake him off, knowing that if I truly were the bull that I am pretending to be, that would have been a sword and now I'd be dead. Simo's scornful smile follows me out the ring, and I don't return.

There are few other amusements. The Minos invites me to a banquet, which is enjoyable, and the women who dance between courses are lovely, but I'm mindful of the warnings of the soldier who escorted me to the palace, and I don't try to touch any of them. No one forbids me to leave the grounds, but on the occasions when I do, I find myself surrounded by men with the cloaks that indicate their military status, and their presence drains the pleasure out of any activity that I find. Also, people treat me oddly. It can't be because I'm a foreigner; Knossos is a port, and ships from all over dock here regularly. They must be avoiding me because I came here to be monster fodder.

One evening, after I show the younger boys some wrestling holds, I see Simo and Enops, one of the friendlier of the young men around my age, leaving the arena together. I pay no attention and am about to pass them, when Enops stops me. "We're going to a tavern in the town. Want to come along?" Simo glares at him, but Enops doesn't appear to notice and talks in a friendly manner about Knossos and Athens (about which I know little) and my voyage here. Winter has made a brief return, and the air is cool. I wrap my cloak around myself tightly.

The tavern is warm and brightly lit. I recognize some of

the palace guards. They appear surprised to see me, but they nod a greeting and return to their cups and their conversation. Enops orders wine and the Kretan pastries I've grown fond of. He's friendly, and before I know it, I've told him the story of my parentage and the circumstances of my trip here.

When I finish, he strokes his chin thoughtfully and then raises his cup for more wine. The tavern keeper fills it and stands waiting for payment. I fish a coin from my pouch. "Leave the bottle on the table," I say. The man inspects the coin under a lantern, and what he sees must satisfy him, because he does as I ask.

"So, Athens is ruled by a king," Simo says. I nod. "Yet the people worship Athena, a goddess."

"She's very powerful." I feel stung by the implied insult to the deity of a city I hadn't felt any connection to until a few weeks ago. "She's a warrior."

"Oh, I know she's powerful," he says. "Everyone knows that Athena is to be feared. But——" He takes another gulp of wine. I refill his cup. Fortified, he lowers his voice and inches over on the bench so that we can talk without being overheard in the hubbub of the busy tavern. Enops leans in closer as well, and his serious face appears thoughtful as Simo continues. "Some people here say that being ruled by a woman is old-fashioned." He looks around, but no one is paying attention. The soldiers appear to trust that my companions will keep an eye on me, and are tossing dice. "And then others say that Goddess"—Simo winces as if expecting to be struck by lightning—"Goddess would never consent to a man ruling. Yet Athena allows it. It's most interesting."

"Your goddess must be very powerful," I venture, not knowing if I am being disrespectful.

Enops nods. "Goddess causes the grain to grow and the lambs and kids and calves to be born in the spring."

"But just as a woman cannot bear a child without a man, Goddess cannot feed the people without Velchanos," Simo says. "It all depends on Velchanos, really. Once a year, at the planting season, Goddess leaves the sky and comes to us. She takes the body of She-Who-Is-Goddess. From that moment until she returns to her home in the sky, Goddess walks among us. She uses the body of She-Who-Is, who for those days *is* Goddess."

"And Velchanos takes the body of the Minos?" I ask.

"No!" Enops sounds shocked. "The Minos is the brother of She-Who-Is. We are not like the foul Aegyptians, whose queen marries her own brother."

"No," Simo echoes. "Every spring, Velchanos is born as a bull calf. The priests seek him out after the Planting Festival. We know him by his strength and by certain markings. Our priests bring him back to Knossos, where he is treated as the god and king he is. He lives with us for two years and accepts our worship. And then, at the Planting Festival, we free Velchanos from the bull's body."

I know what that must mean: they slaughter the bull, who for a while has been their god. Well, I've heard of stranger rituals, and whatever they do here must make the gods happy. Everyone I see appears content and well fed and, aside from a few beggars at the port, relatively prosperous.

"Where does he go, your god, once he is freed from the bull?" I ask.

"Velchanos chooses a man," Enops says, "a man whose body the god will inhabit for the length of the Festival. Then She-Who-Is-Goddess is subjected to a test. She must recognize that man from among all the men present."

Some small villages near Troizena have a similar custom, where the king steps down for a day or three days or a week at planting time and another man, usually someone of no importance, takes his place in the palace and in the queen's bed. At the end of that time, the replacement is presented with gifts and is sent back to his regular life. Sometimes he is also given a blow with a green stick or is slapped across the face. I've heard that in one place he's even whipped until he bleeds. I'm not sure why; perhaps this is meant to remind him that he is not really the king and must not boast later of his temporary elevation to that office.

"Any children born to She-Who-Is-Goddess nine moons later, near the next Festival of Birth of the Sun, are the children of Goddess and Velchanos," Enops says.

"And if it's a boy, he'll be your king?" I ask.

Simo sighs, sounding exasperated. "We have no king. She-Who-Is-Goddess is something like what you call a queen. The Minos is the lawgiver, but he must obey his sister in all things. She-Who-Is-Goddess trains the women who attend to childbirth, and she blesses babies by being present at their birth. She decrees when sacrifices are to be made, how to appease a deity who has been offended, what an omen means, when the crops are to be harvested."

So, the Minos is not a ruler, just as Prokris told me, but if Simo is telling the truth, he has even less power than she thinks. I wonder what this will do to Prokris's plans. Her Kretan informant was not very accurate.

Evidently, Simo feels he's said enough. He drains his cup and stands. "I'm going home." He stumbles out the door, followed by Enops. I finish the wine and follow them, the soldiers trailing behind me, obviously annoyed at having to leave their game.

That's the last time one of the other boys offers to go to town with me, and in fact my fencing lessons and bull practice are not repeated. The days are long and dull. My only real pleasure is imagining the ways I'll avenge myself on Aegeus, if I ever return to Athens. In some daydreams, I content myself with blistering him with my tongue. In others, I imprison him in his own palace. In the most satisfying fantasies, I battle him to the death and install myself on his throne.

It's getting difficult to find Prokris alone, as she doesn't want the Minos to become suspicious about her frequent absences. If he thinks she's found a lover, he'll have her put to death, even though he is clearly infatuated with her. She and I are not lovers, but the Minos has no need to prove his wife's infidelity. His decree would be enough.

When we finally manage to find each other outside the women's compound one warm afternoon, Prokris's feathery brows are drawn together. She pulls me aside, away from the wall, in more than usual concern of being overheard.

"Something strange is going on," she says. "The women are leaving."

"What women?"

"The wives of the Minos. Not all of them. Orthia, the one he married when he was a boy and who has turned back into a child, she's still here. But the rest of them, the ones who live nearby—their families keep arriving and taking them away, and the foreign ones are packing, planning to take ship."

Prokris is a wife from a foreign land, and I wonder if she, too, will have to leave. My heart lifts a little at the thought of becoming disentangled from her schemes.

"Nobody tells me what's going on. The old man does nothing but weep and strew ashes in his hair. He hardly eats. He doesn't play with the children."

"He's in mourning for his sister."

"Yes, I know he loved her." She sounds impatient. "But this is more than mourning. He seems frightened."

"Of what?"

"How would I know?" she snaps, and then softens. "I don't know. But I mean to find out."

CHAPTER 27

PROKRIS STAYED away from me, out of delicacy, I assumed. At first I didn't notice, bound as I was in so many hours of study and practice, and nearly sleepless from grief, but when she appeared one afternoon shortly before the dark of the moon, I realized how much I had missed her.

She ran to me from the end of a corridor. I rose and returned her embrace. She pulled back, and her cheeks were wet. I touched a tear. "Why are you sad?"

She shook her head, holding me at arm's length. "I'm sad for *you*—you poor thing, to lose your mother!"

That she who had lost mother, father, brothers, sisters, home, could still spare some pity for me melted the rock of my heart a little. I even managed to look outside my own grief to notice that she wore a gray tunic like a peasant woman, instead of the fine robes of the Minos's prettiest wife.

Her hair was knotted into a simple bun instead of being dressed in elaborate plaits and twists in the Athenian style. Still, she made the shapeless garment look graceful, and the plain hairstyle brought out the beauty of her face and the length of her white neck.

She saw me looking at her and made a comical little frown. "I suppose that I'm to mourn the death of the sister-in-law I hardly knew," she said. My face must have betrayed my surprise, for she added hurriedly, "As of course I do, you know, dear Ariadne. But your customs are different, and I don't know exactly how to behave. Why are the wives leaving? How long will the Minos sit in the hearth and weep? He hardly notices when I'm there. When will he resume his regular life?"

"Why, never." I was too startled to frame my answer more delicately. "He is no longer the Minos. Or, at least, in a short time he will not be."

"He—he's *what?*" One hand flew to her heart.

"But, Prokris, how could he be? The Minos is born of the same body that gave birth to She-Who-Is-Goddess. Soon *I* will become She-Who-Is. Your husband will remain Minos until the Planting Festival concludes, but then he will lose his power."

"His power? You mean his position?"

"No—well, yes, he'll lose that, too."

"What do you mean, 'He'll lose that, *too*'? What other power will he lose?"

"Why, his power as Minos. He won't be able to summon

Velchanos. As soon as I become Goddess, he will cease to be Minos and there will be a new one." How could I explain that Asterion, the "monster" she had risked her life to see on her first day in Krete, who lived confined in two tiny rooms and who killed children with his blundering attempts at play— that this damaged man-child would soon be the Minos?

I needn't have worried; her mind had already moved on. "But what about *me,* then?"

"What *about* you?"

She gasped, suddenly realizing something. "Is this why the other wives have left?"

"Why, yes, of course." It was worse than talking to a three-year-old. At least a child would know that once the Minos becomes merely Minos-Who-Was, he can no longer support a large family, even with the charity of his sister-niece. The children would be married off, if possible. Being related to She-Who-Is-Goddess is a valuable asset in a spouse. The few who could not find suitable marriages would be sold as slaves, but not for field work, much less working in the mines. Their refinement and education would make them excellent companions to young nobles. Some of my own childhood friends had been descendants of Minos-Who-Was, a kindly old gentleman who had tended an orchard near the palace and had died in my tenth year.

I started to explain this, but Prokris wasn't listening. "Must I leave too?" she broke in. "And where should I go?" The hand clutching my wrist suddenly felt cold.

"But don't you *want* to go home?"

She shook her head vehemently. I was at a loss. Surely she missed her home—didn't she? Did she want to remain with the Minos, who would soon be stripped of his abilities and his rank? Did he even want her to stay? He seemed enchanted with this pretty young wife, but he would be living in a small house, and Orthia, as first wife, would remain with him. The Minos was fond of the bride of his youth.

"They treated me like a servant back in Athens," she said vehemently. "Old Aegeus and his witch-wife. They made me tend to their brat, and then, when they needed to send someone to marry an old barbarian, they chose me. Oh, I know now that he's not a barbarian!" She stroked my cheek until I felt the frown go away. "But that's how the Athenians think of the Minos, and they didn't care that they were sending me so far away. Besides, to be thirteenth wife isn't much more than being a servant to the other twelve, even with a good husband."

I doubted that the Minos could keep Prokris as his wife. I would, of course, see to his needs and Orthia's. Custom, though, forbade Minos-Who-Was from living in luxury at the expense of She-Who-Is-Goddess (my stomach twisted at the thought of how soon that would be me), and a young Athenian wife was certainly a luxury.

"If I go back to Athens, the witch-queen will find ways to torment me. She hates me because she thinks I'm a threat to her precious child, just because Aegeus is my uncle and I'm

Athenian through and through, not like that little half-Kolkhian brat of hers."

"What kind of threat? And who is this witch-queen?"

"Medea of Kolkhis. Aegeus married her after she ran from Iason, and she knows the people don't like the idea of the queen mother being a foreign witch. She killed her brother to get the Golden Fleece for Iason, and then she killed her own children, hers and Iason's, when Iason took his second wife—did you know that?"

"Of course she killed them. She had to."

"She *had* to?" Prokris's mouth gaped open again. "Why would anyone have to kill her own children?"

I was astonished that she didn't know. The story of Medea's courage had reached all the way to Krete. "Medea was She-Who-Is-Goddess of Kolkhis," I explained. "There, the god appears—appeared—in the form of a ram, not a bull, as here. Their Minos dressed in a fleece of gold to summon him, just as ours wears a bronze bull's head. Medea rescued the fleece from her brother, who wanted to use it to usurp her power. But when she ran off with Iason, Goddess was surely very angry at the desertion of her shrine. I know something of Goddess's anger." I swallowed. "She would find ways to punish Medea. They say"—I paused; the outrage was so great that I could hardly repeat what I had heard the priestesses whisper in shocked tones—"they say that he was going to elevate the new wife above Medea."

"I don't see—"

"That would have made Medea's children a threat to any borne by the new wife. Even if Goddess didn't kill Medea's son and daughter in some terrible way to punish Medea for deserting her service, the new wife certainly would, to clear the path for her own children. And it wouldn't be an easy death." I thought of my mother writhing for silent hours on her bed and then soaking the blankets with more blood than I would have thought a body could hold. Goddess's punishment was dreadful, and a new wife would certainly be harsh as well. Whichever one of them killed the children, Iason and Medea's little boy and girl would have suffered in ways that I didn't want to imagine. "Medea slit the children's throats. They died quickly, without pain, and with dignity. It was all their mother could do for them, and the sacrifice would please Goddess."

Prokris still stared at me, this time with what looked like disgust. "What about her brother, then?" she challenged me.

That part of the report had disturbed me as well. Medea's brother had been her Minos (he was called by a different name in Kolkhis, but he served that function) and it must have been hard for Medea to kill him, even if he had been plotting to overthrow her and Goddess. It must have been love for Iason that gave her strength, and now that I knew about my mother and what she had done, how she had dishonored Goddess for the love of a mortal man . . . I closed my eyes.

I had gone to visit Asterion when news of Medea had reached us, while my mother and the priestesses were discussing her actions. I found him in a gentle and sweet mood. I stayed with him for hours, playing games with pebbles and singing him songs while he grinned at me and then fell asleep with his big head on my lap. I stroked his curls as he snored, knowing that I could never harm him, not even for love.

Prokris still stared at me. Then she looked away.

But not before I had seen the same cloud of death and arrogance and betrayal pass over her face, obscuring her pretty features and changing them into something so horrible that I cried out in terror.

CHAPTER 28

PROKRIS GRABBED my shoulders. "What is it?" she asked, but I was sobbing. The cloud passed by, leaving nothing more than a shimmer in the air and the faintest whiff of something rank. I was in a cold sweat, and my mouth was as dry as the sand of the dancing floor.

"What did you see?" Prokris asked, darting quick glances around the room. "Did someone come in? Was it—did you see your mother's spirit?"

I grunted a negative as the room swam around me. Prokris lowered me onto a sofa before the blackness had a chance to swallow me. Footsteps thudded down the corridor, and someone burst in. I didn't dare raise my head, but out of the edge of my eye, I saw the flash of striped cloaks.

"What happened?" It was Gnipho, and I heard the clean *slish* of a sword being drawn.

"It was my fault," Prokris said before I could answer. "The princess was overcome with grief as we talked about her mother and was taken with a fainting spell."

"Mistress?" Gnipho sounded doubtful. I had never been subject to fainting.

I raised my head and tried to smile. "I'm fine. My brother's wife is seeing to me." Gnipho's concerned face swam in front of my eyes, and I lowered my gaze again. After a moment, I heard the guards leave, but I noticed that their footsteps did not go very far down the corridor.

Prokris asked again, "What did you see?"

The vision gripped me once more, but faintly, and as I tried to examine it, it fled. "You must be careful," I said. "There's something evil near you. I don't know what it is, but it's very powerful. And I think it's threatening Theseus as well."

"Something evil, you say?" She cocked her head, and a smile played around her lips.

"Please," I begged. "Please be careful."

"You don't have to worry," she said. But I did worry. The Athenians didn't take things seriously, and my life had suddenly become very serious.

As if to remind me of this fact, a shadow appeared in the doorway. I knew without looking that it was Thoösa and that she was coming to take me back to my lessons. I sighed and stood. Only two days remained until the Planting Festival, and I had not eaten since the day before. I could have told the priestesses that fasting was not necessary. I had no need to create a space for Goddess; the loss of my mother had left a huge, gaping hole in me. But I had no appetite, so fasting was not causing me distress.

"Come see me when you can," Prokris whispered as I embraced her.

I didn't know how I would find the time, but more than anything, I longed for a few hours' peace with no lessons and no old priestesses screeching at me when I turned to the right instead of the left or when I forgot the ancient words of the prayers, whose meaning was hard to grasp and thus almost impossible to remember. So I whispered back, "Yes," and then followed Thoösa to the room where my mother had died and where the other eleven priestesses were now waiting.

They were still at their midday meal, dining on roasted waterfowl. I wasn't tempted at the sight of the crisp brown skin on the ducks and geese or the sounds of the women sucking morsels off the bones. The smell of the herbs and rich fat sickened me. My mouth didn't water, and my stomach remained silent. Damia glanced at me with what looked like surprised respect.

Don't admire my restraint, I thought. *It's not due to self-control. I couldn't eat if you forced it down my throat.*

After the meal, the next step was for the priestesses to practice dressing me in the robes of She-Who-Is-Goddess. Each had a task, from taking off my everyday slippers to putting on the new hard shoes, from pinning up my hair to tying my sash in the ritual knot. I could not wear the real garments until the actual ceremony. The women stripped off my ordinary clothes and pretended to re-dress me in the stiff linen-and-wool skirt embroidered with golden thread and encrusted with gems, and the vest that would leave my breasts uncovered in front of all those people.

"Don't worry," Damia said, who was looking at me as I stared down at my chest. "When the time comes, you won't care. You won't really be *you*. Your body will be there, but what makes it move will be Goddess. You will feel what Goddess feels, not what a girl feels." I was unconvinced.

Thoösa barked her unpleasant laugh. "You'll see." She rummaged in a cloth bag on the table. "Here, take this." She held out a ball of undyed yarn the same size as the white Goddess ball that lay in its special casket inside the box at the foot of my mother's—now my—bed. I held the practice ball in my right hand. I turned to the left and took the thirteen steps that would, on the night of the Festival, lead me into the inner chamber, where the Goddess stone would have been anointed with oil and draped in precious cloth.

And then we stopped. This is where we always stopped. What came next I didn't know. I didn't ask, and they didn't offer to tell me. Once I was inside the chamber, the Minos would come in wearing his bull mask. This I had seen at every Planting Festival. When I later emerged holding a snake in each hand, I wouldn't be Ariadne. I would be Goddess.

But this night, I was impatient and tired of secrets. "What

does the Minos do in the chamber?" I asked no one in particular. The priestesses exchanged glances but said nothing. Surely they knew. They had to leave the inner chamber when the Minos arrived, but they must have learned something about that part of the ritual.

I tried again. "What is the Ordeal of the Snakes?"

"Where did you hear about that?" Thoösa snapped.

"Never mind." I tried to imitate the tone my mother had always used when dismissing complaints or questions from the priestesses. "It is enough to know that I *have* heard of it and that I want to know what it is." I looked around at them as they stood mute. "Damia?" She stared at the ground. I turned to the others. "Zita? Kynthia? Will no one tell me?" Nothing. "Perialla?"

She raised her eyes and glanced at the others. I thought I caught a shrug from Thoösa. "We can't tell you, Mistress," Perialla said. "Goddess-Who-Was should have told you. I'm sure she would have if she'd known she would be leaving you so soon," she added hastily, clearly not wanting to cast aspersions on my mother's memory. "But it isn't our place. The Minos will have to explain it."

"Very well," I said. "I'll just go ask him." They protested, and Thoösa even tried to block my exit, but I pushed her aside and strode away. If I didn't breathe air that hadn't already passed into and out of the bodies of so many people, I would burst like an overripe pomegranate.

CHAPTER 29

THE PRIESTESS'S DEATH changes *everything*."

I look at Prokris, surprised. I've never heard something so close to a whine from her. She wears a frown that on any other girl would look sulky but which on Prokris merely shows how pretty her mouth is.

"I don't see how," I say. "The mother was never part of your plan."

"No, not directly. The daughter is now the one who holds the power. And I've just realized something. She told me that my husband will no longer be Minos after their Planting Festival. Do you know who will be priest in his stead?"

"Her brother."

"You *knew?*" Her voice must have come out louder than she expected, for she flinches and looks toward the garden wall.

I say, "I don't see how he can perform the rituals. He can't even keep himself clean!" Once, I overheard a girl in town say that someone should have "taken care of him" long ago and that if the Kretans were real men, one of them would have slit the boy's throat. I've grown fond of Asterion, but I can understand her point.

Prokris's next words take me aback. "All you have to do," she says haltingly, her words reflecting ideas coming to her as she speaks, "is marry the girl."

"*Marry* her?"

Prokris keeps her eyes fixed on me. "Make sure you are the one she chooses at that Festival. You can drip some blood on the field or whatever it is—and then, instead of stepping down at the end, you declare that since there is no Minos, you're taking charge."

"Why would they listen to me?"

"Krete needs someone strong in the palace; they've been ruled by priestesses and that old man for too long. Ariadne will be the most important person left, and her husband will be the natural one to assume power. There will be no Minos to get in your way."

I don't much like the idea of participating in their ritual. For one thing, I don't know how they extract blood from the man chosen by the priestess. From what I've seen of Krete, it's likely to be uncomfortable, not a mere prick on the fingertip. For another, we don't observe many religious ceremonies in Troizena, and I don't know how to behave.

Besides, I have no intention of marrying the girl, and I say so.

"You don't have to *stay* married to her," Prokris reminds me. "Just long enough to get established as king. Once they see how a real kingdom operates, they'll be happy to leave off their barbarian ways."

I ponder this and see a flaw.

"How am I to make sure she chooses me at the Festival?"

Prokris lays a hand on my knee and smiles. "I don't think you'll find that difficult," she says.

I HAD NOT visited my brother since I had attempted to introduce him to Phaedra two days after the baby's birth. He had erupted into such a jealous rage that I hurried away with my sister while she screamed herself purple. This time I came alone, and Asterion's joy made me weep with shame at my neglect of him. This frightened him, so I quickly forced back my tears and sat next to him and held his hand.

I spent all afternoon there. I sang him songs and told him tales. He loved to try to sing with me, mouthing meaningless syllables in his surprisingly tuneful voice. I never knew how well he followed my stories, so I recounted my own favorites, not the warlike ones that most boys preferred.

I told my brother about Medea and her bravery in sacrificing what she loved the most. I told him about Medusa, who was so powerful that snakes crawled in her hair and so beautiful that men turned to stone at the sight of her. I told him about Moera Krataia, so mighty that even her brother Velchanos bowed to her, and about how she spun the thread that apportioned every mortal's life. I described how she measured each life thread into its appropriate length, weeping when she had to cut one short, rejoicing when she was allowed to leave another long and strong. I lowered my voice to tell him how her scissors finally sliced through the indicated spot and the person died.

When Asterion drifted off to sleep, I placed his hand on his broad chest and left my own there for a moment, feeling him breathe, and then slipped out.

Even before I reached the Minos's residence, I could tell that things had changed. A soft rain was falling in the courtyard, so it was not surprising that it was deserted, but everything about this place looked so different that it took me a moment to orient myself. There was the Minos's bench under his favorite fig tree. Tight buds along its branches looked ready to burst open and turn into the huge leaves that the children enjoyed playing with. Green crocus spears poked their tips through the soil. All this was the same as always, but the rest took me aback. The only other seat that remained was a stool missing one of its three legs. No toys littered the pavement; no awnings were pulled over seats to allow the wives to get a little fresh air even in the rain. The wind picked up some rubbish and swirled it around. The bird cages were empty, their doors ajar.

No sounds of quarrels or laughter came through the columns, no clash of cooking pots, no thud of shuttles banging on looms, no whirring spindles. No babies cried, and no mothers scolded. Even the eunuchs were absent.

A distant voice was all I heard. It was a woman, and she was clearly issuing orders and becoming impatient as they were not followed to her liking. The voice grew louder, and then a portly figure strode into the courtyard and stopped short at the sight of me. A look of annoyance crossed her face. This was the Minos's third wife, who had come with a shipment of tribute from Aegyptos before I was born. No one could pronounce her Aegyptian name, so the Minos had renamed her Ino. Although she had been in Krete for decades, she still kept to her Aegyptian ways, shaving her head and wearing a heavy wig in public, insisting on filmy linen clothes instead of good wool, speaking her strange language to her many children. These children were now all grown and gone, and it looked like Ino was leaving too.

"What are you doing here, mistress?" she asked me in her deep voice, which had retained most of its Aegyptian accent. A servant appeared behind her, dragging a wooden case. She stopped and sat down on the box.

"I'm looking for the Minos," I said.

Ino shrugged. "He's probably in his chamber. I haven't seen him for days."

Indignation swelled in me. She seemed utterly indifferent to the man who had been kind to her for twenty years. "What do you have in there?" I asked, pointing to the case.

"Merely my personal items," she spat. "A wife is allowed

to remove her cooking pots and weaving supplies when she leaves."

I knew that the box contained more than that—and in any case, I had never seen Ino holding anything that looked like a cooking pot or a spindle or loom in her pudgy hands—but I didn't care. Let the wives strip the palace bare, just as long as they left.

As though in answer to my thought, the servant said timidly, "The ship leaves at sundown," and the Minos's wife snapped back at her, "Then why are you sitting there? Take that box to where the cart awaits."

The servant grasped the leather handle and jerked the case along the paving stones of the courtyard and out the gate. Ino swept by me without a farewell or even a backward glance.

Once her haranguing voice disappeared, all was silent once more. Or almost. I caught a low sound, as of someone murmuring, and then a pause, and then an answer in a deeper tone. I recognized both voices, despite how muffled they were, and I made my way to the corner of the garden where the little-used door was open a crack. I took a deep breath and closed my eyes. *That was an illusion,* I told myself firmly. *There was no blood pooling at Theseus's feet that time. It was a shadow.* I pushed the door open.

They were seated under a tree. Theseus leaned back, his eyes half-closed, and chewed on a long stalk of grass. Prokris had her arms clasped around her knees; it was cool in the shade, and she must have been trying to keep warm. She rose gracefully and extended a hand to me.

"However did you manage to get away?" she asked as we settled next to each other on the ground.

"I just left," I said. "They didn't try to stop me."

"Good," Prokris said. "They fear you."

I considered. The priestesses, of course, knew how limited were the powers of She-Who-Will-Be-Goddess, and they also knew that my mother had not finished teaching me, yet they were treating me with more deference than they ever had before. Perhaps this was why I craved the company of Prokris and Theseus—they were still relaxed and friendly.

I was about to respond when Prokris held up her hand. She cocked her head, listening.

"What is it?" Theseus asked, but Prokris was already on her feet.

"The Minos is calling me. Poor thing, he's practically alone in there now."

I hadn't heard anything, but Prokris seemed sure as she trotted to the door. Her feet in their fine leather shoes tapped on the paving stones as she crossed the courtyard.

After a moment, Theseus asked, "How are the preparations coming?"

"Well. I should be there practicing." I felt a twinge of guilt, but it wasn't strong enough to make me return to the chamber where the priestesses were surely discussing my bad behavior in their shrill tones. Stronger than the guilt was fear. Why did they stop the rehearsal each time after I removed the Goddess ball from its chest? What would happen when I was alone with the Minos? And what was the Ordeal of the Snakes? I bowed my head and willed my fears to retreat. *He loves me,* I told myself. *He won't let any harm come to me.* But I knew that he was just the Minos, not Velchanos, and he didn't control what happened there.

"And tomorrow is the ceremony?" Theseus asked.

I nodded, not trusting my voice. I could perform it in my sleep. Grudgingly, I admitted to myself that the repeated rehearsals had served their purpose; no moment was unscripted. Nothing unexpected would happen to make me falter and thus render the ritual ineffective. I remembered the year that my mother had stumbled over the threshold to the inner chamber. After she held a long consultation with the Minos, the ceremony was allowed to proceed, but the crops that year had been so bad, the storerooms under the palace were emptied long before the next fall's harvest was in, and many people had died.

That was the year my brother had been moved into his prison. When those forgotten inner rooms were stripped of their contents to feed the people, ancient, fading paintings of a Minos-Who-Was wearing his ritual bull head had been discovered on their walls. Daidalos had constructed more walls, but my brother broke them down—though he didn't seem able to destroy the painted ones—and that was when my mother had finally been forced to tie him there with a spell.

The silence between us lengthened, and I raised my eyes to Theseus. He was looking at me with a half smile. Had he read my mind?

"You'll be perfect." He took my hand and raised it to his lips. They were warm and soft, and I wished their touch to linger. "How could you not be?" He moved closer so that his thigh pressed against mine. A fluttering in my stomach made me tremble. With his free hand, he lightly took my shoulder and turned me to face him, and his mouth moved to my lips, pressing first gently and then more firmly. I was flooded with an unfamiliar warmth, and I found my hand moving to the back of his neck. His tongue lightly flicked on my mouth, and it opened to a sweetness I had never before tasted.

I was gripped by a new fear. I put my hands on his chest and pushed him away, then stood up. "I have to go back," I said shakily. "The priestesses want me to repeat the prayers one more time."

He, too, stood. "I'm sorry. I didn't mean . . ."

I waved a hand to brush away his words. I fled back through the door, across the courtyard, and into the palace, to the safety of the corridors with their damp air and closed-in smell, through the chamber where the painting of Goddess holding the snakes and wearing her enigmatic smile seemed to simultaneously welcome and mock me as I ran past Her.

I burst into the room where the priestesses were taking refreshment. They looked up at me in surprise, some with their mouths full, others taking a sip of wine.

"I still have much to learn." I choked on the words. "Teach me."

CHAPTER 31

I SLEPT HEAVILY the night before the Planting Festival, perhaps because I hadn't eaten in three days; perhaps because the day had been long and arduous.

I had inspected the tiny white lambs brought in for sacrifice, to determine that all were sound and unblemished, so as not to offend Goddess with an imperfect offering. I ordered the loops of garlanded flowers and herbs to be hung in their proper areas, checked that none of the wine had turned to vinegar, decided which children would lead the spring songs, and supervised the cleaning of the inner chamber and the oiling and draping of the Goddess stone, a small ritual in itself. All the while I, and everyone else, kept an eye on the moon as She rose, a tiny sliver against a blue and then a black sky. She would disappear completely when Goddess left Her home and came to the earth to inhabit me.

I had helped my mother with these tasks for several years and had taken over many of them since I had become She-Who-Will-Be-Goddess, so they were soothing in their familiarity. Perhaps it was also this that allowed me to sleep well; I had nothing more to learn, no more choices to make.

Except one, and it wouldn't really be me, but Goddess, making that choice.

When I met the priestesses at dawn, it appeared that I was the only one who had rested. Thoösa in particular looked haggard and hollow eyed. Damia wasn't much better. Even the younger priestesses were pale, and their steps dragged.

Still, Thoösa couldn't seem to stop herself from giving me instructions. She shrilled on and on as two priestesses plaited my hair and then piled it on my head in an elaborate pattern, with knots that were to bring success to the ceremony. I felt oddly dulled, and her words spilled over me like water.

My clothing for the first ritual, the Ceremony of Velchanos, was newly made, unlike the Goddess robes I was to wear later. They had been too small for my mother, so I hoped they would fit me well, as she had been taller than I and lately had been growing stout. I remembered the day exactly one year before when I had tied the laces in the back of my mother's skirt into the complicated pattern prescribed by tradition and noticed that they were barely long enough.

I forced myself to stop thinking about that day and about the Ordeal facing me later. I had too much to do. The priestesses finished dressing me in my new finery and stood back, leaving a pathway to the door. I took a breath, walked between the two lines, hearing the unfamiliar *tap-tap* of my hard shoes rather than the soft slippers I was accustomed to, and entered the corridor.

As I expected, the halls were deserted. Although I would not become She-Who-Is-Goddess until the ritual, on this day nobody would risk a chance encounter with me outside a sanctified area. The priestesses trailed behind. I took one hallway and then another, turning several times, as the noise of many people talking, laughing, singing, arguing, grew louder. For a moment, I hesitated, foolishly hoping that I could still turn and flee, when a hard finger poked me in the back and forced me forward into the arena.

They all fell silent once I entered the stands, of course. Each eye followed me as I climbed to my seat. I was sure that everyone could hear my heart, and my foot in its unaccustomed high shoe nearly caught on my hem as I stepped into the box where the Minos was waiting for me, his two remaining wives, Orthia and Prokris, on his other side. I was so glad to see the friendly smile crinkling his face that I nearly wept.

I didn't, of course, and I was about to say the ritual "You may begin," when I saw Theseus seated next to Prokris. I turned questioning eyes to the Minos. He said, "I thought it fitting that he observe the ceremony from the best seats." He added in a voice just above a whisper, "Show those barbarians a thing or two!"

From the satisfied look on Prokris's face, I thought I knew where the idea to invite Theseus to our box had come from. I could not have them use this sacred ritual for their own purposes, for meeting and being together in public. I leaned around the Minos and said to Theseus, "Come sit by me. You'll have the best view." The Minos nodded approvingly as Theseus, followed by his large dog, stood and inched past the two women and then the Minos and, finally, me. He squeezed between me and a fat courtier. With Theseus seated on my right and Artemis on the floor between us, her head above his knee, I said to the Minos, "You may begin."

The Minos stood. Silence fell as he spoke the ancient words of the opening of the men's ritual, and tension rose. Everyone strained forward. We heard the odd squeaking blare of a conch shell, and then the door was flung open. The audience cheered as the boys streamed in through a path of golden sunlight. They were so beautiful that my breath caught in my throat. I stole a glance to my left; if the sight moved me, what must the Minos feel as he saw this group of the finest boys of Knossos, his acolytes, rise to their proudest moment?

The twelve boys were now parading around the arena, tossing their multicolored banners aloft and catching them by their sticks, to the rapturous shouts of the crowd. I caught sight of Lysias leaning on the rail that surrounded the arena.

He glanced behind himself as someone spoke to him, and his face didn't betray any of the tension that he must feel. Only the tautness of his back muscles and the way he bounced up and down on his toes showed his inner heart.

Enops marched in, his white teeth flashing; he looked even handsomer as a youth than he had as a boy. I caught sight of Glaukos. He had grown; his shoulders were starting to broaden, and his large hands and feet showed that he was about to shoot up in height. I was surprised that he had been considered fit to serve, with his eye that turned out, but pleased that he should have the honor.

I could guess how old they all were by the length of their hair, from Glaukos, whose scalp was nearly visible after his recent shearing when he turned twelve, to the long locks of the oldest boys. Some must be close to the upper limit of eighteen years, judging by the length of the black curls that hung down their backs.

The parade ended with all the boys standing in two lines facing me and the Minos. We rose together, and the Minos blessed them with the ancient words that had been repeated at this moment since time was time, and sprinkled them with dark wine. I knew that more red splatters would mar some of their clothing that day, but before I could do more than begin to think about that, the boys turned as one and faced the door. It opened again, but the light that should have poured through it was blocked by a huge form. The crowd moaned with pleasure as the hot, heavy smell of cattle wafted in.

This year's bull was the most magnificent I'd ever seen, of a rich red-brown with sacred white and black markings, and gilding on his hooves and horns. His neck was broad, and as he strode forward with three trainers holding the rope that ran through the ring in his nose, his shoulders rippled like wavelets at the edge of the sea. He seemed so calm and mild that at first, I was afraid he would not perform as required (which would be a disaster), but then I noted the distance that his handlers kept from him, and I saw how intelligent his eyes were and how his nostrils flared at the scent of the crowd. He tossed his head, and the handlers flinched, but they kept their hold on the ropes. His great-grandsire, I had heard, had been the famous bull that had gored Lysias, and they were right to be afraid.

I had so completely forgotten my surroundings that when a warm hand closed over mine, I almost shrieked. "Sorry," Theseus said, the crowd nearly drowning out his voice.

I swallowed and willed my heart to slow down. It had recovered from the shock of his touch, but while his hand remained on mine, my pulse would continue to race. I slid my hand out and pretended that I needed to arrange the shoulder of my robe. Theseus's half smile told me that I hadn't fooled him, but he didn't try to touch me again.

The conch shell bleated once more, a mournful, haunting sound, and as its discordant note faded, the three trainers stepped forward and hastily slid the ropes out of the bull's nose ring. When the huge animal tossed his head, relieved of the annoyance, they fled to the stands and leaped over the rail, to the laughter of the audience. The Minos uttered a single word in a harsh voice: "Now!"

The boys scattered, whooping, waving their banners— blue and yellow and orange and green streamers like the long fins of the deep-sea fish that sponge divers sometimes found. The bull stood still in the center of the arena, gazing at them calmly, and this either emboldened or infuriated the boys, because the bravest among them darted in and poked at him with the ends of their banner poles.

People shouted encouragement, gasping as a daring youth ran by and slapped the bull's hindquarters. The crowd cried out when one of the boys skipped out of the way just as the bull tossed his head and sharp horns in his direction. The spectators cheered, and flowers rained down on this boy, the first to score a reaction from the beast.

The bull was now trotting in a tight circle. The arena was too cramped for him to be able to move freely, and he must have been agitated and confused by the swirling mass of youths and banners and flowers. One of the smaller boys performed the spectacular move of diving under the bull's belly and coming up on the other side before the animal realized what was happening. I found myself on my feet, applauding and cheering. The Minos shook a triumphant fist in the air, and I recognized Glaukos, of whom he had always been fond.

Glaukos's example was contagious, and soon I lost count of the number of times one of them pulled the bull's tail or slapped him with a banner or teased him into a direct run, only to hop out of the way at the last instant.

A flying hoof knocked tall Enops off his feet. The crowd gasped as the bull wheeled faster than I would have thought possible, his horns lowered, but before he could gore his victim, two of the boy's comrades had seized Enops and dragged him away while others flapped their banners frantically in the bull's face. The beast bellowed in frustration. Several spectators groaned, whether out of relief or disappointment that they hadn't seen the expected glorious death I could not tell.

Enops turned to salute the crowd, which roared its approval as he rejoined the others.

The bull began to tire. He was huge and powerful but clearly more accustomed to spending his days in a sheltered paddock than turning and running in short bursts. Lysias was keeping a close eye on the beast, and he said something to one of his attendants. The man nodded and opened the case at his feet. He pulled out a bristling armful of spears. The boys dropped their banners and armed themselves.

Everyone leaned forward, and a hush came over the arena. Even the bull seemed to know that something was different. He stood still but for shifting his weight from one huge hoof to another, his head thrown back, his little eyes glaring. I could have sworn I heard his heavy breathing as he stroked the dirt with a hoof.

The boys were much more solemn now; their jeering and teasing were over. This was the most important and dif-

ficult part of the ritual. They circled the bull, each boy holding a spear in his right hand. They found their rhythm, and
soon they were dancing in a circle, one foot in front of the
other, that foot behind the first. They bent and dipped. Someone began to clap in time with the dancers' feet, and then
someone else, and then everybody was clapping, smacking
their hands on their thighs, stamping until the stands shook
like a gigantic heart beating. I joined in; I couldn't help it. I
glanced at Theseus. His face was bright with excitement, and
he clapped and stamped with abandon.

The dance continued longer than I remembered it ever
lasting before. Was this because the boys were awaiting a reaction from the bull, or was it because I was so tense, so alert,
that time stretched out for me? Whatever the reason, the bull
appeared to have turned to bronze. Perhaps that is why the
boys grew careless, why they dropped their guard. Or perhaps what happened was the will of Velchanos and no matter
what they did, the outcome would have been no different.

CHAPTER 32

ARTEMIS SETTLES herself and leans against Ariadne's leg. The girl looks different; her hair is piled on top of her head, and its weight makes her slender neck look fragile. Under her enormous eyes are delicate greenish shadows, which make them look even darker.

I recognize the smell of the arena and the excitement of the crowd. The bull baiting at home isn't on such a grand scale, and many people consider it a low-class entertainment. It's never been my favorite sport—I'd rather see a good foot-race or a javelin toss, and it positively sickens Konnidas, so he never took me as a child—but this is one Kretan entertainment, at least, that will be familiar.

Or so I think. It turns out that like everything else here, bull baiting on Krete is bound up in tradition and ritual, and I don't understand most of what is going on. Even so, it's exciting. The boys are well trained and highly skilled, and they are frighteningly bold. The spectators gasp when the gilded horns flash within a palm's breadth of a slender torso or when a powerful hoof stomps the ground where a long foot had danced just a moment before. Enops has a narrow escape, but his teammates pull him out of reach, and he shows remarkable courage by plunging right back into it. His face has gone almost as white as Ariadne's.

Before the bull appears properly exhausted, the boys are suddenly armed with long, slender spears. I nudge Ariadne to ask why they don't wait until the sport is over before the killing, but she either doesn't feel my elbow or is concentrating on the spectacle. I turn to the man next to me, a court functionary who has traveled extensively and has been helpful in explaining Kretan customs to me. I shout my question into his ear over the rhythmic clapping and stamping of the crowd.

He appears unwilling to yank his attention from the scene in front of us, but he is too courteous to ignore me. "They can't wait until he's exhausted, sir," he shouts. "The god has to be given his chance."

The spectators have leaped to their feet as the boys dance faster, still maintaining unity in their steps, circling tighter and tighter around the bull, who appears bewildered at the swirling mass of dancers, their spears pointing directly at him even as they gyrate and crouch and jump and spring.

The bull lunges. It's difficult to imagine something that huge moving so fast, but in an instant the circle of dancers is broken and the animal is hunched over, butting and pawing at something on the ground. The rhythm of both the dance and the applause is broken as the spectators shriek and the boys blunder out of the way, knocking one another down, tripping over their fallen comrades, and scrambling for the fence that separates them from us. Members of the audience reach their hands over, but not, as I had expected, to help the youths to safety. Instead, it is to push them back into the dirt, where they land sprawling, scramble to their feet, and try again to escape, only to be met by the same resistance.

Ariadne and the Minos are standing and clinging to each other. Ariadne buries her face in her uncle's chest as he clutches her with one arm, his other hand over his mouth.

Nobody makes any effort to save the small figure being buffeted by the furious bull. Given the limpness of his body, I doubt that anything can be done. Still, it doesn't seem human to leave him there to be mutilated. The spectators, quiet now, are staring down as though at a dog worrying a rat, or at a hawk plucking a duckling away from under its mother's sheltering wing.

When the bull has spent his fury, he raises his head. His eyes, dull with blood lust, sweep the arena. The man with the scarred chest, whom I had earlier seen training the boys, barks an order. The boys glance at one another. The man shouts at them. One by one, led by Enops, they pick up their spears and re-form their ring.

The dance begins again, but now the audience does not

keep time. Something is more solemn. Even the bull seems to feel this as he swings his heavy head from side to side.

A naked body flashes, and Enops leaps onto the bull's back. With both hands, he plunges his spear between the broad shoulders. A sound between a bellow and a wail trumpets from the huge throat as the bull's head strains upward and the boy leaps down. A hind leg kicks out and lifts him off his feet. Enops flies like Hermes with his winged sandals, black hair streaming, and crashes into the fence, where he lies in a heap while the bull roars and runs and shakes his huge body, to free himself of the weapon that remains in his hump. No one, neither bull nor dancing boy nor spectator, pays any attention to the still form huddled against the fence.

The animal has spent some of his strength, and the dark blood streaming down his sides appears to confuse and madden him. The other boys, emboldened either by Enops's example or by the bull's distress, rush in, and in moments, one spear after another is lodged in the enormous body. The bull moves heavily, ignoring both the boys on their feet who scatter at his approach and the two figures remaining on the ground, one pulling himself up to sitting against the fence and the other motionless in a dark pool.

The beast stops and lowers his head, puffing and scraping the ground, and yet another boy takes advantage of this pause to jump onto his back. I recognize him: it's Simo. His legs aren't long enough to straddle his mount, but he manages to keep his seat as the bull wheels and snorts. The boy yanks a knife from his belt and, bending forward perilously far, in one swift motion cuts the bull's throat. The animal crumples to his knees, his eyes rolling back in his head, and the boy leaps off, lands squarely on his feet, and turns his back to the bull in contempt.

The crowd goes wild, cheering and shrieking, "Simo! Simo! Simo!" He bows to them. The tone of the calling voices changes into one of warning, and the boy glances behind him and then turns just as the bull, blood streaming from the gash in his throat, hoists himself to his feet, lowers his head, and stumbles forward. Simo stands his ground, facing his enemy. The bull drops to his knees again, wavers, and crashes heavily onto his side.

The Minos holds up his right hand. Those near him fall quiet. The silence spreads until the only sounds left are the harsh last breaths of the bull and an occasional groan from Enops, still pressed against the fence. Everyone looks expectantly at the Minos. He stands with his eyes closed for what seems a long time and then declares, "It is done!"

C H A P T E R   3 3

I T WAS little Glaukos whom Velchanos had chosen to join him in blessing the people. I knew I should rejoice for Glaukos and praise him. But I could not shake the sickening feeling that it was not so much the choice of the god as Glaukos's faulty eye and his awkwardness with using a spear right-handed that had caused his death.

A true daughter of Goddess would not think these thoughts, something whispered. *If you feel sorry for the one chosen by the god, you doubt that he died for a purpose. Would it be better if Glaukos had died merely from an accident? Or is it fitting and glorious that his death will make the sacrifice of your consort even more fruitful?*

Down in the arena, people were helping Enops to his feet. He appeared shaken, and he might have broken some ribs, if not an arm or his collarbone. A woman pressed his belly here and there with her fingertips, and like her I watched to see if he winced, which would indicate an injury too deep for healing. He did not, although he grimaced as he stood upright, cradling his left arm. *I should see to that,* I thought before remembering that for a few days I would be Goddess and someone else would have to make Enops comfortable until I had returned to my body.

The Minos's face was shining. "Did you see how brave Glaukos was? And he the youngest of all of them. Velchanos must be very pleased." I felt ashamed, wishing I could join him in his pride. "And Simo!" His voice was thick with emotion. "I *knew* that he was more than he appeared." I watched that same Simo trot around the edge of the arena being showered with golden crocuses. Although I did not like to praise the unpleasant boy, Simo had indeed acquitted himself beautifully, and the Minos had every reason to feel satisfied.

The ritual of Velchanos had had the effect of distracting me from what lay ahead, but the relief was only temporary. Worry and fear settled again on my shoulders, crushing me until it took all my will to stand upright. I turned to lead the women from the stands but stopped when I felt the Minos's hand on my shoulder. He squeezed gently. "It will be all right, Ariadne." The unusual use of my name brought stinging tears to my eyes. I turned back and looked at his face, his dear, familiar face with its lines, and its frame of graying curls. He'd apprenticed to Minos-Who-Was for many years, and when She-Who-Is-Goddess who was my grandmother died and

Minos-Who-Was retired to his orchard, this Minos had served my mother well. Goddess had always found her, and she had never sickened after the ritual. That Velchanos refused to show himself to her was not my uncle's fault.

"I trust you, brother." I couldn't speak what was in my heart: How could Asterion ever perform whatever ritual invited Goddess into my body? And what was that ritual? There was no point in asking, as the first question had no answer, and the Minos would not reply to the second.

The women were still waiting for me. I forced myself to smile at the Minos and kissed his cheek. Then I left.

We had rehearsed the next steps over and over, and yet they felt new, perhaps because instead of stand-in Goddess robes, I was finally being dressed in the actual garment. I stripped down to my skin, and the priestesses draped the various pieces on me. They were heavy and stiff. Perialla had to pull the laces on the bell-shaped skirt as far as they would go to keep it from slipping off. It was made of thick wool and linen squares, dyed yellow with precious saffron and sewn together in alternating plain and striped panels, and it fit tight over my hips and then fell in tier after weighty tier.

Orthia held the brocaded jacket open behind me, and I cautiously slid my arms into its short sleeves, shrugging to settle the garment on my shoulders. It, too, was large, but I was glad of this, as it meant that the edges came a little closer together over my breasts than they had on my mother. I was still embarrassed at the thought of going out in front of everybody exposed like this, but the priestesses acted as though I was dressed as modestly as a farmer's wife.

Behind me, two of them fumbled with the sash that had to be tied in a sacral knot at the back of my neck. They fussed and tugged, pulling me nearly off my feet, before pronouncing themselves satisfied.

"Sit," Thoösa commanded, and I perched on a padded stool, being careful with my garments. A rip or a tear would not be disastrous; the clothes were so ancient that they had been mended often, but the time was short for sewing. It had taken the boys longer than usual to liberate the god from the bull's body, and we had to hurry a little.

Someone settled the gilded cow horns on my head. I closed my eyes, remembering the last time I had seen them on my mother, the new moon before she died. "Be with me," I begged her inwardly. I waited for an answer, but none came, so I opened my eyes just as the women declared that the headdress was on firmly.

"Stand," Thoösa said, and I rose slowly, worried that the horns would wobble. I rotated and saw them all staring at me, Thoösa with her hands on her hips, Damia with her mouth open, and the others with shining eyes. The sisters Pero, who looked so much like my mother, and Kylissa had their arms around each other's waists. Pero's lower lip trembled.

"She has returned," Kylissa said softly. "She-Who-Is-Goddess walks among us."

"Hush," Thoösa snapped. "Don't you know it's an evil omen to call her that before the ceremony has finished?"

Kylissa's head drooped, and she murmured an apology, which I didn't bother answering. All their concerns and worries suddenly seemed trivial. Didn't they know that the little things people did—the automatic blessings of the food, the gestures to ward off evil, the tiny charms that babies wore—didn't they know that none of these meant anything to Goddess? Goddess was greater than any of these trifles.

"What's the matter with her?" Athis asked. Did she mean me?

Thoösa handed me a polished bronze mirror. I moved it up and stared at its wavy surface. I examined my features. They had painted me with white makeup and outlined my eyes with kohl from Aegyptos. The juice of crushed pomegranate seeds made my lips bright red. My eyes looked larger and darker than I remembered, but perhaps this was due to the kohl and to the whiteness of the skin around them. Someone took the mirror from my hand.

"Come," I said, feeling that I was watching a girl who looked like me. "Come with me to the Minos and make me Goddess." Without waiting, I went to the door, enjoying the sharp sound of my shoes on the floor. The left one rubbed my heel. *I'll have a blister there tomorrow,* I thought, feeling like this was an observation made about someone else.

"Wait!" Thoösa rummaged in the chest at the foot of my bed. Her voice was like a slender thread that almost snapped and let me go but at the last moment held me. I swayed, the desire to complete the ritual warring with the irritating feeling that I had forgotten something. Thoösa pulled out one ball of yarn after another, laying them carefully on the bed. Green, red, blue, yellow, a single black one . . . And then I remembered. The priestess lifted out the precious casket and opened its lid.

There it lay: the white Goddess ball. The knots and loops that strayed over its surface looked like the dark spots on the face of the moon. All the priestesses crowded around while Thoösa knelt and held up the box in both hands, as was proper when making an offering.

My right hand moved of its own volition and picked up the ball. It was lighter than I had thought. It was as light as though it were hollow, as though moths or worms—

And just as that thought came to me, the precious ball collapsed in my fingers and crumbled into dust.

CHAPTER 34

I STARED STUPIDLY at the pile of grayish powder
that sifted through my fingers, until the priestesses's shrieks
of horror brought me to myself. I looked up. Pero and Kylissa
clutched each other like drowning women, and Athis's vomit
splashed onto the stone floor.

Perialla supported Damia, whose lips had gone so white
that they were nearly invisible in her wrinkled face. One bright
red spot glowed in the middle of each of the old priestess's
pallid cheeks, and her eyes burned like embers as she glared
at me. "I knew it!" she croaked. "I knew she was no daughter
of the god! See how he shows his disdain!" Her crooked finger
trembled as she pointed at the ugly pile of desiccated wool
fragments mixed with worm droppings that lay at my feet,
and she shook with a weird cackle, torn between laughing
and screaming.

"Silence!" Thoösa was so red as to be almost purple. "There's no one else! Would you have Knossos fall?" Damia fell silent midcackle, her bony hand still flung toward the ruin of the Goddess ball. She lowered it but continued piercing me with her faded eyes. The only sounds were Pero's sobbing and Kylissa's murmurs of comfort. The priestesses all stared at me, their eyes wide with terror.

Outside, the conch squealed. It was not an order for me to appear—nobody could order me now—but a reminder that the people were gathering. I knew that the Minos was standing in the sun, and although the air was merely warm and not yet hot, the heavy bronze bull's head on his shoulders and his red woolen robes must be stifling.

Still they looked at me mutely, and I made a decision.

"Bring me wool," I ordered. "One—no, two—skeins of undyed wool, the whitest and finest you can gather in a hurry." They stood like stones. I stamped, and Kynthia started, looking awakened from a dream, and scurried out the door. I addressed the priestesses. "Show me your hands." Looking dazed, they all thrust out their arms. Athis's fingers were the smallest, and I remembered that she had been skilled at the games we had played as girls, when we would pass looped-up lengths of yarn from one to the other in increasingly complex patterns. "You are to help me," I told her.

Kynthia reappeared, bearing two skeins of decently smooth and decently white wool. I took one and sat on a stool. I held the spindle between my knees. It twirled as I wound fluffy yarn quickly into a sphere. No time to work the central knots; that part would be concealed by succeeding layers, and making it right would have to wait until after I had become Goddess and then turned back into myself. *I'll do it with all reverence*, I promised Goddess. *Just help me now.*

I didn't know what the people would do if I appeared in front of them without the Goddess ball in my right hand, and I didn't want to find out. They would be terrified at the sacrilege. I wouldn't be surprised if they tore me to pieces to please Goddess.

She must be angry with me to have caused such a disaster—or maybe it was a test. This thought gave me a sliver of hope. Maybe the Pasiphaë part of Goddess would forgive me for her own mistake if I could make my fingers do the work correctly. *Someone* had made the ball, and that someone must have been She-Who-Is-Goddess who was my many-greats-grandmother. My mother was now Goddess along with that ancestor, and I had to trust that she loved me too much to condemn me for a sin she herself had committed.

Help me now, I begged again. I nodded at Athis, who was sipping a cup of honey water. She still looked shaky, but she put down her cup and pulled up a stool to face me. She sat on it with her hands out. "Spread your fingers," I commanded. Manners, too, would have to wait. I made a loop and hung it over her middle finger, then made another, twisted it, and hung it next to the first. I closed my eyes, willing my hands to remember my mother's motions as she tried to puzzle out the mystery of the Goddess ball.

The conch sounded a more urgent note. I opened my eyes, smiled reassurance at Athis, and continued.

Soon, a white ball of the correct size lay in my right hand. As far as the people were concerned, this was the same Goddess ball that my mother had held and all our mothers before her. Still, I wanted it to be correctly made, not for their sake but for the sake of Goddess.

I stood. "We must hurry." I was surprised at the firmness of my own tone. "The Minos is waiting."

Once we arrived at the inner chamber, shielded for now from the view of the people, everything moved swiftly, one step following another as smoothly as in one of Daidalos's strange mechanisms. I didn't have to think; I knew exactly what to do.

The air was heavy with aromatic smoke pouring from censers hanging on the walls. It felt harsh in my throat, but with a purifying harshness, scouring something from me. I nodded, and the door to the portico swung open. People would be standing on the festival grounds straining to see in, although it was impossible, outside in the sunshine, to make out what happened inside the dim chamber.

The room darkened further as a form loomed in the doorway. I knew it was my dear uncle, my brother, the Minos— but even so, my courage failed me for a moment. The figure was formless, a mass whose horned head I saw only in silhouette against the spring sky. He moved, taking one slow step, then another, then another, until he stood facing me. He cradled a bronze cup in both hands. I eyed it uneasily and then searched the impassive mask. He could not have been looking through the eyes of the bull, which were set with shining black stones and which in any event were too high up and far apart for a man to use. Then I spotted two small holes in the bull's neck, directly under its chin, and looked at them.

The Minos spoke the ritual words of greeting in the ancient language, "Blessed is Karia," and I answered, as I had been taught, "Blessed forever."

I caught a glimpse of the familiar hands of the Minos for just an instant before he put the cup down on the table, tucked his hands into his sleeves, and stepped back. He opened the door again and the priestesses filed out, only to return almost immediately carrying the heavy clay jars, each woman placing one hand on the pot-lid in case its contents were lively, and taking care not to cover the holes pierced around the top. No sound came through the door, although I had the sense of a large crowd waiting tensely outside.

One by one, the priestesses deposited their jars at my feet. For an awful moment, I was afraid that Damia would be unable to rise again unassisted, but she managed, and then she joined Thoösa, who already waited at the door. Orthia followed, then Kynthia, and then the others, in order of seniority. Athis, the youngest, put down her jar. She seemed ready to faint with relief as she took her place next to Perialla. I reached out my hand, and as I knew she would, Damia placed the cypress branch in it. I dipped it in the sacred water, brought down from Goddess's mountain spring at the last dark of the moon, and shook drops of it over them.

Thoösa spoke, her cracked old voice sounding as loud as a bull's roar in that silent room.

Long, long ago, before time was time, the island of Krete lay dead.

She told the story of how Karia had come to Krete—how *I* had come to Krete. I closed my eyes, hearing the priestesses intone "Blessed be Goddess" at all the right moments. When Thoösa finished, I opened my eyes. Was I Goddess now? How would I know?

The priestesses backed out, careful not to ruin everything by tripping. Athis cleared the door and turned, relief shining from her like a light as she nearly skipped across the portico to the stairs.

The door closed behind them, silencing the noise from the crowd: excited voices, hushed laughter, what sounded like questions. The priestesses would be giddy with relief that their part in the ritual was over. People would be asking them how I had behaved. *Don't tell anybody about the Goddess ball,* I silently reminded them, even though I knew they would not. Someone might proclaim that the only way to cleanse the Goddess stone after such a disaster was with the blood of the priestesses. Even the most pious among them would hesitate to risk this.

Now the Minos and I were alone. This was the moment I

had been dreading most of all; for the first time since my arrival at the shrine, I had no idea what would happen next. I stood with my hands clasped in front of me like a little girl, bowed my head, and said the only words that came to me, "I place myself in your hands."

CHAPTER 35

I SUPPOSE the bull baiting was exciting; as I said, I have little taste for the sport, so I'm not a good judge. I stand outside the door to watch the spectators pour down to the field alongside the palace. Enops comes out, leaning on the shoulder of a companion. His friend is teasing him, and the boy makes a brave effort to smile.

I'm about to follow the last of the thinning crowd, when a dozen solemn-faced men appear wearing only red loincloths. They wield knives, most of them flint but a few that shine with the glint of bronze. Some also carry large baskets woven of rushes. Each man bears a tattoo in the shape of a pair of bull horns spreading over his shoulder blades like sinuous blue wings. In contrast with the gaiety and even hilarity of the rest of the locals, these men appear intent on their business. I lurk a little longer and then peer through the doorway into the arena, trusting that they won't see me.

The men stand motionless around the massive body of the bull. They seem to be waiting for something. The dirt under the red-brown body is dark with blood, and flies are already buzzing near the corpse. One of the men shifts from foot to foot. The others glare at him, and he subsides. Then, from somewhere under the stands, a large figure emerges. Its huge head is crowned with horns that sweep wide, and its shoulders are massive. As it emerges from the shadows, I see flaring nostrils and small, glittering eyes on either side of a broad muzzle.

Artemis whines softly. I drop my hand on her head to quiet her. I see now that this isn't a magic bull walking on its hind legs, as I had first imagined, but rather a person—a man, to judge from the height—wearing a mask in the shape of a bull's head, and long red robes that sweep the dirt up into a cloud as he strides forward. It must be the Minos.

He carries a bronze wine jug. The waiting men bow, then straighten. The priest says something, and the men fall to, butchering the bull so rapidly that despite their apparent skill I wonder if they fear for their fingers as their neighbors slash and slice in grim silence. One of them holds a bowl in which he collects blood, and he then pours it into the wine jug.

Faster than I would have thought possible, the large baskets are heaped with glistening dark red meat, slippery-looking purple entrails, yellow fat, and gleaming white bones. The scent of blood, and of manure that spilled from the intestines, is heavy in the air. All but two of the men depart, carrying the baskets by their handles, the baskets themselves bending and bulging with the weight of what is inside them.

The two men left are now bent over the hide, scraping off the last bits of flesh and fat with long flint knives. The Minos stands motionless, apparently watching them, although it's impossible to tell exactly where he's looking. When the butchers have completed their work, they fold the hide over and over itself until it is a long, neat packet on the bloody ground. They place the bull's horns and hooves on it and pick up the bundle, each supporting his half on both forearms. The Minos turns and leaves, the two men with their burden following him.

I realize that I have witnessed a ceremony that was probably not intended for the eyes of a foreigner—or perhaps even of anyone not consecrated to their god—so I take care not to be seen as I move away from the door and then follow the path in the grass to the large field, a path beaten down by many feet. It's a cool afternoon, perfect for a festival, with a light breeze moving a few clouds across the blue sky. Fires burn under large cauldrons. The sound of chatter and laughter, the sweet smell of wood smoke, and the sight of children running and playing turn this day back into something approaching normal. I wander among the celebrants, exchanging smiles with some, a few words with others.

An undercurrent of unease runs through the busy crowd.

Nerves and worry are always present at a festival, of course; something might go wrong at any time. A priest could forget the words of the ritual; a holy fire could go out. It appears that everything went well with the bull baiting, though. Even Glaukos's death seems to be something to celebrate. I wonder at the tension coming from the people around me.

I'm the one with something to worry about, in any case. I don't know if Prokris's plan has any merit, and I don't share her confidence that shy little Ariadne will choose me as her consort. Artemis seems to pick up on my mood and keeps close, pressing against my leg whenever I pause. She is occasionally tempted by the smell of one cooking pot or another, but she doesn't stray far.

After a while, I see a crowd of men gathered near a fire, around the scarred old man who had trained the boys. They seem to be at the center of the vague sense of unease that I feel. Their voices are tense, and occasionally one man or another speaks too loudly and the others shush him, looking around to make sure no one has noticed. I draw near, unnoticed.

"He's been a good Minos," the trainer—Lysias, I've heard him called—is saying. "His bloodlettings have always been swift and seem painless." This is good news to me, if Prokris's plan succeeds. "And whatever he does to She-Who-Is to bring Goddess to her, he does it just right. I've heard that in past times, sometimes Minos-Who-Was was clumsy and Goddess-Who-Was couldn't perform her duties. But this one hasn't had that trouble."

"Except that one time," puts in another man. He leans forward to poke the fire, and I see his face: Simo. He wears an anxious expression, and he gnaws at the inside of his cheek. I move a step closer, hoping they won't notice me.

"We don't know that for sure," Lysias says sharply. "It might not have been his doing. She—Goddess-Who-Was—was young. They can all make mistakes. If she thought she saw the god, she had to say so."

Simo chews harder at his cheek. "My sister told me. My sister Perialla. She said . . ." He lowers his voice and looks around. I don't move. "Perialla said that after Nikanor was killed by that falling beam, She-Who-Is-Goddess went raving through her apartments saying that it was her fault he'd died shamefully and that she should have spoken the truth."

"I don't believe that," another man says.

"Are you accusing me of lying? Or my sister?" Simo looks angry now.

"Neither. Just—why didn't you mention this earlier?"

"Nothing to do about it while we had the Minos. But he's nothing but Minos-Who-Was after tonight."

"Why didn't he choose a boy to apprentice with him?" bursts out a young man who stands with his arms crossed angrily over his chest. "That's happened before. My grandfather used to talk of a Minos who was not born of Velchanos and She-Who-Is-Goddess, in his own grandfather's time."

"That was only because She-Who-Is of that time bore no living boy," Lysias says with an air of authority. "Asterion was born at the Birth of the Sun in the darkest night of the dark of the moon and he still lives. He *is* Minos-Who-Will-Be."

Simo mutters something. "What?" Lysias asks sharply.

The young man raises his head with a defiant air. "Then that's a mistake, a mistake that someone should correct." A miserable silence settles over them.

"Is there no hope that the boy can be trained?" asks another young man, barely more than a boy himself.

Lysias snorts. "As much hope as there is for that pig there to put on a bull's head and speak the proper words." We all watch as a squealing black and white pig is dragged to the slaughtering area. The block is stained with fresh blood, and the pig seems to know what fate awaits him. He digs his trotters into the earth that has been churned up by the hooves of the creatures led in before him. A man expertly slits the pig's throat, cutting off his protests in midsqueal, and then the portly body is swiftly sliced up, and the pieces are sent off to the roasters.

Just then, Lysias notices me. He salutes. His voice is civil but strained as he asks if there's something he can do to help me.

"Just wondering when we eat," I say.

"Depends," Lysias says. "We have to wait for She-Who-Is-Goddess to show herself." I'll learn nothing more now, so I wish them a happy festival and move on.

It seems that the waiting lasts longer than people are expecting. Men mutter and glance at the sun; women damp down the flames under the cooking pots to slow the bubbling of their contents. A fretful baby is put to the breast, and older children who whine about their hunger are shooed off and told to play.

Then a hush spreads, starting near the palace. It ripples outward until even the children feel it and stop their quarreling or crying, and they all turn toward the door.

Suddenly, inexplicably, I feel the urge to run, to flee down to the harbor and find my ship, to push it into the water and escape back to Troizena. But of course this is foolish. I will myself to hold still, and with the rest of the crowd I stare at the door, which eases open.

CHAPTER 36

I KNEW THAT my dear Minos would never willingly harm me. Still, the unmoving bronze face with its flared nostrils and cold, blank eyes, and most of all, the figure's silence, turned my stomach to water. The Minos was a talkative man, and when not talking, he sang or hummed to himself.

As he turned to the table, I saw the red robes he still wore under the bull's hide, which had a pungency that I would normally find distasteful but whose stench of death seemed appropriate in this place, at this time. It was only when he laid a firm hand on my wrist that I stopped trembling. He touched me not merely to calm me, though—he turned my palm up and placed the sacred bronze cup in it.

When he finally spoke, it was in the archaic language used for prayer, but I had no trouble understanding him: "It is time for She-Who-Will-Be-Goddess to die." For a desperate moment I thought, *I'll throw the cup on the floor and run away—I'll run to Asterion and stay with him forever under the palace.* I hardened myself to stay, but I couldn't move. The cup sat on my open palm, its contents' oily surface shimmering as my hand shook, until the Minos gently curled my fingers up around it and raised it toward my face. A pungent odor, acrid yet earthy, rose to my nostrils. It smelled like rotten leaves and mushrooms and pine needles; it smelled ancient and deadly, yet somewhere in it was the scent of spring and renewal.

"All of it?" I managed to whisper. The huge bronze head moved up and then down. I lifted the cup, and before I could change my mind, I swallowed its contents. I handed the cup to the Minos and watched him as I waited to die.

He removed the lid from the largest of the twelve jars lined up inside the door and reached inside it. He appeared to be moving as unhurriedly as the sun moves across the sky. When his hand came out of the jar, it was holding a long snake, whose tail slashed the air like a bullwhip, but so slowly that I felt I could dance around it.

I tried to speak but made only a raspy grunt, and the big horns swung in my direction. I thought the head gave a little shake, as though my uncle were telling me to be still. I watched the serpent as it moved sluggishly. Was the creature in a holy trance, or had the Minos drugged it?

After a time that seemed interminably long yet infinitesimally short, the Minos's voice said, again in the beautiful language of prayer, "It is time for She-Who-Is-Goddess to be born and to let Goddess enter her." Still holding the snake in his right hand, he grasped my wrist in his left, and before I knew what he was going to do, he had scraped the tips of the serpent's fangs along my flesh.

I squinted; even the light that came through the cracks around the door was now—*When? A moment later? The next day? One hundred years later?*—unbearably brilliant. Then heat traveled from my heart through my body and out my fingers and toes, tingling and burning.

The Minos was speaking, but I had no interest in his words. I stretched out my fingers. My left wrist felt tight, and I saw that it was swollen and pink and that my hand looked like it belonged to a fat baby.

The Minos lifted off his mask and gazed at me, his grizzled hair sticking to his head with sweat. To my mute astonishment, I saw tears spilling out of his eyelids. Then he did a very strange and unexpected thing. He bowed, so low that I thought his forehead was going to knock into his knees, and said in the ancient language, "My lady Karia."

Then I understood. Ariadne was gone; She-Who-Will-Be-Goddess would be dead until my own daughter, born at some future Birth of the Sun, became a woman. Now I understood my mother's loneliness. I was alone, even though I would always be surrounded by people, because unlike me, they were all fated to die, while I would live forever and one day would look down on them from the sky.

The Minos slumped a bit, exhausted. I understood that now that his duty was done, now that he had summoned Goddess, he had turned back into the old, familiar Minos. He would laugh and talk and eat and drink and play with babies and flirt with girls for the length of the Festival. And then, afterward, he would move to his cottage with Orthia and with someone else—who was it? I racked my brain trying to remember if he had another wife who was going to share his retirement with him. Then I gave up. It was not important.

What was important was this: My mother was with me. I could not see her, but I felt her presence as strongly as if I were lying on her lap, as I had when I was a baby, or as if we were sitting companionably together knotting wool into intricate patterns for a particularly difficult healing, or as if I were standing behind her, massaging her head to drive away a pain.

And not only my mother, but her mother and all our Mothers since time was time were suddenly with me, invisible but present nonetheless. I turned to the Minos to ask him where they had come from, but he was no longer there—at least, not to my eyes. Instead, I saw the moon, full and white and bright. It didn't occur to me to question why She was there, in that small, windowless room, and especially how I could see Her now, during Her dark phase. Nor did I wonder when She hovered over the edge of the sea, making a brilliant white path that stretched toward me. She dipped her edge into the water.

And now I saw my mother. She looked as she had when I was a child, her shining black hair untouched by gray, her grave eyes, and only a hint of a smile. Behind her was one I knew to be She-Who-Is-Goddess who was her mother, although I had never seen my grandmother while she was alive. She was shorter than my mother and had a laughing countenance and thick hair like mine that escaped from its fastening. Her own mother was behind her, a woman with a withered arm and a gentle face. On and on they stretched in a line, and they didn't speak, but all looked at me with an expression that I couldn't read. Compassion? Pity? Fear?

I wanted to ask them why they were there, but as one they turned from me and started dancing in a line. The Goddess farthest from me, whose features I couldn't make out, took a step toward the moon. At first I thought she was dancing in the water, and then I realized that she was *on* the water. She trod the silver path that the moon made, moving straight toward the white disk. The next woman followed close behind, and the next and the next, until they stretched far away, looking like a line of ants, purposeful in their parade, bending and straightening, twirling and prancing.

My mother glanced over her shoulder at me. I took an eager step toward her, but she held up her hand, her face serious.

"No." Her voice was as I remembered it from my girlhood, lighter than in her later years. "No, Ariadne, my darling, my dearest, you are not to come."

"I am not to come now?"

"You are not to come," she repeated, and then she was far away, dancing along that bright road, and in an instant she was swallowed by the last shining sliver as the moon sank below the horizon, leaving the world, and especially me, in darkness.

Someone was saying the same words over and over. I didn't want to listen. I wanted to follow my mother. Was I *never* to go with her? Was I not meant to join her and our mothers and live eternally in the moon? Or was it that I was not yet ready and could not go now but would at some later time?

The voice was insistent, and reluctantly I made myself listen. "You must meet your people, my lady Karia," the Minos was saying patiently. "You must show yourself to them." I turned obediently toward the door, but he stopped me. "You have forgotten something." I wrenched my thoughts and remembered the rehearsals, and the white Goddess ball.

There came to me a sickening feeling that made Goddess retreat a bit and Ariadne try to reveal herself. Ariadne had something to tell the Minos, but Goddess wouldn't let her. Goddess was too strong; She was ancient and powerful, and She was not only my mother but all our Mothers since time was time. Goddess choked off the speech in my throat, Goddess turned my feet; Goddess opened the richly carved wooden chest and pulled out the sham ball.

The Minos gave an exclamation, but I couldn't tell what the sound meant—surprise or dismay or something else. No matter. The ball was heavy, far heavier than it had been before, and it lay cold and inert in my hands. Some ancient memory told me that it should feel alive and should glow. It had always glowed like moonlight during the ceremony, ever since I had first become Goddess, back when Knossos was no more than a collection of huts by the river Theren, with the Goddess stone that had fallen from the sky in their midst. But now it felt dead.

I could do nothing about it. I turned left and paced the thirteen steps that took me to the Goddess stone. It gleamed white under its draping of red garments. I knelt and held the ball of yarn up to it. I counted to thirteen in my head and then stood and nodded to the Minos. He hesitated a long moment before he bowed and pushed the door open.

My eyes clamped shut against the brilliant light, and my arm felt like it would break with the weight of the ball I held out in front of me. The cheering that reached my ears was sweet, and I was tempted to look, but even a crack in my lids was painful. Behind me, the Minos shouted, "Goddess walks among you!" I doubted that anyone heard his words over their own noise.

Far, far inside me, I was still Ariadne. I wondered what to do next; I worried that I did not know how to find my husband. Something in me even felt hungry when the smells of roasted meat and hot bread reached my nostrils. But mostly, Ariadne was gone. Dead, as the Minos had said? Or merely hiding? Almost all of me was Goddess, and as my eyes adjusted to the light, I half opened them.

I looked out over my people and felt a rush of love. They were so imperfect, and different one from the other, yet so similar. They were beautiful, even the old ones deformed with stiffening bones and the tall, young ones whose faces bore the angry red marks of youth. My eyes passed over tiny Phaedra, who was cradled in her wet nurse's arms, and she was no more or less dear to Me than any of the others. They were all My children, and they were all beautiful.

Yet at the same time, they were hideous, because every one of them was dying. As I gazed at them, I saw rotting corpses, even the babies, even the rosy maidens and the youths hanging over them. I found this neither frightening nor disgusting; instead, I felt renewed love, as well as pity for their fate. None of them would be alive for more than a few years, while I would look down on their children and their children's children forever from the night sky, except when I descended and lived among them for a few precious days.

I had been Goddess since time was time, and I would be Goddess forever.

CHAPTER 37

CHOOSE YOUR attendants." The Minos and I
were back in the Goddess chamber. He indicated the largest
jar, which rattled on the floor as the snakes that he had tipped
into it struggled with one another.

He lit a small torch, and the room felt even stuffier. I
reached for it, but he shook his head. "They'll flee if you approach with fire. Choose." I almost asked how, and then I
realized: I would know. I was sure of it. I closed my eyes with
relief; maybe this meant that I would know Velchanos as well.

The Minos removed the lid, and I stood over the mass of
dark, writhing serpents. My two hands shot out together—
they acted without my will—and each grasped a snake square
behind the head. I stood with my arms stretched out in front
of me, a wriggling snake in each hand. They knew their fate;
I could feel this in the way they arched and flailed, trying to

escape. *Too late, sisters,* I thought as I turned toward the door. *You have been chosen as I have been chosen.* I stepped outside a second time. The people cried out and fell to their knees, weeping with joy and terror.

I gazed on them until they quieted. "Choose me!" some men were saying wordlessly, and "Choose my son!" some women were telling me, their thoughts as clear as actual words. Others hoped that I would pass over them, over their brothers and sons and lovers and fathers and husbands. It made no difference. It was not I, but Velchanos, who would choose; it was up to Velchanos to reveal himself—or not. I was amused but not irritated at their error, any more than I would be irritated at a child who stubbornly tried to catch a moonbeam, refusing to see that her hand would pass through it, no matter how many times she failed.

My gaze swept through them as they stared up at me, high on the top step. Ariadne inside me asked, "What are we looking for?" but Goddess inside me told her to hush, that We would know.

And We did. Near the cooking pots, someone stood a bit apart from the others. I stared in his direction, and some people in the crowd craned their necks and turned around. I knew who the solitary figure was, and the recognition made my heart lurch.

I climbed down the steps, half floating and half about to trip over my heavy skirt. Both my hands clutched the snakes. As soon as I stepped down from the portico, I lost sight of the figure, but I knew that I was walking directly to it as surely as one of Daidalos's lodestones turned toward the north. In the days when I had been free to wander outdoors, I used to love to watch fields of grass divide and bend under the force of the god who made the wind blow through them. I remembered that now, as people moved silently out of my way.

He was standing in front of the fire tended by Kylissa, priestess and birth sister of my mother. She held a long wooden spoon in one hand and cradled her little grandson in the other arm. She took a step backwards, away from me. I hardly noticed her, for I had my eyes fixed on the other figure.

I knew who it was. I had known even before I took my first step down from the portico. Something had drawn me to him, and I searched myself. How would I know if the force pulling me to him was the divine love of Velchanos for Goddess, or if it was Ariadne's love for Theseus? I had felt something when he kissed me. Was that love?

I needed time, and I needed someone to ask. I had neither.

The Minos was suddenly at my side. I didn't know if he had moved quickly or if time had changed its pace yet again. I was glad to see him, because a part of me was aware that my hands were cramping. I gave him the now-limp snakes. Soon, they would be in pieces in a stew, along with the others, who still lay coiled in their pots.

I looked up at Theseus's bearded face, which was staring at me in confusion. Velchanos had been testing me; he wanted to see if I would make the same mistake that my mother had made. I smiled and thought, *I've passed your test. It's not one or the other: Do I love Theseus? or: is this Velchanos? It's both. You'll see, my lord; I'll do what is necessary.*

I took the sash from my attendant and wrapped it around his waist, drawing him close to me. I felt his breath on my face and his warmth on my chest. "Welcome back, my lord," I said, and smiled up at my lord Velchanos, who had returned to me as surely as a dove returns to its cote, in the person of the Athenian prince Theseus.

⇀ THESEUS ↽

CHAPTER 38

I NEVER REALLY believed that Ariadne would choose me. Athens is subject to Krete, so she wouldn't have anything to gain politically by marrying me, even if my father were to recognize me as his heir. This appears doubtful as long as Medea's son is alive. Prokris insists that the choice has nothing to do with politics, though, and that Ariadne's mother chose a simple blacksmith last year.

In any case, at first I'm not really sure that she *has* chosen me. She looks odd—pale, and with staring eyes—when she comes out to stand on the top step of the palace portico for the second time. She's followed by the Minos. He no longer wears the mask, but the bull's hide is still draped over his red robes.

The two stand there until I wonder if Ariadne's arms, stretched in front of her for so long, are tired. She's clutching something, but I can't see what. She hardly moves; maybe a little back and forth of her head, but that could be fatigue. I hear that she hasn't eaten for three days, and the smell of the lambs and kids simmering in their pots of milk and the roasting pig's and bull's meat are enough to drive my stomach to rumbling like a volcano.

She stands there for a long, long time. Nobody seems surprised, although they do appear tense. A muscle works in the jaw of the woman next to me, who occasionally dips her spoon into the pot at her side to stir its savory contents. In fact, the only motions I see are those necessary for cooking.

Even the babies are quiet. The little children have stopped their games and their noise and have joined their elders in staring at the small figure of Ariadne, who wears a huge skirt and not much else and is perched on the top step as though she's about to take wing.

Her head has stopped moving. I turn to see what she's staring at, and just as I realize it's me, she takes one tottering step forward, then a step down, and another step, and another, and then she's making her way through the crowd, coming as directly to me as an arrow. Her arms stick out in front of her, and now I see that she is clutching two writhing snakes. From the whiteness of her knuckles, she must be holding them so tightly that the squirms are their death throes.

The Minos is close at Ariadne's heels. She doesn't seem to notice him but walks steadily until she's standing in front of me, looking up with eyes so black that I see tiny copies of myself reflected in them. She stands without moving for so long that I wonder if I should do something. I'm about to stammer a greeting when she hands the limp snakes to the Minos, who in turn passes them to one of his acolytes.

The woman next to me puts down her spoon and hands her baby to someone. She comes to stand near Ariadne. The old woman named Damia hobbles up, leaning on the shoulder of a little boy, who winces as she digs her claws into him. Damia takes her place in front of the woman who had been holding the spoon. A girl who looks very much like Ariadne joins them, and then another old woman, and a comfortable-looking chubby matron with streaks of gray in her hair, and more and more until, soon, a dozen women and girls are ranged behind Ariadne in two lines, with the oldest at their heads.

Damia unties a sash that is knotted behind Ariadne's head. Ariadne takes it without looking away from my face. She reaches forward and wraps it around my waist, retaining hold of both ends so that we are brought face to face. One of her arms is puffy and red. "Welcome back, my lord," she says. I stammer something about being glad to be there, like a polite child at a party.

The Minos turns to the crowd and shouts, "Velchanos recognizes his bride!" and they all erupt into cheers. It seems like something dead has leaped to its feet in front of my eyes. The very air seems alive as men embrace, children squeal and jump up and down, and women turn to each other with shining faces to exclaim their joy.

In the middle of this whirling chaos, Ariadne and I stand with our eyes fixed on each other. This is what Prokris has planned; this is what we've worked for. This is why I kissed Ariadne—although, I must admit, that part of Prokris's plan was not unpleasant. But I know that I have deceived the girl, and I'm desperately uncomfortable as she gazes at me with her bright eyes.

The Minos is carrying the huge bronze bull's head. Before I'm aware what he's about, he lifts it with an effort and places it on my shoulders. I'm not prepared for its weight or for the way its edges, padded though they are, press into my flesh. But I understand that this must be an important moment, and I stand as tall as I can. I wish I could see more than the tiny field of vision afforded to me through the small holes in the bull's neck, because the noise is deafening. If the crowd was wild before, it is twice as enthusiastic now. Conch shells blast, women shriek, and men bellow.

Adding to my discomfort is that I don't know what to do next. The Minos holds out his hands to us. Ariadne takes one and motions at me to take the other. I comply, and the priest leads us to a long table. Finally, blessedly, he removes the bull's head from my shoulders and motions to us to take our places.

I start to whisper a question, but Ariadne shakes her head as the two lines of women, who have followed us, fill in the benches, six on her right, six on my left. Across from us, the eleven remaining bull baiters sit down too. A twelfth boy, looking both terrified and proud, joins them, evidently to replace Glaukos. I wonder what happened to that small body.

The twenty-six of us sitting at the high table are motionless as all around, people snatch flat slabs of hot bread and pile them high with meats of all descriptions. They drink deeply from the leather flasks that are passed from hand to hand, emptied, refilled, and passed again. Mothers dip their fingers into the grease puddled on the wooden carving boards and stick them in the mouths of the babies on their hips, who suck eagerly.

The Minos stands behind Ariadne as serving men bring out large platters of roasted meat. At the smell of beef, my stomach whines. No wonder the butchers cut the bull into such small pieces—it had to cook quickly to be ready for this feast. The platters and a large bronze pitcher are placed in front of me. Everyone looks at me expectantly. I glance at the Minos.

"Tell them to eat," he prompts.

"Eat the body of your god," I say, hoping that my words are close to what the ritual demands. They must be, because everyone reaches in and takes a handful.

"Now pour for them," the Minos says. The pitcher is heavy, but with so many cups to fill, its load lightens quickly. The meat is rich, but strong in taste and tough, coming from a bull and not a steer. I take a swallow of wine to wash it down. The drink has a metallic taste that I don't think is due to the pitcher. I look up at the Minos with a question in my eyes.

"It is mixed with the blood of Velchanos."

Strange people, I think, *to mix their wine with bull's blood and not with water,* but although the flavor is odd, it's not strong enough to be unpleasant, and I continue eating and drinking. Soon, I hope, I will undergo my ceremonial bloodletting, the feast will break up, and I can get out from in front of all these eyes. I can't read their expressions. Most people seem happy, but some look at me with what appears to be pity, and I squirm inwardly as I remember the evil-looking instruments that had been used to torment and then kill the bull. Whatever they use on me will certainly be less painful. I'm sure they wouldn't dare to hurt their god, even a temporary one, too badly. Still, I think of the whipping that I've heard sometimes accompanies these rituals, and I wish that Prokris had managed to learn more about it.

The crowd has quieted a great deal. Little girls dance to a flute, and children sprawl all over in sleep, as do many adults. A drunken brawl breaks out, and people part the antagonists.

I notice the Minos looking at Ariadne with concern. I have drunk a fair amount of wine but not enough to dull my senses, and I'm startled by her expression. She winces as she looks down at her arm, seeming surprised at the red streaks on it, and then she huddles her shoulders to bring the two edges of her bodice together over her breasts.

I ask, "Are you cold?" She shakes her head and drops her gaze, but not before I see her lip quivering.

I stand to tell the Minos that she is not well, but he has

seen it too. "Don't worry." He helps her to her feet. "It's wearing off. I'd hoped it would last another hour . . ." He lets his voice trail off as he supports Ariadne and helps her step out from behind the table. They have taken a few paces when the Minos turns around and calls over his shoulder, "Why aren't you coming?" I stumble around my own chair as each face at the table stares at me, and now everyone in the large field is looking in our direction. A man snickers. Someone shushes him with an angry whisper.

"You want me to go with her?" I ask as I hurry to catch up with them. Ariadne is hunched over, cradling her sore arm, her long skirt dragging.

The Minos looks surprised. "Of course. Where else would you go on your wedding night?"

"I'm so sorry," Ariadne says as tears slide down her pale cheeks. Her eyes are red, either from weeping or from the drug her uncle has given her, or both. "I'm sorry, I'm sorry."

We're in the middle of a huge bedchamber. I put an arm around her shoulders in an attempt to help her stop trembling, taking care not to crush her elaborate bodice. She feels like a bird, with a fluttering heart and tiny bones. She trembles, and I wonder if she's cold or frightened. Someone brings a pad of cloth that has been soaked in sweet-smelling herbs, and I hold it on the angry red streaks on her forearm and kiss the top of her head. What a strange girl, to apologize for making me a god!

"Don't be sorry," I say. "I'm honored. I never thought that you would choose me, a foreigner." I fight back the guilt; it's hard to continue to deceive this trusting little thing with the huge dark eyes that glitter with tears.

I lead my little bride to the ornate and ancient-looking bed, only the second I have ever seen that was raised off the ground, and ease her down onto it. Artemis stays so close to me that I tread on her paw, but she doesn't whine. I sit next to Ariadne, keeping one arm around her shoulders. She whispers something that I can't make out. I bend in closer. "What was that?"

"You are very noble." She leans her head against my chest.

The guilt becomes even more painful. "Perhaps not as noble as you think."

"Oh yes. To give your life for the Kretan people, when you are an outsider, that is a noble thing."

I try to laugh, but my throat has closed. "I don't plan to give my life for anybody."

She pulls back and stares at me. "But that's what you're here for. That's why there's a Chosen One at the Planting Festival. He has to die for the people."

It's like she's speaking a foreign language, one where I understand only one word in three. "What do you mean, 'Die for the people'?" It must be some way of talking that they have here, some ritual where the king's bloodletting is seen as a kind of death.

Ariadne looks down. "The Minos will open the pathway

of your blood. Your blood will go on the fields, and the harvest will be good."

"How much of my blood?"

"All of it." Her voice is so low, I can barely hear it, but the words are all too clear.

I'm shaking. I remove my arm from around her shoulders. "You people aren't barbarians. You don't do things like that. You even allowed that monster to live, who would have been exposed at birth anywhere else." The look on her face increases my agitation, and I leap to my feet, preparing to flee.

"Please," she begs. "Please sit down."

"Are you talking about the bloodletting ceremony? Does someone . . ." I'm too horror struck to go on. Rage heats me. Prokris couldn't have known this; my death would ruin all her plans. She should have learned more about Kretan customs. How dare she be so careless with my life?

"And you ch-chose *m-me* for this?" Outrage makes me sputter.

"*I* didn't choose you. Velchanos did. He took your body. He is in you. I saw it—I saw him when you were standing in the crowd. I couldn't choose another. It would have been a great sacrilege. It would have been the second time, and this time would have meant the death of my people." Her tears have dried, and her face is more composed.

I don't know what she means by "the second time," and I don't care. All I know is that I have to get out of here. I don't know where I'll go, but surely there is someone on this island with some sense. I'm strong, and now I have experience on a boat and can work my passage—not to Athens, but to another land where women don't control things and where the king isn't slaughtered by his barbarian subjects.

Ariadne is silent as I run to the door and fling it open only to see two large guards blocking it, with spears crossed over the opening. Artemis growls.

"You require something, my lord?" one of the men asks. I can't see his eyes through the slits in his boar-tusk helmet, but I hear his amusement. I can tell he knows that what I require is escape.

"Wine" is all I can think to say. I close the door and retrace my steps.

⇝ ARIADNE ⇜

CHAPTER 39

SOMEONE MURMURED outside the door. It opened, and Prokris entered, carrying a tray with a wine flask and two cups. The Ariadne part of me, which was growing stronger at every heartbeat, wanted to run to her, but the waning Goddess in me insisted I sit still and not show my weakness to a mortal.

"Prokris," Theseus began, but she interrupted him.

"I know." She put the tray on a low table. "I heard. They plan to do it in three days."

"You seem very calm." His bitterness startled me and allowed Ariadne to push Goddess aside a bit more. "I'll just have to stop them," Theseus continued. "I'll tell them that as a foreigner, I didn't know what it meant to be chosen and I refuse the honor."

"No," I said. They both looked at me. I was weary to the

marrow, my arm ached, and thirst raged in my throat, but I forced myself to speak. "It's not something you can accept or refuse. If you're Velchanos, that's who you are. You have no choice."

"But I'm not Velchanos!" he protested.

"You are."

"I would know it if I were."

I shook my head and reached for the wine. There was no point in arguing. I drained the cup and lay back on the pile of cushions, exhausted, my head whirling. *I should have done something,* I thought miserably. But what? It had not been my choice to be She-Who-Will-Be and then She-Who-Is-Goddess and, finally, Goddess; it had not been my choice that Theseus had come to Knossos so close to the Festival; and it certainly had not been my choice that the god would pick Theseus to host him. I had not chosen him. I might have been momentarily shaken by his kiss, but now I felt nothing more for him than I did for any other man. Pity, certainly; friendship, perhaps; gratitude that from our first meeting, he had treated me as myself and not as She-Who-Will-Be-Goddess; but nothing like what my mother had said about Nikanor: "the one I loved above all others."

No, it had been the will of Velchanos that Theseus should be his incarnation on earth. Everything important in my life had been willed long before I was born, as was everything that would happen from now on. Theseus would be my consort for three days, and then he would make the fields fertile. The Minos would—

I sat up in a panic.

"What is it?" Theseus asked.

I tried to calm myself and to answer evenly, but my voice caught in my throat. "There is no Minos." My uncle, who had just become Minos-Who-Was, must even now be planning the removal of his belongings from the palace to the cottage, with its orchard that had lain untended since the last Minos-Who-Was reached the end of his earthly days. A new Minos was going to have to open the pathway to Theseus's blood and would have to make me Goddess again at Harvest and then Birth of the Sun. Someday, that same Minos would turn my future daughter into She-Who-Will-Be-Goddess and then She-Who-Is-Goddess.

Asterion could never, never do any of those things, and Knossos would fall.

Every Minos was a mortal man; at his death, he would be richly buried and deeply mourned, but his body would rot, and his spirit would go only where the spirits of all virtuous women and men go, not to the eternal moon. The Minos's business was not my business, and until recently I had never worried about the problem of his succession. Surely *he* had, though.

Prokris stirred uneasily and stood. "Someone will wonder where I am," she said. "I'm supposed to be feasting with the other wives." I strode to the door and flung it open. The startled guards leaped to attention, crossing their spears again.

Prokris ducked under the long shafts and hurried down the hall. "Bring me Minos-Who-Was," I commanded.

"Minos-Who-W-w-w-?" stammered the taller of them.

The shorter guard, evidently cleverer than his colleague, nodded comprehension. "Immediately, mistress." He knocked the back of his hand on his forehead and sped down the corridor. Theseus looked bewildered as I paced, supporting my left wrist with my right hand. I felt more clearheaded than I had in a long time—maybe since the day my mother had gone to join our Mothers.

For only the second time in my memory, my uncle ran into the chamber of She-Who-Is-Goddess, but this time *I* was She-Who-Is-Goddess, not my mother, and I was alive, not lying drained of blood on the bed. "What is it?" He looked from me to Theseus. "Has it gotten worse? The effect should be almost gone by now."

I held out my wrist for his inspection. "I think it's getting better," I said, and relief spread across his face. He sat down heavily on my mother's stool and rested his face in his hands.

"Uncle." He didn't answer. "Uncle, I need to know— have you been training a new Minos?"

"This is not a matter I can discuss, not even with She-Who-Is-Goddess." His voice was muffled behind his hands, but even so, I could tell that he sounded uncertain, and I pressed my advantage.

"You must tell me. For the next three days, I am not

She-Who-Is, but Goddess Herself." He lifted his head and looked at me with respect and a little fear. Love he had always shown; pride, too; but this was new. I went on. "I know that some doubt my parentage, and I will need a strong Minos to defend me."

"My successor has proven himself the chosen of the god," he said. *Oh no. Simo.* "But I'm afraid the people will never accept him. Not while Asterion lives. I was planning to tell them during this year's Festival. Your mother had approved it. She was going to adopt him as Her son while she was Goddess, and then he would have been as legitimate as Asterion, and when the time came for him to become Minos, it would have been an easy transition. But then . . ." His voice trailed off. *But then she died before she could do it,* I knew he was going to say.

"Couldn't you announce it now?" Theseus asked.

"Pasiphaë can no longer adopt him, now that she is with her Mothers." He sighed heavily. "It would have pleased her. The boy was born of her, although he was not the son of Goddess and Velchanos. Still—"

"He *what?*" His words drove all traces of Goddess from me. *Simo? Born of my mother?* He must be the boy born before Athis. So he hadn't died, as I'd assumed. Why had she never told me? I tried to absorb this as the Minos continued. I hardly heard his words.

"And I am no longer Minos," he told Theseus. "I stopped

being Minos the moment Goddess appeared in front of the people bearing the white ball in her hands."

"But I—" I stopped.

The Minos looked keenly at me. "But you what, child?" I couldn't tell him about the Goddess ball, so I shook my head and poured another sip of wine.

He kept his gaze on me while he addressed Theseus. "We can't make such a change now. You must have your time as Velchanos, and then, before the final ritual"—he delicately avoided saying what that was—"while Ariadne is still Goddess, she will announce the adoption. As Minos-Who-Was, I can continue to counsel and train the boy." He laid a gentle hand on my arm. "I will do what I can to protect Asterion, but afterward . . ." He shook his head.

Theseus had grown red. Now he broke out, "I know what you mean by 'afterward,' old man, and you're going to have to change your plans. I'm not going to submit to having my throat cut by you or some boy or anyone else. You'll have to find a Kretan who's willing to die for the people of Krete, because it won't be me."

Minos-Who-Was stood. I suddenly saw him as a stooped, tired old man, as Theseus had called him. When his power left him, he seemed to have lost a palm's width in height. He rested his hand on the door handle, and before he opened it, he said, "I'm afraid you have no choice. Not every man chosen by Velchanos has gone willingly to the altar, and over time we have developed ways of making sure that the god's will is done."

He pushed the door open. The guards uncrossed their spears to allow him to pass. Theseus started to bolt after him, but the shorter of the guards shoved him square in the chest and sent him sprawling. As the door closed, we heard them break into raucous laughter.

Artemis laid her head on my lap, and I stroked her soft fur. The marks she had left on my wrist were long gone, but I could almost see them still, ringing the bone in a perfect crescent. I bent over and whispered into the cream-colored ear fringed with long hairs, "You weren't trying to harm me. You were warning me, weren't you? Warning me to keep away from him?" Her tail waved gently, but whether it was an answer or merely a response to my attention, I'll never know.

"You people are determined to kill me one way or another." Theseus was red with rage. "And when your Minotauros showed no interest in eating me, you hatched this plot."

"That's not how it is," I said helplessly. "I'm sorry." My apology sounded pitiful even to me, and I didn't take offense at his derisive snort. "Why would we want to kill you? I thought you understood—and even if you didn't, there was nothing you could do about it. The god led you to Knossos. He chose you to be the one to take his body. There was *nothing* you could do about it."

He glared at me. "Do you really believe that? Do you believe that everything happens because it's willed to happen? That nothing we mortals do can change what the gods have ordained?"

I almost said, "I'm not a mortal," but I didn't want to risk his scorn. Instead I said, "But that's what the gods do, what the gods *are*. Your life is fated to end three days from now, and even if you run, it *will* end then. You'll drown at sea or be eaten by lions, or you'll be killed by the guards. Your destiny demands it. Surely it's better to end your life in this way, honoring the gods and giving life to the people of Knossos, rather than in some pointless accident." *Like Nikanor,* I thought, and my heart lay heavy in the hollow of my chest.

"How do you know my life isn't destined to end three *years* from now? Or thirty years? Or fifty? And if I run, I'll be able to fulfill *that* destiny."

I touched his arm. He shook me off and flung open the door. The guards must have been expecting this, because they were crouched in the opening with their spears pointing inward. "You can't kill me," Theseus said with a sneer. "I have to live for three more days. Don't you know that? If you kill me now, how will your god fertilize your fields?"

The larger guard, in one swift movement, pinned Theseus's arms behind him while the other whipped a long piece of rope out of the pouch on his belt. Theseus shouted curses at them, their mothers, their grandfathers, their children born and unborn. Silently and expertly, they bent his knees so that they could tie his ankles together with his wrists at his back. They wrapped the end of the rope around his neck in such a way that if he moved his arms more than a hair, it would tighten, strangling him. Even I, who had much expertise with knots, admired their skill.

They laid Theseus on the bed. He propped himself up on his elbow immediately, his curses never slowing. They pushed him down again. Their contempt was obvious. "He's not from Krete," I wanted to remind them. "He didn't know." But of course they were aware of this, and of course they didn't care, as long as the god performed his duty.

Clearly, I had no chance now of bearing the god's child at the next Birth of the Sun. This was not unusual; my mother, after all, would not have conceived a child this year, if she had lived. Goddess sometimes prefers She-Who-Is-Goddess to wait. It didn't matter. Many years stretched ahead of me to choose a man and then watch him die, choose another man and watch him die too, every year for the rest of my earthly life. This was how it had been since time was time.

The guards didn't bother to gag Theseus. Why should they? As long as he stayed here until the final day of the Festival, there was no danger in what he said to anyone, especially me. The guards knew that Goddess would not be swayed by anything said by the imperfect body that Velchanos had chosen. Of course the mortal part of my husband would fight against dying, would be reluctant to leave the world in its perfect spring, in its promise of many more springs to come. Unless he was a very pious person who accepted his fate with no question, the chosen man would try to persuade me to let him go. This was to be expected, and Goddess, much as She might pity the mortal part of Her husband, would never help him escape.

And even if I wanted to help Theseus, untying him wouldn't accomplish anything. The guards would be relieved by two others before these were tired. The men of Knossos considered it a great honor to keep vigil over the bridal chamber of Goddess and Velchanos, and it was not difficult to find volunteers.

Theseus appeared to grow weary of cursing and lay with his back to me. After a moment, he said quietly, "Would you mind loosening the ropes around my ankles? My feet are going numb."

I felt like I weighed twice what I had that morning, and like I had aged twenty years since then. Wearily, I bent over my husband. The restraints did appear too tight, but my attempts to loosen them were futile. My left hand was still useless, and the rope was thick and hard. "I can't," I said. He didn't answer.

I sat down helplessly, wishing I could do something to ease his pain, both in his body and in his heart. I heard voices and running feet from somewhere far away, in the depths of the palace. I was transported back to a time long ago—no, it had been only the length of a few moons—when my mother and I had walked under Goddess and Her stars, back from the hut where the woman and her tiny babies had died. I swayed as the memory rushed over me. That night, too, hurrying feet and muffled cries had disturbed the darkness.

I raised my head and listened. Theseus appeared not to hear anything out of the ordinary, but then, unlike me, he had not lain awake night after night here, growing to know the sounds of the palace the way a midwife knows the sounds of a woman in labor and can tell by a change in her breathing that something has gone horribly wrong.

Once again, the door opened. I stood, dreading what I would see. Didn't they know that Goddess and Velchanos are to be left alone unless a visitor is summoned, as I had summoned the Minos? Who would dare to disturb us now?

The wrinkled old face of Damia peered around the door, looking like the turtle I had always thought must be her sister. Her lashless eyes blinked, and then she snapped at the guard, "Push the door farther, can't you?" The door swung inward. Like Prokris, she carried a tray on which sat two cups and a flask. She came in, her steps uncertain even with that light weight, and set down her burden. A folded cloth ran along the tray's long end, concealing food, I supposed. I felt that I would never eat again, but I grudgingly acknowledged that it was a kind thought.

"Thank you," I said, "but . . ." I indicated the nearly full flask of wine already there.

She shrugged and filled her two cups with the wine she had brought. "Open the door," she said loudly. One of the guards did so, and she handed the cups out to them. "Might as well not waste it," she said, ungracious as always, and the two men took the cups with muttered thanks.

"The Minos—Minos-Who-Was, that is—he invaded the sanctuary of the priestesses," she announced without preamble. "He demanded to know what had happened with the Goddess ball." Her beady eyes fixed me with an unblinking stare, making my throat close over my voice. "What did you tell him?"

I shook my head. "N-nothing," I managed. "I started to, but I stopped."

"Whether you stopped or not, he knows."

"No . . ." I moaned.

"He has questioned us, and Perialla told him everything. *Everything*," she said emphatically as I tried to protest again. "The priestesses are terrified. It is up to the Minos to decide whether they live or die."

"No! I won't let him. Only Goddess—"

"Goddess's days are over." I put up my hand to ward off the blow, and she seized it, pulling me close. "Listen to me! In the time of She-Who-Is-Goddess who was Pasiphaë's mother, Goddess lost four cities." *So that's why my mother wouldn't tell me their names,* I thought. I couldn't speak, and the old woman's scratchy voice continued inexorably. "A few years ago, Medea fled for her life from Kolkhis, leaving her Minos dead and the city in an uproar. I doubt that the rituals of Goddess are being observed there now. That makes the fifth. And just a few weeks ago, we received confirmation of a dreadful rumor we had been hearing for some time: She-Who-Is-Goddess of Delphi has been forced by priests of the sun god to serve him and not Goddess." I gasped in horror at this desecration, and again when I realized that I myself had seen the messenger who had brought that news. "That was the sixth city to be lost of the thirteen, and we have learned that her worship on holy Naxos has ceased. If Goddess wanted to stay here on Krete, in Knossos, why did she destroy the ball just a moment before it would have made you She-Who-Is?"

There was a rustle outside the door. Damia cocked her head as if listening, and then went on. "Minos-Who-Was sent me here with wine he prepared *for the guards*"—she said those words with an odd emphasis—"and with this." She nodded at the tray where the cloth-swathed bundle still lay. She rose creakily to her feet. "You must hurry." Then she was gone. My mouth was hanging open. I snapped it shut. *Hurry?* What did she mean?

"Old fool." I had almost forgotten Theseus. "She didn't bring wine for the guards. She brought it for us—for you, anyway—and it was only because we already had some that she gave it to them. And what did she mean that the wine had been prepared by the Minos? How do you *prepare* wine?"

Something was different. I closed my eyes to think. Then I opened them. The guards—where were they? When Damia had left, they should have been standing in the opening, their spears crossed, but I had seen no sign of them. I opened the door.

The men were there, but they lay on the floor, one of them twitching in sleep, and the other snoring. I picked up the wine flask and put my nose to its opening. A sweet scent rose to my nostrils. Wine may be sweet, and wine may have honey added to it, but this smell was neither sweet wine nor honey. It was extract of poppy, and anyone who drank wine laced with poppy essence would sleep for a long time.

Theseus started to speak. "Hush!" I said, and to my surprise he did. I closed the door softly and opened the bundle on the tray.

In the torchlight, three gold figures on the blade of a short sword blinked coldly.

WHEN I FEEL the cold metal, I'm sure that Ariadne has decided not to wait for the ceremony but to kill me right here. Then I realize that the blade is not slitting the veins on my wrists but slicing the knot that holds them together.

"What are you—" I start to ask, but once again she orders me to hush, and somewhat to my own surprise, I do.

I sit up and rub my wrists.

"Can you walk?" Ariadne grabs my heel and waggles my foot.

I yelp as the blood burns back into my feet. "Stop! Stop!" I hiss.

She shakes her head. "No time. I don't know when the guards are to be relieved, but it can't be long." She grabs my arm, and with surprising strength, she hauls me to my feet.

Too late. Footsteps are padding down the hall. They're light but moving fast. I take my sword from Ariadne and swing it up as the door flies open, then lower it at the sight of Prokris. She cowers, her arm over her head.

"The old lady, that one who looks like a turtle, she sent me," Prokris says between gulps of air. She drops onto a stool, and her shoulders shake with the effort of catching her breath.

Ariadne isn't listening to her. "I'll get my brother," she says, "while you two go to the ship and make it ready. Then I'll bring him to you and you can leave. I'll—"

"Slow down. Wait a minute," I say. "Get your brother? What are you talking about?"

"Don't you understand?" She turns wild eyes on me. "They'll kill him so that no one will object to Simo being Minos, and they won't be kind about it. He has to go with you. Once you're gone, I'll declare that Simo is My son, and he can do whatever he wants. But you *must* take Asterion."

"But what about you?" I ask. For the first time, she hesitates, and I take advantage of her indecision. "You can't stay here either. I don't know what the old woman meant about the goddess ball, but it seems to me that she doesn't think you're truly their goddess. Am I right?" Ariadne has gone even paler than usual. "What happens to someone who says she's the goddess when she isn't?"

Even her lips are white now as she falters, "I . . . I don't know. It's never happened—at least, I never heard of—"

"Come with us!" She hesitates, and I press my advantage.

"I'll help you get your brother to the ship. He likes me; I can make him come. There's little enough to make ready. We'll go to Athens—I have a score to settle with my father—and we can stop at some island on the way and get provisions. I can easily find men at the dock to help me sail her."

"Wait!" I'm afraid Ariadne is going to argue, but instead she throws open the lid of a wooden chest at the foot of the bed. She tosses out one moth-eaten ball of yarn after another until they litter the floor like blue and green and yellow and white rocks.

"What are you *doing?*"

She pulls out a ball that's as black as squid ink and lumpy with knots. For an instant, she clasps it to her chest, her eyes closed. Her lips move, and just as I'm about to shout that there's no time for prayer, she thrusts it at me. "You'll need this to get him out. Unravel it, or he'll never be able to leave the chamber. I'll find honey or preserves or something to tempt him away."

"And will you come with us?"

"I can't." She stands upright, and despite her small size, she looks strong. "I'm a priestess of Goddess, and I always will be."

"All right." I give up. I don't know what she means, but I don't care, as long as she hurries. "Let's go." We slip out the door and down the corridor. Prokris pries a torch out of its holder as we run past it.

It's quiet, but distant, agitated voices and weeping echo

so strangely that I flinch every time we turn a corner, expecting to encounter a guard or at least a servant who will raise the alarm. But we see no one. "They're frightened," Ariadne whispers. "If Perialla has told them about the goddess ball, they will be terrified, and they know that they don't have a Minos." She looks frightened too, and I reach for her hand. I hold it as we approach the stairs. She stops, bringing me up short. "Tell my brother where I've gone, and why. He remembers—I *think* he remembers about the kitchen. Hurry! And don't forget to unravel the ball as soon as you get there."

I grip the clump of wool and wonder what the boy's reaction will be. Prokris hands me her torch, and the two girls run in the other direction.

Even with the flame, the dark is heavy. The stench and a soft sound coming from Asterion's den make my stomach clench. He's eating something, and the sucking and slobbering make the hair on my arms prickle. He must hear me or see or smell the torch, because I hear his "Ah!" and blessedly, the chewing stops. Another "Ah!" and I round the corner and see him.

He stands with the leg of a lamb or a kid dangling from one hand, while with the other, he points at me, a grin showing his yellow, crooked teeth. Someone must have brought him a portion of the festival food, a kindness even if he's been left alone while everyone else celebrates in company with their families, with music and dancing.

He catches sight of the ball of black wool. He shrieks and

flings himself backwards, slipping in the filth and falling, then fleeing from me on his hands and feet, scrabbling like a gigantic crab. "Oooooh!" he wails. "Ama! *Ama!*"

"It's all right!" I tear at the yarn with my fingernails, then with my teeth. I dig my thumbs into it and grasp an end and yank at it, but the mass knots itself together even tighter. "It's all right, Asterion." I approach him. He whimpers, looking up at me through the curls that fall on his forehead. I reach out a hand, and he flinches.

"Come with me." I raise my voice over his moans. "Your sister—Ariadne is waiting for you up in the kitchen. She has some honey. You like honey, don't you?"

His sobs slow, and he tentatively rises to his knees and then to his feet. I tug his hand, but I might as well be pulling at the rock that had lain on top of my sword and sandals. For an instant, my mind's eye sees the bull with spears projecting from his hump, his eyes glazing as he's brushed by death's wing.

I slice the ball of yarn open with my sword, untwisting the center, and throw it to the ground. I trample it into the urine and feces from the overturned bucket. "See? The magic is broken. It can't hold you here anymore!" The boy gasps and leans toward the door, twisting his body to distance himself from the matted wool, but he doesn't step out of the ring of white paving stones.

"Ama!" he calls. "Ama-a-a-a!" For the first time, I see his resemblance not to a bull but to a calf that has been separated from its mother. His huge eyes, as he glances at me, blaze with confusion and fear.

"Ama!" He stretches his big hand to the door. Then he screams and shrinks back, shuddering, his arms crossed protectively over his naked chest. An instant later, I hear it too: the tramp of feet. Then there's the hot, greasy smell of torches, and three men are suddenly in the doorway. Enops, leaning on a companion, with bandages wrapping his chest, is in the lead. Behind him is Gnipho, the guard who threatened Artemis's life when she bit Ariadne. He is heavily armed, and at his side stands Prokris. She throws me a defiant look. I'm too amazed to wonder what that means or what she is doing with them.

The men do not bear decent swords and spears. Instead they carry an assortment of hooks, branding irons, and barbed implements with narrow points that look like they are intended to enter a body and then be pulled out along with some of what should never be seen. Enops's expression is grim, and as I watch, he sticks the tip of his vicious-looking weapon into the flame until it glows red.

The two men with him look frightened but determined. Behind them, Ariadne and Artemis have appeared. Asterion is weeping. I imagine what will happen if these men work their will on him—his bewilderment, his terror, his prolonged suffering—and I make up my mind. I grip his shoulder, and he turns and wraps his arms around me, burying his face, slimy with tears and snot, in my neck.

Ariadne squirms between the men, who appear frozen. She stops short and claps her hand over her mouth. Then she fixes me with a stare and raises her right hand, the first finger and thumb curled into a semicircle. She holds it above her head as tears spill out of her eyes in an unending stream. Then she nods at me. I hesitate, not sure I understand, and she nods more firmly.

Asterion's large body is between me and the soldiers, and I doubt they can see me pull the sword out of my belt. With my free hand, I stroke Asterion's hair, remembering how Ariadne soothed him that day, his head on her lap while she sang to him. I keep my gaze on Enops, who has narrowed his eyes, wondering what I'm up to. Prokris grabs his arm and leans in to say something in his ear, but he shakes her off.

"Hush, now." I grip the hilt tighter, and Asterion's sobs slow a bit. "Hush, now."

And then it is done.

CHAPTER 41

ARTEMIS POINTS her nose at the ceiling and howls, long and low. I ease my burden down gently, even though Asterion is past feeling any hurt. He lies on his back, his restless limbs finally still. One dark eye is open, and it stares at me mildly, without accusation. I close its lid and rest my hand on the boy's damp face.

The men huddle together in horrified silence. Even Enops appears shocked. Behind them, Prokris is bent over, her hands covering her face. Only Ariadne looks at me, her eyes shining with tears. She takes a deep, shuddering breath and steps inside the circle of white stone that used to mark the limits of Asterion's domain. She stoops over her brother's body and smooths the curls off his bumpy forehead while her tears drip onto his face.

Two more figures join the crowd in the doorway. One is

the Minos, or Minos-Who-Was, as Ariadne now calls him. His face is as impassive as the bull's mask that he wore a short time ago. With him is the bent-over old woman who brought us the drugged wine—and my sword.

The man glares at Enops. "You!" he spits. "Traitor! And to think that I thought you worthy of being Minos!"

Ariadne wheels on her uncle. "*He* was your chosen one? I thought that Simo—"

Enops thrusts his chin out at her. "No. He chose *me*. And now I'm going to be not only the Minos of Knossos, but its king as well." His voice is shaky. "I am Pasiphaë's son as much as *he* was." He glares at the motionless body inside the circle of white stone. "As much as *you* are her daughter. Why should I have to risk my life in the bullring? Why am I of no consequence, when a monster is called the son of the god, and Minos-Who-Will-Be?"

Ariadne stares at Enops before turning her back on him. She bundles the filthy yarn into a mass, which she carefully deposits on Asterion's chest. She crosses his hands over it and stands. She and her uncle lock gazes. I can't see her face, but something in it makes him bow his head in submission.

He is the first to speak. "Take the body and give the boy a decent burial."

"No!"

At Ariadne's voice, the guards look up. Gnipho glances at the man, then at Enops, and finally at the girl, who is still in her finery. He salutes Ariadne. "Mistress?"

Ariadne says, "Take the body of Minos-Who-Will-Be to the sacred valley. He did not live long enough to be made Minos, but is there any among you who will deny that he was the true son of Goddess and Velchanos?"

Apparently there isn't, and Gnipho signals to his men. They come forward and pick up the lifeless body. As they shuffle toward the door, one of the boy's hands drops off his chest and trails in the muck. Ariadne stops them and replaces it gently. She follows the group with her eyes as they ease their burden through the narrow door.

"And what of you?" The old woman's voice is thin but full of power, and everyone turns to look at her. She leans on a staff, addressing Ariadne.

"Of me?" Ariadne seems bewildered. "What do you mean, Damia?"

"What of Ariadne? Are you Goddess, or are you not? Were you born of Goddess and Velchanos, or of Pasiphaë and"— her voice cracks, and a tear running down one of the ridges in her face sparkles in the torchlight—"of Pasiphaë and Kilix?"

Ariadne appears unable to answer. Flies buzz as they congregate in the dark pool. I remember that it was meant to be *my* blood that was shed, and my stomach wrenches uneasily. If Ariadne is not who she has claimed to be, this might mean that I'm not the god they think I am. I don't know if that means they will let me go free or if they will kill me even more horribly than they would have on the altar, as punishment and to cleanse the sacrilege.

"You must go," Damia tells Ariadne. "You must leave Knossos. Goddess has lost six cities, and the rest are crumbling, even the holy island of Naxos. She will lose Knossos now. The people will still obey Minos-Who-Was, at least for a short time, and he will not allow anyone to harm you if you leave. But if you stay, they will kill you. They will kill you slowly to drive out anything of Goddess that found its way into you—or they will keep you down here, in your brother's chambers, to show everyone how strong they are and how debased Goddess is."

The cunning look on Enops's face tells me that what the old priestess predicts is accurate. I take a firmer grip on my sword in case he decides to put one of those plans into operation now.

"And, child"—the old woman raises her face, and even in its ancient decrepitude, something noble shines from it—"child, I couldn't stand to see that. I gave my son to Goddess; I cannot give Her my granddaughter."

I'm bewildered, but Ariadne looks as though she finally understands something. "Kilix was your son? The man my mother named as Velchanos the spring before I was born?" When Damia nods, her old face wrinkles even more, and Ariadne folds her in her arms. The two women stand there for a moment, breathing as one.

Ariadne steps back. She glances at me, and I think I see what it was that made her uncle submit to her will. She no longer looks like a frightened girl. Instead, she is a woman who wears a firm expression. "I'll go. Goddess may be finished here, but I'll find a place where she is still revered." The old woman wilts—with relief, it appears.

Enops stands in the doorway with the wooden shaft of his barbed weapon still clutched in his hand. Although the red glow has faded, I know that its tip is still painfully hot. I wonder what I will do if he tries to prevent us from leaving. Then he steps aside, and Ariadne, and then I, and then Artemis pass through the door.

WE WERE at the first turn when Minos-Who-Was caught up with us. "Don't go. Let *him* go, but you stay with me. I'll protect you. Somehow, I'll keep you safe. Don't leave me alone." His voice was so humble that it made me wince. This man had so recently worn the great bull's head; he had performed the ritual to make me Goddess; for a few hours, from the time when he put on the bull's hide until Velchanos revealed himself to me, he had been the god. And now he was begging.

I realized that my whole life had been preparing me for this. "This is something I must decide for myself, Uncle. I can't let anyone do it for me. Goddess's time here is over, and She-Who-Is-Goddess has no more place on Krete."

Minos-Who-Was let a sob escape. "I lost my sister—I lost myself as Minos. I can't lose you, too."

"You still have me," Prokris said. I hadn't noticed her approach us, and now I whirled to face her.

"You!" My voice shook with rage that temporarily chased away my wrenching grief. "You!"

"Yes, me." She tried to slide her hand into the crook of my uncle's elbow, but he kept his arm clamped to his side.

"You betrayed us." My throat felt thick. "You told Enops what we were planning. If it hadn't been for you, Asterion would be safely on the ship, instead of—" A sob wrenched itself from my core.

Theseus asked harshly, "Is this true?" For once, Prokris was speechless. Theseus went on. "When you saw that I wasn't going to become king, you found a replacement. Is that right?"

She raised her chin and glared at him. "That's right! I found a *real* man, someone who will take the throne—"

My uncle cut her off. "Enough." He turned to Enops, who glared at us from the doorway. "Remove her from my sight. I am no longer Minos, or I would order her walled up in the Goddess shrine, but I *am* still her husband, and if she shows herself in my presence again, I will sell her as a slave in the limestone mines." We watched in silence as Prokris fled. Enops pressed his lips together in a tight line, bowed curtly, and followed her.

Theseus shifted on his feet behind me. "We have to go," he said softly. But my uncle stretched his arms to me.

"I must," I said. "I must find a place where Goddess still lives."

Tears slid from his eyes as I entered his arms for one last, long embrace. He was the first to step away. He stared searchingly into my eyes, attempting to decipher something he saw there. "Child, during the ritual—did you? Did you become Goddess?"

I remembered the moon with the line of Goddesses dancing into it. I remembered, too, how I had been denied entrance. "I think I did," I said. I wanted to tell him that if I had truly become Goddess, it was only by my mother's grace and only for a short time, and that I was the last one. But I couldn't. I couldn't break my uncle's dear heart. I raised my hand over his head in blessing and then moved to where Artemis waited, the waving of her tail increasing in speed as I led her out of the basement.

My mother's tomb was broken open, all too soon after she had been placed in it. Ordinary people might be laid in caves, but only a chamber dug into the cleft between the two holy mountains would serve for one who was divinely born. The ceremony for the burial of Minos-Who-Will-Be was performed, but hastily. I tried not to worry about Enops and Prokris and whether they would gather their courage enough to defy the will of the people and attack me.

I made sure that all the rituals were performed meticulously. I could not permit my brother to leave his confinement only to face eternal imprisonment in a tiny grave, and I had to do what was necessary to ensure that his spirit would roam freely. I sacrificed thirteen white lambs, some so young that they tottered on their tiny legs, and a yearling bull that would otherwise have danced and died in the great palace arena the next spring. Minos-Who-Was and his men brought in vase after vase of wine and olive oil, adding them to the ones left for my mother, which had been deposited there so recently that hardly a whisper of dust lay on them.

At the last, I handed my uncle one more item to sweeten my brother's journey. He glanced at it, then smiled even as a tear trickled into the corner of his mouth: a small stone pot with a honeybee stamped into the wax that sealed it.

Asterion's bulky linen-wrapped body was showered with crocuses, and women wailed and screamed as it was closed in a heavy stone coffin. I had paid them for their mourning, but I knew that terror at their future, with no She-Who-Is-Goddess and no Minos, added to their cries.

I myself did not weep; I had no time. I returned to the palace to pack a few belongings for myself and my sister and to bid a hasty farewell to Athis and those among the priest-esses and servants who had once been my friends.

Then, almost before I knew it, we were on board the long black ship that I had seen pull into the harbor bearing Theseus and Prokris and Artemis, and along with them, the beginning of the end of the life I knew. I held Phaedra close as Theseus struggled with the nanny goat that was to provide her milk during the voyage, and tried not to laugh as he cursed at the stubborn beast.

To my surprise (and I think to Theseus's as well), I took to the sea as easily as if I had been born the daughter of a fisherman. The salt spray on my skin made me feel more alive than I ever had before, and breathing the cold air that rose off the water at dawn made me realize why so many peoples of the lands of Hellas worship Poseidon, god of the ocean, above all others. Dolphins kept pace with us almost constantly, delighting me, as I had never seen them close up before. When the sailors threw fish guts into the water, the dolphins swallowed them and then rose upright and cackled at the ship as though asking for more. The contrast between their voices, so like Damia's that I expected them to tell me to behave myself, and their smooth, shiny skin and wide grins, so unlike her wrinkles and habitual scowl, made me burst out laughing. I held little Phaedra up to see them, but she was too small to notice.

It was exhilarating, to be sure, and I was finally fulfilling my longing for travel. Still, I felt empty. The knowledge that at the first oar stroke of our ship I had lost whatever divinity I had possessed mattered little to me now. I could not return to Krete, yet the thought of Athens was not appealing. I could never be subject to a king.

So I lay awake in my hammock most of that first night, with Phaedra in a smaller one within reach. I imagined my mother's arms encircling me, rocking me gently. I even thought of Asterion without pain. My life on Krete had belonged to another person, like someone whose story I had heard sung in tales. The girl who would be Goddess and who longed to see other lands and to have a friend was a stranger to me, and she had died down in a dark, smelly chamber, along with her beloved brother. I was still Ariadne, daughter of Pasiphaë, priestess of Karia, and sister of Phaedra, but I was no longer She-Who-Is-Goddess—if I ever had been— and no longer She-Who-Will-Be-Goddess.

A worry made my sleep restless. On the third day after the ritual, what would happen to Theseus? If he had become Velchanos during the ceremony, that meant Moera Krataia had measured out the thread of his life and would cut it on the appointed day. Or would she? If we were far away from any land where Goddess ruled, would Moera Krataia put down her scissors and measure another, longer lifeline for him?

And was Theseus still my husband? He had married Goddess, or I thought he had. If I was no longer Goddess, was I still his wife? When we met for meals, we were courteous with each other, but no more. I felt no special love for him; nor did I harbor ill feelings toward him. Theseus had done what he needed to do, as had I. What had happened was the will of Goddess, and perhaps of Theseus's gods, Erechtheus and Athena, as well.

On the second day, we moored in the harbor at the lovely island of Thera, where Theseus bought several barrels of water and enough food to last us the rest of the trip. Even though I longed to see the palace's famous wall frescoes and the hill-top city, I remained on board with Phaedra, too timid to meet so many strangers all at once. Theseus stayed on land overnight, and when he returned the next morning, he had a headache and was in a sour mood, so I avoided him. After that, things between us eased a bit, and we talked together like friends.

The next day, I woke early. I slipped from my hammock, checked that Phaedra was sleeping soundly, and tiptoed to where Theseus lay, his hammock swaying gently as the boat rocked. I laid a hand on his chest and felt a warm wave of relief wash over me as it moved up and down. The whole third day still lay ahead of us, but at least for now, he lived.

I went on deck. The sky was gray, and a cool wind blew spray on deck. The dolphins were absent and the screech of the gulls annoying, so I was about to go below, when a sailor in conversation with another said a familiar word: Naxos. I leaned in and listened attentively.

It appeared that we had sailed past the tiny island of Ios, and we were on track to skirt the islands of Paros and Naxos. Naxos—she was a famous She-Who-Is-Goddess, born on the island that was then named for her. A sudden longing to see the holy site flooded me like the waves washing over the prow of our ship, and a tiny seed of an idea was planted in my heart. I was still the daughter of Pasiphaë, and Phaedra and I would be honored at Naxos for our mother's sake, if even a tiny vestige of Goddess worship remained in that most holy spot. I picked up a length of rope lying on the deck. My fingers flew, making one knot after another.

As I firmed up the last knot, there came the roar of something large tearing. The sailors stared at our mainsail; a gust had hit it, and a hidden flaw made the cloth split in two and flap uselessly. Theseus appeared from below and strode to where I stood, glared at the ruined sail, cursed, and told the sailors to man the oars. I hid the knotted rope behind me.

"Can we row all the way to Athens?" I was hesitant, since Theseus kept telling me that the smallest child in Troizena knew more about boats than I did.

"Of course not. Or we could, but it would take too long. We'll have to stop and have it fixed." We passed a fishing boat, whose occupants hailed us with friendly waves and directed us to Naxos. I maintained a calm demeanor, while all the time the beat of my heart shook me more than did the waves pounding our bow. I didn't know if my knots had caused the sail to rip or if a lucky gust had just happened to find its weak spot at that moment.

"I'd like to see the island," I told Theseus.

He appeared surprised. "It's smaller than Thera, and less grand." Looking pleased, he helped me into the boat. He rowed well, but still I clung to my seat as the small craft bucked and shook over the choppy waters.

My first steps onto the beach felt unsteady after the rolling of the ship. I was afraid I would drop the baby, so Theseus carried her. Everything looked strange. I knew, of course, that other places were different from Krete, but something about this island was unsettling. Then I realized. "Look, Theseus!" I pointed at the sand underfoot. "It's yellow!" He laughed and took my hand. We walked on the golden sand, Artemis leaving a neat line of rosette-shaped paw marks behind us.

Up in the town, local leaders, alerted to our arrival by the heralds along the shore, welcomed us with a ceremony and what passed for a feast among them. We sat outdoors, eating roasted fowl with herbs and bread dipped in honey. As the sun set, I glanced across the table at Theseus.

"What?" he said, but I shook my head. When the last red edge of the sun had disappeared, I took a huge breath of relief that escaped in a laugh which surprised me as much as him. Three days had passed, and yet he lived. I raised my cup to him, and he returned the salute with a grin, then turned back to the pretty serving girl who was finding the tenderest pieces of meat to put on his plate.

That night, I thought I would finally sleep well, with the worry of Theseus removed from my mind. Instead, I lay awake on a soft pallet on the floor of the king's tiny palace for a long, long time. What was preventing me from sleeping was that seed of an idea, and I felt it growing into something that would change my life yet again.

The seed grew to a green plant the next morning. Theseus slept late, and the wife of our host worried that I would be bored, so she took me on a tour. The town was small, but bright and clean, with cheerful inhabitants, and the queen was proud to show me their Goddess stone in the palace's tiny sanctuary.

"Dionysos is our most important god," she informed me as her hand stroked the gray lump that showed signs of years of anointing with oil. "But I've always loved Selene"—one of Goddess's many names—"I've always loved Selene best." The green plant grew a flower, and I told the queen who I was. Her kind eyes widened, and we conferred until the sun had risen fully and beat down on us as we walked back to town.

"I'm staying," I informed Theseus when he finally sat down to breakfast. He nearly choked on his bread.

"Staying? Here?"

I nodded and reached for a fig. They had been expertly dried, and even now, months after the harvest, they were moist and sweet. "Your Athens is no place for me. I can't go where the people don't know Goddess. Besides, you're unsure of how your father and stepmother will receive you. You don't need me there complicating things." I told him about the Goddess stone and how Her worship had fallen into decline here. "I'll always be a priestess, you know. Goddess's days may be numbered, but I can still venerate Her. Besides, I've always wanted to meet new people and see how they live, and now that I'm here, I want to stay for a while and learn from them. And they can learn from me. They have forgotten most of the ways of Goddess, and the queen is anxious to relearn them."

He looked doubtful, so I added, "If it turns out I don't like it here, I'll send word, and you can come back and take me away." He finally seemed convinced, and when the sail makers came and said with a thousand apologies that they couldn't fix his sail, that they could sell him another, one ready-made of just the correct size and dyed an elegant black, he purchased it for more than what they had been asking and went down to his ship to supervise its installation.

The next day, I accompanied him to the harbor to say farewell.

"I'll send back a boat to see how you're doing, after I'm settled in Athens," he told me. "I have some business to take care of first."

Tension in his voice made me look at him more closely. "What 'business'?"

He threw a stone into the harbor just as his men shouted that the sail had been hung properly and that the wind was freshening. If they wanted to make the tide, they would have to leave soon.

"What business?" I asked again.

He threw another stone. "My father. He won't like to see me return. And his wife—she'll think of me as a threat to both her husband and her son."

"*Are* you a threat?"

For the first time since that last, awful night in Knossos, he looked me in the eyes. "He's the king, and he's within his rights to order me to a certain death, but I don't like that way of ruling. Maybe it's because I grew up in the country, with a king who let people decide most things for themselves, but I want to do something about it. And I don't think he'll like it.

I can't change anything while he's on the throne, and he knows that."

He kissed the top of Phaedra's little head and held me in a long embrace. In a way, we were married, so it was proper, and we were friends, so I allowed it. I remembered the first time I had seen him, his broad back to me as he watched the boys in the arena, and I remembered his kindness to my brother. He would always be dear to me, even if I never saw him again.

I watched the black sail until it dipped below the horizon, and then I went in search of twelve intelligent girls to train in the ways of Goddess.

THE GUARD tries to stop me, but I sweep him aside and stride into the king's dining hall. Once again, my father is there; once again, Medea sits opposite him, with their son on her lap.

The king freezes at the sight of me, but his wife springs to her feet, clutching little Medus. "My quarrel is not with you," I tell her, but her eyes are wide and fixed on me, "nor with my brother." She glances at my father and then scuttles across the floor, the little boy protesting that she's hurting him, and disappears out the door.

The king rises, looking at the sword in my hand. "Come to slit my throat at my own table with my own weapon?"

"It's better than the death you planned for me," I say. "But as it turns out, it was I who killed the monster, not the other way around."

"Oh, indeed." His sneer is audible. "As you killed the man who tried to cut off your feet? And as you fed the thief to the turtle?"

I flush. "The blood of the innocent Minotauros fouled this blade. I need to clean it with the blood of a king."

He looks shaken for a moment but then draws himself upright and spreads his hands, palms upward. "I am weaponless," he says.

"Don't worry," I answer. "I have no intention of fighting a defenseless old man in secret. Arm yourself; we will meet outside, in full view of your people, and only one of us will walk away."

I quail at my father's look of confidence, but then I harden myself. True, he has many successful fights to his credit; he is taller than I, and his sword is twice as long. But I'm younger, and I have my rage, bottled up in Krete and on the voyage home. That, and the hours I spent practicing with the Kretan soldiers.

We circle each other in the arena formed by pine boughs, looking for a weak spot. Before I can see more than that his right leg moves stiffly, he lunges at me, shouting a battle cry. His men join him in a raucous chorus. The king swings his sword, but it moves slowly, and I duck under it. I come up behind him and thrust my own weapon at his kidneys, but he flings himself sideways.

We face each other again. He is sweating and panting,

but I know better than to assume that he is tiring already. Gray beard or not, this is a warrior.

His sword flashes again, and this time I feel a hot pain as he slices my left thigh. It's not enough to fell me, though, and I bring my own sword up hard and fast under his, and his weapon flies from his hand. It sails through the air and over the heads of his men, who turn to watch it disappear off the cliff and into the sea.

A groan rises from the soldiers, and for the first time, the light of fear shines in the king's eyes. I advance two steps in his direction, and he falls back one step before clearly forcing himself to stand still.

My breath feels harsh in my throat. I spit a glob of snot and dust into the dirt. "Do you yield?" He doesn't answer, so I raise my sword.

"Yield or die," I say, and this time he says, "I yield."

I expect to feel a surge of joy, of triumph, but something holds it back. Perhaps it will come when he bows to me as victor. I lower my arm and advance to him warily, feeling the pain in my thigh at each step. "Drop your sword," he says. I hesitate. "I don't trust you," he goes on. "I won't submit until your hand is empty. I have no weapon, and it's cowardly of you to approach me armed when you have defeated me." The men around us murmur agreement, so I stoop, lay my sword on the ground, and advance.

The king stands with his head bowed. When I'm an arm's length from him, he moves faster than I would have thought possible, and bronze glints in his right hand. I seize a pine bough and thrust it at him. His dagger cleaves it nearly in two before its blade shatters. I reach back blindly, and my fingers close on the hilt of my weapon. I swing it up and bury the blade to a hand's depth in his belly.

Nobody moves. My father looks at me, then at the sword protruding from his midsection. He pulls it out, and blood spreads across his robe. "You haven't killed me," he says hoarsely. He turns and takes a stumbling step, then another, and then he's trotting, blood dripping and then pouring from his belly, his mouth, his nose. The men part to let him through.

"Father!" I call, but whether to stop him or to curse him, I don't know. "Father!"

He says again, "You haven't killed me." He throws his arms wide and shouts, "Poseidon, take me!" as he flings himself off the edge of the cliff. I pull to a stop and lean over. His body bounces off the boulders and splashes into the water. Then there is no sound except the scream of the seagulls and the crash of the waves.

A shuffling behind me makes me turn. Aegeus's men, all of them, are on their knees, and as I watch, they bend and press their heads to the ground. The soldier at their front stands, approaches, and prostrates himself in the dirt. "My lord," he says.

"Get up," I say. He scrambles to his feet, and as we proceed on our way he tries the delicate balancing act of telling me how the people are all rejoicing that the king is dead without insulting the new king's father.

It has been a most interesting homecoming.

I feel a pang—a small one—at the thought that I'll never really know my father. Then I remember Konnidas, and my heart warms. I'll send for him and my mother as soon as I'm settled. She'll be perfect as mistress of the palace, issuing orders and countermanding them just for the fun of it.

It's not long before the poets are telling the tale of my adventures. They misunderstand a great deal. Before I went to Krete, I, too, believed that the Minotauros was born of the unnatural union of a bull and the queen. I believed that he ate people, that he lived in a maze so bewildering that the only way to find your way out of it was to follow an unwound ball of yarn. If I were to tell people of the Planting Festival and about the bull's head worn first by the Minos and then by the man chosen as the god, they would be disappointed. I agree that the truth is not as good a tale.

Some even say that my father, seeing the black sail on my ship, thought I had died on Krete, and that in his grief he committed suicide by jumping off the cliff. I find it absurd that anyone would believe such a tale. He tried to send me to my death, after all, and would have rejoiced rather than been stricken with despair if the monster had eaten me, and the many witnesses to our final battle could contradict that nonsense, but I don't mind what people say.

It does sadden me that they think I killed the harmless Asterion in order to escape from him and that I abandoned sweet little Ariadne on Naxos against her will. I've tried to explain, but mercy killing and leaving behind at her request a woman they see as the spoils of war are not actions they deem worthy of a king, so I let it be.

For although I am a different kind of king than my father, a king is what I am, and I will rule my people.

➵ EPILOGUE ➴

Tonight is the new moon, and I dance.

My feet remember the complicated patterns that my mother taught me. I guide my little daughter through the steps, and her mouth grows round as she gawks at my cow-horn headdress, which mimics the shape of the crescent above us. She holds my hand, and I laugh encouragement. My bare feet mark the golden sand of the beach, and the signs they form mingle with the smaller patterns made by hers.

I don't need to wait until morning light to read the marks. They will repeat the news I hear from passing sailors, who say that Theseus is well, that his kingdom prospers and his people adore him. The marks will tell those who can read them that Medea and her son fled from Athens and that no one has heard of them since. They will say that Minos-Who-Was died peacefully in his sleep after the last Birth of the Sun Festival and that Damia terrorizes the servants and tends to Orthia as she would a favorite child, spoiling her and giving her everything she wants.

They will say that my husband, a quiet and gentle priest of Dionysos, loves me and Phaedra and our daughter and that he will love the child I am to bear near the Harvest Festival. My husband's sister is a priestess of Selene and was my first friend on Naxos. She can tease a laugh out of me at any moment, and she has done much to teach me the ways of the people here.

Now that I know what love is, I know I felt nothing like that for Theseus. Friendship, yes; gratitude for his kindness to Asterion and for seeing me as a woman and not a goddess in training, yes;

but not love. That is something different, and something I hope my friend Theseus will find.

What the marks do not tell me, what they can never tell me, is whether I could have prevented my brother's death and whether I became Goddess that spring evening in Knossos. Sometimes I think I did and that if I had stayed home instead of crossing the sea, then one day I would join my mother and her mother and all our Mothers in the moon. At other times, I think that I never was Goddess, or I would have been able to read the warning signs that She sent me. In either case, at the end of my days, I will lie in the ground next to my husband and our son, who died while being born, a year after I came to Naxos.

Phaedra is being trained to worship Dionysos. She has a sunny disposition, and my husband treats her as his own. Our little daughter is not She-Who-Will-Be-Goddess. Even if I had a Minos to initiate her, I could never bear to watch her survey the silent crowd seeking her husband, knowing that her actions would mean a man's death. She will be a priestess and will serve Selene, but I wonder how long it will be before even that simple worship disappears.

But for now, it is enough that I am here on a warm spring night, dancing under the new moon with my daughter, and up in our small house up the hill, my husband and Phaedra are waiting for us, with Artemis keeping watch.

I dance.

It does sadden me that they think I killed the harmless Asterion in order to escape from him and that I abandoned sweet little Ariadne on Naxos against her will. I've tried to explain, but mercy killing and leaving behind at her request a woman they see as the spoils of war are not actions they deem worthy of a king, so I let it be.

For although I am a different kind of king than my father, a king is what I am, and I will rule my people.

→ EPILOGUE ←

Tonight is the new moon, and I dance.

My feet remember the complicated patterns that my mother taught me. I guide my little daughter through the steps, and her mouth grows round as she gawks at my cow-horn headdress, which mimics the shape of the crescent above us. She holds my hand, and I laugh encouragement. My bare feet mark the golden sand of the beach, and the signs they form mingle with the smaller patterns made by hers.

I don't need to wait until morning light to read the marks. They will repeat the news I hear from passing sailors, who say that Theseus is well, that his kingdom prospers and his people adore him. The marks will tell those who can read them that Medea and her son fled from Athens and that no one has heard of them since. They will say that Minos-Who-Was died peacefully in his sleep after the last Birth of the Sun Festival and that Damia terrorizes the servants and tends to Orthia as she would a favorite child, spoiling her and giving her everything she wants.

They will say that my husband, a quiet and gentle priest of Dionysos, loves me and Phaedra and our daughter and that he will love the child I am to bear near the Harvest Festival. My husband's sister is a priestess of Selene and was my first friend on Naxos. She can tease a laugh out of me at any moment, and she has done much to teach me the ways of the people here.

Now that I know what love is, I know I felt nothing like that for Theseus. Friendship, yes; gratitude for his kindness to Asterion and for seeing me as a woman and not a goddess in training, yes;

but not love. That is something different, and something I hope my friend Theseus will find.

What the marks do not tell me, what they can never tell me, is whether I could have prevented my brother's death and whether I became Goddess that spring evening in Knossos. Sometimes I think I did and that if I had stayed home instead of crossing the sea, then one day I would join my mother and her mother and all our Mothers in the moon. At other times, I think that I never was Goddess, or I would have been able to read the warning signs that She sent me. In either case, at the end of my days, I will lie in the ground next to my husband and our son, who died while being born, a year after I came to Naxos.

Phaedra is being trained to worship Dionysos. She has a sunny disposition, and my husband treats her as his own. Our little daughter is not She-Who-Will-Be-Goddess. Even if I had a Minos to initiate her, I could never bear to watch her survey the silent crowd, seeking her husband, knowing that her actions would mean a man's death. She will be a priestess and will serve Selene, but I wonder how long it will be before even that simple worship disappears.

But for now, it is enough that I am here on a warm summer night, dancing under the new moon with my daughter, and that in our small house up the hill, my husband and Phaedra are waiting for us, with Artemis keeping watch.

I dance.